Love THAT Counts

TWO WAYS
Home

DISCARD

June '17

Love that Counts

TWO WAYS Home

SONDRA KRAAK

Trail House Publishers

To Marci
My sister and friend.
Thanks for laughing and dreaming with me and supporting me on
my writing journey.

CHAPTER ONE

Pine Creek, Washington Territory, 1884

"He loves me. He loves me not." Twelve-year-old Mary Smith dangled her legs over the bough of the cherry tree in which she sat. Leaning her head against the trunk, face to the sun, she plucked at the daisy. "He loves me. He loves me not." She threw the petals into the breeze and watched them float the seven feet to the ground. "He loves me—"

"I doubt it."

She gasped, nearly losing her balance. Luke Thomas's taunting voice grated worse than a raven's caw. She scowled down at him. He thought he was so grown-up at sixteen.

"In fact, I guarantee it." He poked her boot with a stick, and she seized the branch as she teetered. Luke's smile held a bucketful of mischief. "Whoever he is, he can't possibly love Dairy Mary, the girl who spends more time with cows than with people." He tipped his head back, his grin encouraging her to lash out.

"You're a pest." She wished she had something other than a daisy to throw at his suntanned face. "Go back to the picnic and bob for apples. You could use the wash. Looks like someone dipped your hair in mud."

He glanced over his shoulder toward the meadow, where families picnicked for the Fourth of July, sprawled on blankets, and children chased each other in a game of tag. "Why aren't you with my sister? Thought you two were inseparable."

"Grace is picking violets." With someone else, a fact

7

that had set Mary into a mood.

Luke jumped up, grabbed the branch she was sitting on, and swung back and forth. A show off in every way. As if he needed to prove he was the strongest of the boys. He'd already shed his lankiness and donned the muscles of a man, and every girl had noticed, including Cecily Reynolds.

Mary stretched out her legs and landed the heel of her boot square on his fingers.

Crying out, he dropped to the ground and cradled his hand.

She rolled her eyes. "Stop being a baby."

Hunched over, hand to his chest, he moaned. The invincible Luke Thomas could not possibly be hurt. She prayed he wasn't. She'd meant to hassle him, not maim him.

He shook out his hand. His *right* hand. If she'd hurt his best shooting hand, he'd never forgive her.

She swung down from the tree. "Come on, you're fine." She didn't need one stupid move costing him a chance with the Texas Rangers — and everyone this side of the mountains knew how much he wanted that, thanks to his wagging tongue.

"You're fine, aren't you?" She nudged his arm.

He straightened and laughed.

She punched his shoulder, but he blocked it with one hand. Wiggling his eyebrows, he tightened his grip on her fist. She swung out her foot, attempting to undercut his legs. With a laugh, he jumped back, and she tumbled to the ground.

He bent over her. "I hope you treat your cows nicer."

Her cows cared more for her than Luke, the Duke of Pine Creek. She crossed her legs in front of her and smoothed her calico skirts.

Snickers sounded from behind. She whirled around to see a small crowd of classmates had gathered. Ears-too-big Preston, squirrely Davis, Prince Matthew, and Perfectly Perfect Cecily, who'd switched from braids to buns at age ten. That had been five years earlier. Scandalous, but no one was brave enough to tell her so.

Preston placed his arm around Luke's shoulder and speared her with a look. "Forget the cows. You should treat your future husband nicer." He thumped Luke's chest.

Luke shrugged away and swiped his shaggy hair from his eyes. "Go away."

Preston did, his grating laughter trailing behind. The others remained, probably wanting to see another clash between her and Luke. Not today. They'd have to wait for next week. Or at least until school tomorrow.

Matthew prodded the toe of her boot. "My money's on you like it is every time you and Luke go at it." He tussled the top of her head before sauntering after Preston.

From the corner of the meadow, their teacher rang a bell and announced the three-legged race. Luke raised his brow. "Don't you and Grace like to make fools of yourselves at this thing?"

She and his sister did everything together, but today Grace seemed more interested in picking flowers with the new girl, so Mary had climbed the cherry tree with a pocketful of daisies.

Luke grasped her upper arm and pulled her to her feet, kindness replacing the mischief in his eyes. He was like that. All joking, and then polite. A real helper of the people, as he liked to say so humbly of himself. He'd make a good Ranger.

He picked something from her braid and waved it in her face. A piece of hay. "You sleep with the cows, too?"

And then, quick as lightning, he was all teasing again. She hated lightning.

Mary huffed and retrieved her basket of honeysuckle vines from the base of the tree. "You think you're so funny."

He snagged a daisy and plucked the petals, mouthing words she didn't need to hear to understand. Everyone claimed, wrongly, that she liked this boy. Couldn't they see how she barely restrained herself from letting her fists loose on him? *You should treat your future husband better.* Ha! She'd rather marry a cow.

"He loves me. He loves me not."

Luke's singsong words ground the last bit of patience from her. "Let me tell you a thing or two, Luke Bradford Thomas."

He raised his eyebrows, a mocking attempt at surprise. "Be my guest, crazy girl. I could use some wisdom from a—"

"You are the last person I would ever marry. And no other sane girl would marry you either." Her heart pounded. "You're skinny as a broomstick, and you look like someone turned you upside down and swept the floor with your hair."

The grin that edged up his face spurred her on.

"You're like . . . like cream that won't churn to butter. Seed that won't grow." She fisted her hands at her side, hating the taunting of his hazel eyes. "A boy that won't get married."

He laughed, spun around, and whistled as he walked away.

She flung her basket after him. "I mean it."

CHAPTER TWO

———————————————— ✤ ————————————————

Eight years later, April, 1892

Darkness lapped up the last light from the sky as Luke rode into Pine Creek. How fitting that night veiled his return. He prodded Gabriel around the edge of Smith property, which jutted beneath Thomas ranchland. Even with darkness encroaching, the landscape bore a familiar presence.

On a whim, he veered off the path in the direction of town and scrambled up the rise. His shoulder ached as he pulled to the top and started down. He'd pass through Smith property and pay Father's grave a visit. Then he'd be ready to face his brother.

He adjusted the bandage around his shoulder. Three weeks since the trio of bullets had peppered him, and despite the stitching, one of the wounds still oozed.

Below, pastures stretched across the valley, a milky blanket of moonlight covering them. With the Wenatchee River serenading in the distance, he dipped down and led Gabriel along the fence line of the main pasture. Reining in, he stared at the homestead, the place he'd worked as a thirteen-year-old boy the summer after Father had died. The summer of stupidity and shame.

Though it neared milking time, the barn appeared dark. He wondered if Mary had already finished, if she'd adjusted to being back in Pine Creek after leaving her musical studies in Portland. His sister Grace had fed him information through pages of letters, as if he'd cared about Mary.

Of course he had. Still did. Mary had been a part of his

childhood, and Grace loved her.

His gaze traced the dark shadows at the corner of the structure. Sensing movement, he straightened in the saddle and blinked, his Ranger instincts suspecting the worst.

Relax. This is Pine Creek.

Darkness blurred his perception, and he squinted, certain he'd seen a figure outlined against the tall, two-story barn, pushed against the wall.

Thomas, you're some kind of crazy.

Mary or her father was bound to be moving about their dairy at milking time.

Nudging Gabriel onward, he stared harder. At the maple tree in the center of the pasture, he slowed, hugging the trunk and surveying for further movement. A soft light appeared through the open doors of the barn. Someone had lit a lantern. The shadowy figure he'd seen scrambled along the side wall and curved around behind. Not likely a hired hand, since he knew from Grace's letters that the Smiths had been forced to let go of their hired help. And a hired hand wouldn't have need to conceal himself against the side of the barn or slink off around a corner.

Hand on his gun, Luke led Gabriel in a wide circle around the barn but didn't see anything that resembled a person. His exhausted mind must be seeking its own adventure, making things up for the sake of excitement—and maybe to distract his heart from his homecoming.

It couldn't hurt to check on the Smiths.

Back at the front of the barn, he slipped off Gabriel and peered inside and down the two rows of open-sided stalls. Only half of them were occupied tonight. Mary sat with her back to him, milking. Even from this angle, he noticed how she'd vacated the cusp of womanhood and was now securely in the midst of it.

A lantern sat on a stool beside her, vulnerable in its place low to the ground. She knew better. Then again, conventionality wasn't one of Mary's guiding principles.

He stepped inside the barn doors, confused at the way his heart quickened. "Dairy Mary."

Yelping, she leapt to her feet and spun toward him. Her foot struck the stool beside her and sent the lantern toppling to the ground. Hay sparked, and he rushed forward, but Mary was quicker, diving on the flame to smother it. Darkness captured the barn. Luke fumbled his way to the water trough. His foot knocked against a bucket, and he snatched it, feeling the heaviness of liquid.

"Mary!"

A faint sight of orange robbed his breath. Was that a spark? He threw the water in the direction of the flame on which she'd fallen.

She gasped.

He snatched another lantern from its hook, felt along the shelf for a match, and restored light to the chaos.

And what beautiful, albeit angry, chaos. Mary stood before him, mud streaked down her cheek, hair mussed, and the middle of her dress singed. Other than the searing glare souring her face, she seemed unharmed.

Back not even an hour, and the nightmare of his past had confronted him. He and Pine Creek didn't mix well, which was why — *Lord, please* — this visit had to be kept short. "I'm sorry."

"For what? Scaring me, nearly burning down my barn, or dousing me with dirty water?" Her voice trembled.

"For all of it."

The fury in her eyes underscored the severity of what had almost happened: another fire, his responsibility.

"What made you think walking into a barn at nightfall and calling out a hated nickname was wise?" She clenched her hands at her sides. "This business is all Papa and I have."

Smoothing the front of her dress, she examined the burnt area which stretched no more than six inches. She'd fallen on that baby flame before he'd had a chance to move three steps into the barn.

13

"Are you all right?"

She tilted her chin. "I suppose."

He strode to the trough, scooped water, and emptied it on the scorched hay for good measure. "No harm done," he said, attempting to convince himself. He glanced at her disheveled appearance and smiled. "Except you look like you wrestled a cow."

In addition to looking . . . good.

That's right, Thomas. Keep it ambiguous.

Ambiguous was safe, and his thoughts as he took in her curves, the dark hair that waterfalled around her shoulders, and the lips that were frowning at him, were anything but vague. Or safe.

This is Dairy Mary. Spirited, witty, sharp-tongued, playful, hardworking . . . *How long are you going to stare?*

He smirked, stepped across the mess, and plucked a piece of straw from her hair.

Mary jerked from Luke's touch. Only a few inches taller than she, his presence somehow shrunk the barn to weird, dream-like proportions.

Luke. Home in Pine Creek. She let the knowledge of his homecoming penetrate past the terror of the lantern rolling across the ground, sparking. His family had prayed for the day he'd return, and here he was: shaggy-haired, scruffy-faced, his chest as broad as what she'd imagined a Texas sky might look like. Too handsome for his own good.

She pushed aside the leftover energy that hummed through her from the almost fire. A hug seemed out of place, no matter the urge to throw her arms around this childhood friend.

"Welcome home." She settled for a pat on his shoulder.

Sucking in a breath, he seized his arm.

"What's wrong?"

He stripped the grimace from his face. "I'm on the

14

mend."

"From what?" A glance didn't reveal any wound.

He'd not lost any legs and arms, and it remained to be seen if he'd lost any brains down south, something she'd teased him about when he'd left. Not to be a doubter, but he'd taken pleasure in fooling her before.

"I was shot in the shoulder."

"Shot?" Her eyes widened as she examined both his shoulders. The faint line of a bandage showed beneath his shirt on his left side.

"Just three times."

Just? Her gaze slammed into his. "Is that all? What a relief."

He grinned and looked around the barn, apparently in no rush to leave. Outside the entrance, his mount released a breath and shifted his weight. Full saddle bags indicated he'd likely not been home yet.

"Your family know you're here? Grace is going to cry her eyes out over you, or at least bake you a pie."

"I was on my way. Cut through your property and thought . . ." His eyes narrowed, and he looked away.

"Thought, what? How about I scare Mary by setting fire to her barn?"

"I didn't realize the girl who picked on boys twice her own size and climbed trees taller than the schoolhouse, got scared." A smile hinted beneath his short whiskers. "Except during thunderstorms."

She ducked her gaze and perched on the stool next to her favorite jersey, Mud. Her chest stung from where she'd fallen on the flames. Thankfully, she'd been wearing her thick chemise beneath. Better a mild burn than a lost livelihood. Nothing a little salve wouldn't cure.

Not sure how to respond to Luke's lingering, she returned to milking. "Did they get tired of your shenanigans and kick you out of the Rangers?" She bit her tongue against the banter that came too easily.

Luke shoveled the burnt mess to the side. "A man doesn't need a reason to come home."

"Calling Pine Creek home." She smirked. Luke had never been shy about wanting to leave. "There's something I didn't expect to come out of your mouth."

"Witty comments. Something I *did* expect to come out of yours."

Fresh into town, and he was already drawing the snappy from her. *Settle down.*

Luke settled on the stool in the stall across from her and tossed his hat five feet. It landed on a post, and he winked at her. "I—"

"—don't miss." She finished the statement with him, words she'd heard him say numerous times, primarily referring to his shot.

Keeping the flow of milk going, she stole a look at him. He hadn't changed, apart from having gained an air of ruggedness, which she supposed was what being a Texas Ranger did to a man. It grew the gruffness along with the cockiness.

He situated the pail and began milking. The grimace she'd seen when she'd patted him, returned.

"You don't have to help," she said. "It can't feel good for your shoulder."

"The shoulder's fine."

Arching a brow, she emptied her pail into one of the cans on the cart in the middle aisle and moved to the cow roped next to Luke. She squeezed back-to-back with him, careful to maintain several inches of space between them.

"I take it your father's not doing well, since he's not helping?" he asked.

Mary glanced back, gaze hooking onto Luke's.

He must have read the question in her eyes. "Grace writes me long letters."

She wondered how many lines in those letters had been dedicated to telling her news. "It takes all his energy to shuffle around. When he does, he gets out of breath. The doctor thinks there's a separate issue aside from the achy joints."

Luke stopped milking and stared at her.

"Don't look at me like that."

"What?" His eyes held a knowing, despite his pretense of ignorance.

"You're pitying me."

"Heaven forbid."

She issued a glare meant to subdue his mockery and returned her attention to milking. Behind her, Luke remained still and quiet.

"Are you going to work or not?" she asked.

Five seconds later, Mary heard milk shoot into his pail. She finished milking her cow before he finished with his, though she'd started later, and settled next to the last cow.

Scuffling sounded, and Mary jerked around. Luke pushed against the antsy cow and mumbled something she couldn't make out.

"How you doing over there?" she asked.

"Milking a cow is more intimidating than facing down six guns."

A boy who'd idolized the Rangers and left to claim his adventure wasn't intimidated by milking a cow. Her response rose, unbridled. "I suppose that makes me braver than you."

"Think about those words next time it thunders."

Five years he'd been gone, but they'd slipped into their customary repartee as if they'd practiced every day. She hid her smile as he emptied his pail and snatched his hat from the hook.

She could think of only one reason he delayed going home—other than making up for scaring her and almost setting the barn on fire. "Go home to your family. Paul doesn't bite."

His smile grew in mischief as he leaned back against a post. "Not like you."

"Don't hassle me, and I wouldn't have to bite."

17

Cool spring air snuck through the open front doors, stinging her chapped hands. She shivered, the wet fabric across her middle rubbing against her singed skin. She had good reason to bite tonight.

She glanced sideways at Luke. Light gleamed off the metal of his six shooters. She'd never forget the first time he wore them to church, a fifteen-year-old with too much to prove. When Paul had realized the bulge under Luke's jacket had been guns and not a Bible, he'd dragged his brother out during the middle of the sermon. They'd all learned the truth of sibling rivalry, not from the morning's text of Joseph and his brothers, but from the Thomas brothers' demonstration.

Stifling a yawn, she swatted the Jersey on the side. "You're done, girl."

Luke took the pail from her and emptied the milk into the third can. He checked to make sure the lid was secure before pulling the cart toward the door. When she tried to take the handle from him, he resisted.

"Your shoulder—"

"Is fine."

Carrying the lantern, she walked ahead the forty feet to the springhouse and opened the door. The trickle of the creek soothed like a lullaby.

"Let me." She nudged Luke aside and hopped into the back of the cart, not wanting him to lift the eighty pound cans when he was on the mend. She'd trained her body to shift the loads the several feet from cart to trough.

"How many times do I have to tell you I'm fine?" He snatched her around the waist and set her on the ground as if she'd had Grace's delicate figure instead of a sturdy one fit for a milkmaid.

He finished unloading the cans into the troughs. "Seems like yesterday."

She'd been nine the summer he'd worked at the dairy.

"What's this?" Luke pawed the ground with his boot, and she held the lantern closer.

A string of yellow honeysuckle spread across the back of the springhouse floor. She picked up the vine and breathed in the sugary scent. "First blooms of the season." She wound the twelve-inch strand around her wrist twice and tucked the ends together. Papa must have tracked in the vine earlier.

Yawning again, she moved toward the door. As interesting as it had been, this reunion had to end. She stalked across the yard toward the house where Papa likely was already sleeping.

"Good to see you again, Luke." She called the words over her shoulder, waving.

"Sorry for the surprise."

She turned at the door. "A surprise from you isn't a surprise at all."

He swung onto his horse. "Everyone needs a good surprise now and then."

Spoken like a Texas Ranger. She opened the door.

"'Night D—Mary."

She grinned. That Luke had stopped himself in the middle of her nickname was a surprise to beat all others. Maybe he'd grown up a bit while he was away.

CHAPTER THREE

Luke rode thirty seconds before turning to survey the now dark barn and the soft glow of light in the front window of the house. He scanned the shadows around the barn, the house, the springhouse, the trees. The homestead was wrapped in stillness, but if he stared long enough, maybe he'd see something like he'd thought he had before. In his exhausted state, he couldn't recall how convincing that initial movement had been.

Seeing things. Next, he'd be hearing things. Or worse, thinking things—the kind of things that had entered his mind after dousing Mary in water and taking her in, curves and all. A man didn't need thoughts like that to distract him.

Five years hadn't seemed like a long time while he'd been on the move in Texas, but judging by the changes in Mary, five years had been a tick shy of eternity. The rounded face of a child had slimmed into that of a woman, and other round things had . . . become rounder.

Lock it up, Thomas.

He was in Pine Creek for one reason. *Only* one reason.

He turned from the Smith land and kept Gabriel at a walk. No more delaying. Time to face the place where Father's voice haunted the barn and Paul's voice rang out all too real.

Luke's mother would fuss over him when she discovered he'd been wounded. Paul would look at him with that resentful glare that could kill a man if aimed right. They were equally skilled at aiming, Paul with his glare, and Luke with his guns.

And Grace would shoot her peacemaking skills at them both.

Luke directed Gabriel across the east pasture and down the ravine that led to the old fire pit where he and the boys had carried out their midnight roasts. Gabriel shook his head, let out a breath and increased his pace as he meandered the ridgeline. Night cloaked the view of the Thomas ranch, but Luke sensed the quiet life, the simplicity of the place. The hominess. Those things were good for Paul, his mother, Grace. They thrived on the establishment of home and all that it meant. Luke thrived on adventure.

He followed the western pasture up to the homestead and dismounted between the barn and the house. Light shone through the crack of the barn doors, and a faint whistle indicated Paul at work. Luke strode toward the house. He'd put up Gabriel in a bit.

The porch boards squeaked his presence as he crossed to the door and knocked. A small pair of boots lay haphazardly next to the door. He strained to remember the age of his niece, Helen. Four?

Footsteps sounded beyond the door. He prayed for it to be Grace. She admired him in a way every brother envied. Not that he'd proved worthy of that admiration, but Grace was generous like that. Loving. Kind-hearted . . .

The door opened. Grace squealed and leapt into his arms.

. . . enthusiastic.

He clenched his jaw, holding in the grunt that ripped through his chest. The tenderness of those wounds robbed his breath.

He pushed her back and lifted her hands from around his neck. Though her face had matured, she remained slender, dainty. He couldn't help comparing Grace's petite frame to Mary's full-figured one. "More beautiful. Just like I knew you'd be."

Her grin shone through her tears. "What are you doing

21

here? How long can you stay? Forever?" She moved to hug him again.

He shifted, letting the impact of her embrace hit his right side, and put his arm around her.

"Grace?" His mother swept around the doorway from the kitchen. Her eyes connected with his, and she stopped. She lifted floured hands to her mouth before letting out a laugh and running the rest of the hallway. She flew into his other side.

He staggered back. "Whoa."

Something about his tone must have alarmed them, for they pulled away, smiles gone.

"What's wrong?" His mother's gaze raked his body.

He needed to keep this simple; otherwise his mother might set foot on a path of worry that would veil his entire visit. "I'm recovering from an injury."

Grace's eyes widened. "As in, you fell off your horse?"

He cocked his head, reached out, and tweaked Grace on the nose.

She swatted his hand. "I'm too old for that. Answer the question."

His eyes shifted from his sister to his mother, who clasped her hands in front of her chest, rubbing, churning them.

He worked for a steady expression. "I was shot."

Grace frowned and threw herself at him for another hug. This time, he put his arm out to stop her. "The left shoulder's tender."

She drew back. "Oh."

"Grace, go get Paul." His mother nudged his sister. "Paul will be thrilled to see you."

Debatable. Paul wore his commitment to the ranch as a badge of honor and lorded it over Luke. After Father had died, things had gone south.

Really south. And not just figuratively. Luke's fascination with the Rangers had grown into an obsession, a vision for his future. Paul couldn't swallow it.

Luke turned to smile at his mother but froze at the apprehension in her eyes.

"Shot?" Her whispered question brought back the image of his father ten years ago. The simple wound in his foot had become infected.

"I'm fine. Look at me." He'd have to hide the way his shoulder burned when overused or bumped wrong. "The doctor told me I could travel."

He'd not wanted to come home and dredge up the past for his mother, but Captain Finch had demanded he pay a visit to his family, recuperate, and let the questions concerning the Fowler arrest and all that had gone wrong dissipate. Questions didn't dissipate. They built, like thunderclouds, until they broke loose overhead and drowned you. He should be in Texas to defend himself.

"Luke?"

The gentle voice from inside the door drew his attention. His brother's wife, Abigail, stood at the base of the stairs, the same charming expression on her face as when he'd left. Figured that his brother would sweep a sweet girl off her feet. No one else could put up with Paul's intensity.

Abigail moved forward and hugged him. "Welcome home. We've missed you."

He didn't doubt her genuineness, only her claim of *we* implied his brother.

Three times in five years his brother had attached a note to the bottom his mother's letter. A few stiff, awkward sentences.

Luke's mother took his cheek in her hand, and he felt like a mud-caked boy again. "Ma." His brows furrowed.

"Oh, stop. You'll always be my boy." She rubbed his whiskers. "Don't they believe in clean faces in Texas?"

"It's not exactly comfortable to lift my arm."

Dogs barked from across the yard. He spun around before Gus and Maggie took out his legs, but it wasn't Gus and Maggie that bounded up the steps with Paul jogging behind. These mutts were unfamiliar.

"I can't believe it." Paul wrapped him in a hug gentle enough to convince Luke that Grace had mentioned his wounds.

Luke pulled back, looked into Paul's eyes, and waited for the initial welcome to be replaced with something like *the prodigal has returned* or *look who took time from his important work to visit family*.

Two collies turned circles around his ankles, noses riding up and down his boots and pants. "Who are these newcomers?" Luke sidestepped the activity.

"Couple friends we picked up that love ranch life." Paul shooed the dogs. "Tripp and Kat, go lay down."

That loved ranch life. Implying, Luke didn't. Growing up, he'd sweated over this land and stock as much as Paul had.

"Come inside." Grace took his hand and pulled him across the threshold, across one season of life back into another.

He dug deep and claimed gratitude: for being alive after having bullets rip into him; for getting to see his family and visit his father's grave. And even for being able to face the memories resting in Pine Creek. Luke Thomas wasn't a hider, no matter that being here felt like walking back into a life he wasn't meant to live. Like hanging up his guns and settling down.

Settled was for old people in their rocking chairs on the porch. For new families setting up their homes. Not for twenty-four-year-olds who strapped guns on each morning and fought for justice.

"Apple or cherry?" Grace rushed ahead into the kitchen.

His stomach growled. "Both. And add huckleberry."

"No luck there."

He took his chair at the table, the ladder back with the

broken slat from when he and Paul had wrestled Christmas morning of '77. "Gus, Maggie."

Rustling sounded from around the corner. Maggie limped into the kitchen. Luke held out his hands. "Hey, girl."

Gus knocked Maggie to the side and reached Luke first. Luke ruffled his ears, and when Maggie caught up, did the same to her.

Paul sat across the table and ran a hand through wavy brown hair that seemed thinner on the top. Weather and hard work had aged his face, unless the lines across his brow were from the intense concentration he was paying Luke. Abigail pulled a chair close to her husband and snuggled her hand in the crook of Paul's arm. All Paul had sought in life had been marriage and the ranch.

What other people hunted after should be their own business.

Paul nodded toward Luke. "Tell us about those injuries."

Grace set a plate loaded with two pieces of pie in front of Luke. He studied the goodness to avoid meeting Paul's gaze. "I was apprehending some criminals."

"I could have guessed that."

Luke didn't want to offer more and get into the leave of absence or the investigation into his actions.

Grace sat between the brothers and swiped her finger through the cherry filling on Luke's plate. She licked it with an exaggerated slurping noise. Thank heavens for Grace, whose playful sweetness was keeping this awkward conversation from tipping out of control.

And where was his mother? She'd not followed the family in to the kitchen.

"How have things been around here?" Luke asked.

"Over east of Wenatchee on the other side of the Columbia they're having issues with rustling." Paul rapped his knuckles against the table. "If any of that comes our way, I'll dish out justice with a vengeance."

Truth to that. Paul and vengeance were inseparable. Luke swallowed his bite.

Grace pulled the pins from her light brown hair and fingered through the mess. "I don't like what you do."

He'd read that line at least once in each of her letters. "It's terrible, isn't it? Keep peace. Work justice. Serve others." He pulled his plate away from Grace's greedy finger.

"That's not what I meant." Grace lunged across the table, snatched his fork from his hand, and licked it. "I hope you can't be disarmed as easily."

If Mary had pulled that stunt, he'd have pasted his plate on the middle of her face, but the pie was too good to waste teasing Grace. And he wasn't fifteen anymore.

His mother whisked into the kitchen. "Have you eaten yet?"

"I'm trying." He retrieved his fork from Grace.

"If my son eats like he used to, I'd best get cooking." She opened the stove and shoved in two pieces of wood.

"How long you staying?" Paul finally spit out the question Luke had been expecting from the moment he'd set eyes on his brother.

"Don't know exactly." Not longer than necessary.

"Through the summer? You can't have traveled so far for only a week." Grace scooted her chair closer and laid her hand on his arm.

"I didn't sail from China. The Union Pacific takes me all the way to Umatilla, and then it's a day's boat ride up the Columbia to Wenatchee and two day's horseback to Pine Creek. Or one if you have a mount used to traveling long distances." Luke shifted his gaze to Paul. "Maybe you all should visit sometime."

For as much as Paul talked about family, valued family, and breathed family life like air, he'd hardly written. Unlike Grace, whose letters Luke had answered page for page.

His mother circled around behind and placed a hand on his good shoulder. "We'll take you for as long as we can."

"No we won't," Grace said. "We'll take you longer."

"How about you?" He elbowed Grace. "You've been back, what, four weeks?"

"And I don't plan to leave ever again."

Convincing her to study under a French seamstress in Seattle had taken some creative letter writing on his part, but with sewing gifts like hers, she'd needed to find a mentor beyond what Pine Creek could offer.

"You're all the more better for studying with Mademoiselle Froufrou," Luke said. "And if I were you, I'd consider staying where your gifts have a chance to shine." Nothing shone in Pine Creek, save unwanted memories. "What do you plan to do here? Sew outfits for the cows?"

"I see Texas hasn't dimmed your wit." She rose and poured herself a cup of tea. "I want to open a shop in town."

He waited for her to laugh at her joke. A town the size of Pine Creek didn't need a dress shop. Rod's Mercantile carried pre-sewed items for the families who didn't sew their own clothes. "You're not kidding?"

"Why should I be? Mary says it's a good idea." Grace smiled at him over her cup, as if she knew a comment about Mary might draw his reaction. "I don't need to make a fortune. There's plenty of work with the ranch. Unlike some" —she swatted him on the back of the head—"I'm content to live a simple life at home."

Luke's bite lodged in his throat. Despite the shine in Grace's eyes, her words sounded influenced by Paul.

"Grace is right. Plenty of work here." Paul leaned back in his seat and folded his arms across his chest. He opened his mouth to speak, but Abigail cleared her throat.

"We'll catch up more in the morning. You must be exhausted." Abigail stood and pulled on Paul's hand. "Helen will be thrilled to meet her uncle. We talk about you every day."

Luke raised his brows.

"Don't look so surprised. You're one of us." Paul's four

words should have offered acceptance but came off more like a sentence from a judge. He placed his hand on Abigail's back and guided her toward the stairs. He turned back, and with a tight grin, nodded once. "Welcome home."

Two words had never carried so much weight.

CHAPTER FOUR

Stars spilled across the center of the sky, lighting Mary's way from the woods into Clifton, a town an hour and fifteen minutes to the southwest of Pine Creek. Laughter from the Gold Mine Inn interrupted the otherwise quiet street. She slid from Holly in front of the establishment that served as an inn, saloon, restaurant, local gathering place . . . and who knew what else.

Don't think about what else.

Papa didn't know about her performances at the Gold Mine the past three Saturdays. When she earned enough money, she'd tell him. The dairy's loss of business, combined with Papa's declining health and talk of selling, had required her to dig for a creative source of income. She'd not had to dig far. Since leaving her musical studies in Portland last August, she'd mourned the loss of opportunity to perform.

The Gold Mine offered an audience and a supplemental income. But it was the nature of that audience that had her not wanting to tell Papa.

He'd want to know.

She shook her head at the whisper of her conscience as she secured Holly in front of the two-story building. By keeping information from Papa that would cause him to worry, she was helping him. She'd been the cause of enough hurt in his life already.

She gulped one last breath of fresh air before plunging through the double doors into the pungent odors of alcohol, sweat, and musk. The hinges squeaked, announcing her presence and drawing looks that spanned her body length. She dismissed the frankness. The men worked in mines and lumber camps twelve hours a day, six days a week, cut off from the softer gender, and their eyes betrayed their loneliness. She could put up with rude manners if doing so allowed her a stage on which to perform and a few extra dollars for the dairy. Contrary to what most might imagine, the rough crowd had offered appreciation and respect for her abilities.

Simon, called Old Si, dusted his overalls, set aside his mug, and pushed from his chair. Beneath a yellowed beard, his lips formed a grin. "Been hummin' one of your tunes all week. Something from that Pach man, I think." He tipped his straw hat, sending a few loose strands of straw floating to the ground. A chestnut-sized hole on the side offered a window to wavy, gray hair that looked coarse as a horse's tail. "Got that there piano pushed out and ready. Even brought out a small pillow for your . . ." His face flushed. "You know."

"That was thoughtful of you."

Sarah Jane, the middle-aged proprietress, glanced up from serving customers at the bar and greeted Mary with her customary nod and a twitch of a smile. Rhett snatched his glass from Sarah Jane and swaggered toward Mary in a way that warned her he'd probably worked harder at drinking this evening than he'd worked in the mine all day.

Suppressing a groan, she turned to the piano and tried to look busy by smoothing her skirts and dusting off the piano keys.

Circling to her side, Rhett came close enough she could count the cracks in his dried lips. "That pillow wasn't Simon's idea." He puffed his chest. "Was mine."

Oh, heavens. She barely restrained herself from rolling her eyes.

Rhett's attempts to be suave annoyed with the strength of an inharmonious chord. His bushy hair framed a youthful face, which he'd not bothered to wash after a dusty day below the surface of the earth, and the whites around his pale eyes were yellow-tinged like eggs after she used the beater on them.

His gaze traveled down her body. "Wanted to make sure we kept that backside of yours nice and soft."

Her spine stiffened. This had gone beyond eye-rolling annoyance. "That's not appropriate." His boot toed hers, and she squared her jaw. "The comment, that is, not the consideration of my comfort." Gratitude had a way of appeasing people, and she'd use her manners to make up for the lack of his.

He squinted at her, and she refused to show weakness by looking away.

Stepping back, he crossed his arms. "You're right. I apologize." He returned to the counter, where she assumed he'd appease his unending thirst for liquor.

Confidence solidified, she exhaled, smiled, and sat on the piano stool. Papa had no need to worry about her. Not that he was worried. How could he be when he didn't know?

Mary lifted her hands to the keyboard, and the room hushed. She relished the anticipation. Rachmaninoff's melancholic tones pushed from her fingers, each note settling her further into the joy of sharing music with others.

As much as music had been kin to her heartbeat, she'd wept when she'd left the dairy for Portland. Then again, when Papa had called her home, she'd wept to leave the ornate concert halls. She wanted Portland and Pine Creek. The dairy and the piano. At the Gold Mine, she'd found the balance. An audience, applause, and a home not more than a horseback ride away.

After Rachmaninoff, she played a Beethoven sonata, and following that, several pieces by Grieg. Schubert, Bach, and an etude by the contemporary, Chopin, finished her concert.

After Mary's performance, Sarah Jane shoved an envelope into her hands. "Here you go, Miss Mary. These men sure do like it when you come."

Sarah Jane, a woman of many *almosts*, almost smiled, same as she almost complimented Mary every week in a vague way that started with 'these men." Same as she almost looked content, in a resigned sort of way. But the woman couldn't mask the discouragement and weariness that forced its message past tight expressions and slumped shoulders.

"Thank you. May I come back next week?"

"'Course you're coming back next week." Old Si pushed between Sarah Jane and her, taking hold of her elbow. "We've come to expect it. Now I be escorting you to your horse."

Mary laid her hand on Simon's. "You're a fine gentleman. Thank you."

"Simon!" The call barreled across the room.

Old Si grunted. "Maybe I won't be escorting you. That man's got an argument to pick with me ev'ry time I turn around." He nodded goodbye, then turned toward the voice. "I'm comin', you old coot."

These were harmless people. Rough around the edges, rowdy sometimes, but not dangerous. True, some were misguided . . . those who drank too much or . . . she blocked the thought but couldn't stop her gaze from lingering at the foot of the stairs where a scantily-dressed woman flirted with a miner.

Mary fingered the envelope and made for the door. Her purpose here wasn't to condone behavior but to use her gifts of music and earn money.

Leaving the stuffy room behind, she pushed through the doors onto the deserted boardwalk. The chill of the mountain stung her throat. She'd have to dig into her pack and pull out a blanket for the ride home.

"There you are."

She gasped and spun around, preparing herself for Rhett's unwanted attention, but Matthew Bridges stood there instead, hands in his pockets, grinning.

"Matthew."

She threw her arms around him. His stiff hug exemplified that quiet disposition of his that made him come off polite, albeit aloof. He released her and stepped back.

She poked him in the arm. "Shy about embracing a neighbor and childhood friend?"

He flushed. "You look fresh as the spring."

"A compliment. That makes up for the bad hug."

A neatly trimmed beard covered Matthew's square jaw. Of the boys in the schoolhouse, he'd been the one who'd consistently combed his hair and washed his face. He'd looked the part of small town royalty, not surprising since his father owned and operated the largest lumber company in the county.

"How are things at the camp? I haven't seen you for a month." Twice a week she meandered around the backside of the mountain and up the half-cleared hillside to deliver milk to the lumber camp.

"Father's got me working hard." He ducked his head. "Been staying down at the south quarters." Matthew's dependable, hardworking, and quiet ways had made him a favorite childhood friend. "You performed wonderfully tonight."

She smiled. Two compliments. Luke hadn't thought to offer any. He'd chosen the welcome home surprise. The burn-your-barn-down approach.

And why was she thinking of Luke?

Matthew shoved his hands into his pockets and raised his gaze back to hers. The light from the Gold Mine shone through the windows, illuminating his soft expression. He had eyes that looked as if they understood, the welcoming eyes of a gentleman who encouraged a woman to trust. Matthew's kindness paired with Luke's adventuresome nature would issue the perfect specimen to fall in love with.

"What brings you to Clifton tonight?"

"Some of the boys wanted to hear the new piano

player, and I wanted to make sure they didn't get into any trouble."

If someone as proper as Matthew could enjoy an evening with friends at the Gold Mine, then for sure, she wouldn't let doubts of propriety prey on her opportunity here.

"Papa doesn't know I'm playing here to make extra money."

Matthew rubbed behind his neck and shook his head. "Mary . . ."

"It's only temporary."

He put a finger to his lips, and she took it as a promise to stay quiet.

"Thank you."

"Can I see you home?"

How like Matthew to ask. "That's not necessary. You know my independence."

"I know your mischief." He grinned. "Listen . . ." Shoving his hat over his blond curls, he backed down the steps in front of the Gold Mine. "Father's wanting to expand. I know things have been hard with the dairy. Selling to him might be an option, you know, if things get worse."

"Things aren't that bad." She might be struggling to keep up with the work, given Papa's inability to help every day, but they had the help of neighbors and the town. And, besides, this had been Mama's dream, and one didn't sell a dream.

He shifted his feet. "Keep us in mind." Backing into the darkness, he unwound the reins of his horse. "I have to catch up to my crew. Good to see you, Dairy Mary."

If she and Papa sold the dairy, she wouldn't be Dairy Mary. As much as she'd hated that nickname as a child, it was who she was. The name went along with her home. Without Dairy in front of her name, she'd just be Mary.

And who was Mary?

The one who'd lived when Mama had died.

CHAPTER FIVE

They'd killed the fattened calf for him. At least that's how it felt to Luke.

A hundred townsfolk swarmed the Thomases' yard, and they'd brought enough food to make it a feast worthy of the prodigal son's return. Paul played the role of the elder brother with ease.

One would think fifteen hundred miles would be enough time to prepare for a visit home. It hadn't been.

He wiped the sweat from his brow and focused on the game. Thirty minutes of playing bat and ball with the children had saved him from the questions that had assailed him since he'd set foot in church that morning. He turned the dense, cloth ball in his hand and narrowed his gaze at little Rebecca Randolph, whose determined stance, wild eyes, and status as the only girl allowed to play with the boys, reminded him of another time he'd pitched to a brown-haired girl with an overdose of spunk.

You're home for one reason, Thomas.

He'd had to remind himself of that every time that spunky girl—woman—bounded into his thoughts.

He tossed the ball, and Rebecca smacked it over the fence into the pasture. Eli Pearson scrambled after it amidst pleads from his teammates to hurry. Rebecca pumped her arms and sped back to her original place near the oak at the west corner of the barn. "Home safe," she yelled.

The innocent cry wrapped fingers around Luke's heart and yanked. *Home* and *safe* weren't words that belonged in the same sentence.

Luke adjusted his hat. "Nice smack."

Rebecca smiled up at him, chest heaving for breath. He waved to the boys who looked defeated, and made his way to a shaded table where Mrs. Lunsford was serving mint tea.

The elderly woman winked as he approached and waved a newspaper clipping in front of his face. "Wonderful news. Simply wonderful. We're all so proud of you."

He should never have showed that article to his mother. She'd passed the clipping to each family as they'd arrived, and in two instances had shed tears at the smiles and congratulations others had offered. Was it any wonder he'd slipped off to play ball with the children?

Mrs. Lunsford picked up a glass and poured the tea. "What a hero we have here in our little Pine Creek."

She didn't know the falsehood of her statement, and if he pulled up his sleeve and showed her the scars on his arms, told her the story, the town would send him back to Texas before he could say *remember the Alamo.*

"It's all part of the job," he said.

"Not many of us have jobs that require us to be heroes."

The article had been published a year ago when he'd brought in the leader behind a ring of cattle thieves. By doing what he'd been hired to do, he'd landed in the newspaper. Ironic, since it had been clippings that had turned his attention to the Rangers in the first place. As a fascinated youth, he'd kept those stories in a box under his bed and read them daily. They didn't get old. Stuff happened in Texas. Good stuff. Justice. Adventure. Opportunity to be a better shot than you thought you could be. To be stronger than you were yesterday.

Opportunity to forget the past.

Mary strode by with a plate of food — not an opportunity to forget the past.

"When does the parade start? I think I know who'll be

leading the band." She tipped her head toward Cecily Reynolds, who'd been his mother's self-assigned assistant hostess that afternoon.

Mary marched on before he could spit out a response.

He stepped after her, but two barefoot boys darted in front of him, one wielding a stick in pursuit of the other. He pulled back to keep from tripping. The only thing that had changed about Pine Creek since he'd been gone, other than the hotel construction, was the amount of little ones running wild. These people had taken the commandment to multiply seriously.

"Used to be us." Barrett Clarke leaned against the porch post, a plate of food half gone.

With average height, average brown hair, and an above average personality, Barrett had been a friend worth hanging around when Paul wasn't demanding that Luke work. Though a few years older, Luke had experienced more camaraderie with him and Cam than with the boys his age.

Luke jutted his chin toward the two rowdies. "We weren't that wild."

"I wasn't. But you were, when Mary was chasing you." Barrett popped half a biscuit in his mouth and grinned.

Luke smirked and leaned back against the porch railing next to Barrett. The chaos of the gathering itched under his skin. From the moment he'd stepped into church that morning, a sense of obligation had mantled him, as if others expected him to express how much he'd missed Pine Creek and dreamed of the day he'd return.

"Uh-oh." Barrett took another bite of chicken and licked his fingers.

Luke's senses alerted, and he examined the crowd with a hand to his gun.

Barrett thumped him across the chest. "Hold the panic." He nodded toward the other end of the porch. "But the mayor looks like he's about to give a speech."

Johnston Brown straightened his suit coat and let out a

two-fingered whistle that silenced the crowd. Luke placed a hand across his belly to quell the sudden indigestion.

The mayor smiled at Luke. "I'll keep my comments short. First, on behalf of Pine Creek, welcome home."

Applause rippled through the yard, and Luke nodded his thanks.

"I'm sure you've many stories to share."

None that he cared to mete out. He hadn't done the things he'd done to bring glory to himself. They'd been the right things to do, not to mention, they'd been the things of his job. A job he prayed still existed.

"In turn, we've got some exciting things happening in Pine Creek. With the town expanding and new industries arriving, we find ourselves at an interesting crossroads. Your visit, I'm convinced, is not an accident. As our dear pulpit supply mentioned this morning"—Johnston directed a smile at Cam—"The Lord's purposes are beyond our understanding."

Barrett chuckled beneath his breath. "Johnston will seek to explain them anyway."

"I would be so bold as to say that your reason for being here is to help Pine Creek move forward into the future with confidence." Johnston looked over the people, an implication of ownership in his broad smile.

Luke elbowed Barrett. "He doesn't know what he's talking about."

"You're the man, Luke," Barrett whispered, imitating Johnston. "We need you."

Turning a glare on Barrett, Luke straightened. The last thing Pine Creek needed was him.

"In the coming days, I hope we sit down for some long conversations as the town explores new opportunities." Johnston smiled at him. "Once again, welcome."

The people applauded, and Luke struggled for breath as he ran a hand through his hair. The attention stifled him more than the summer sun on the Texas plains.

"Don't look now, but here comes Claire, marching across the yard wearing her determined look." Barrett's eyes honed in on his wife.

"Does she have an undetermined look?"

"I'll let you know if I ever see one."

Snagging a chunk of chicken from Barrett's plate, Luke relaxed and watched Claire waltz across the yard, book in one hand and dragging Grace with the other. He'd met Barrett's wife that morning, and after ten minutes of conversation, had pegged her as the most sophisticated woman in Pine Creek. As if her vocabulary and diction weren't enough, her getup, which included black and white flounces and a high ruffled neckline, had sealed his conclusion.

No competition from Mary who sported dirt on her dress, hay in her hair, and mischief in her smile. Yeah, she was beautiful without the stuffiness of sophistication.

Claire dropped Grace's hand and thrust the book at Barrett. "This," she said, modeling her teaching voice, "is what Grace is going to sew for me. She designed it herself."

"I knew you were up to something." Barrett put his arm around his wife and rested his hand on her shoulder.

"Bear." Claire glared at his messy fingers. "You know I'm not accomplished enough with laundry to remove grease stains. Kindly remove your hand."

Kindly remove. Luke made a note to try that phrase on an outlaw.

"That's no fun." Barrett shoved his hands into his pockets, his pretended frown coming off more like a pout.

No man needed an expression like that, even a man so in love he'd lost his reason, and Barrett and Claire had clearly lost all rationality.

"And see here?" Claire pointed at the drawing. "The outer skirt splits and forms an inverse v from the waist to the ankles. The top layer will be pale blue, like the sky, and underneath will be a juniper color."

The enticing look Claire sent Barrett earned her a kiss

on the cheek. This lovesick behavior was why Luke had hunkered into his job. Texas didn't bat eyes at him.

He peered over Claire's shoulder at the detailed sketch. Grace's patience and precision showed in each line. Admiration swelled his chest. He put his arm around her shoulders. "Impressive work."

The grin she sent him was warm enough to melt snow. He loved that girl and her kindhearted spirit, her love for beauty.

He excused himself, claiming the need for dessert, and set his dish on the porch. Mary had disappeared, and for all he knew, she'd decided to take a nap on Grace's bed, gone home to tend her cows, climbed a tree somewhere, found someone to lecture . . .

A small body tackled his legs from behind, and a tender hand slipped into his. Sweet Helen's. Luke's back went rigid. He didn't do handholding.

His niece smiled up at him. "I had cake."

"Sounds delicious." Luke pulled his hand from Helen's grubby fingers and tousled her thick brown hair.

"Do you like my hair? I'm growing it to look like Grace's."

A tangle stuck up on top, and Luke tried to smooth it down.

Helen reached for his hand again and rubbed her fingers over his calluses. "But I want my hands to look like yours."

Luke pulled his hand back and fisted it. "You don't want calluses. They're not feminine."

"What's fenimime?"

"Feminine." He repeated the word slowly. "It means ladylike."

"Mary says rough spots are the gift of hard work."

Mary said a lot of things. He could fill a dime novel with the list of all the bizarre things she'd said to him. "It's not conventional for a woman to want calluses."

"What's conventional?" Helen grabbed both his hands and climbed his legs to turn a somersault, something he'd seen her do with Paul.

He tightened his hands on Helen's and helped her flip. When her feet hit the ground, he pulled his hands free and shoved them in his pockets. "Conventional means usual or normal."

"Grandma calls Mary special, but she won't tell me why."

Luke didn't need to engage a four-year-old in an analytical discussion about what made Mary special.

Helen trailed him to the desserts and pinched off a bite of piecrust while he measured the assortment. The women from church had baked as if he'd come back from the dead, not Texas. He could hear Mary saying, *same thing.*

Stop hearing Mary, thinking of Mary, looking for Mary.

Helen ran off after a boy with floppy red hair, and Luke allowed his hands to relax. He needed an open-range moment away from the crowd that had made him feel like his homecoming would save Pine Creek from natural disaster. The barn's wind vane hailed like a steeple, and he aimed his steps toward the structure with the white peeling paint. He'd find peace by his horse.

The smell of fried chicken that lingered near the house gave way to animal sweat and soiled hay. Contrary to the sunshine that had warmed the yard, the interior of the barn was refreshing with its damp, cool air.

"Fed up with your admirers?"

His head jerked back, and he peered toward the ceiling. Hopes of peace faded. Mary sat on the rafter above, legs dangling back and forth, probably swinging in time to Beethoven.

"Why are you hiding in the barn?"

Parties like this were ideal for a person like Mary, who loved chattering with friends.

"I needed a break." She scooted to the edge of the beam

41

as if she might jump.

"What are you doing?"

"Coming down."

He gauged the distance between the beam and the floor. "Not wise." But not surprising. He'd seen her fly from swings, wagons, and fences, but this was a little much. "Come down the way a normal person would. By using the ladder."

"That's not how I got up."

He took a fraction of a moment to guess at how she'd gotten up but decided it wasn't worth the mental energy. This was Mary, not Grace, meaning her ways were beyond understanding, like the Lord's. Was that sacrilege? "Suit yourself."

He turned toward Gabriel, waiting for the thud, wondering if he'd have to carry her to the wagon while she fumed about the inconvenience of a busted ankle. That was the problem with Mary; *one* of the problems. She was unstoppable. Mary's mind didn't budge anymore than his Colt missed.

A rustle of skirts sounded, and then soft footsteps. He spun around. Mary was climbing down the ladder. So she could be swayed once in a while.

His Colt still didn't miss.

"How long until—?" She slipped. Her dress caught between the wall and the ladder and ripped.

He rushed forward, and she fell onto him, knocking them to the ground. Her elbow pushed his left shoulder into the hard dirt, and he groaned at the grinding sensation in his wound.

She jumped off and knelt beside him, her hand reaching for his shoulder before he could shift out of range. Tender fingers prodded beneath his collar bone.

He brushed her hand off. No one coddled him. "Number fifty-three."

"What?" She twisted her braid and tucked it inside the collar of her dress.

"The times you've landed on me . . . from trees, swings" — he scrolled the memories — "the roof of the school."

She chuckled. "I can't help it if you're underfoot."

Dogs got underfoot, not people.

Her hand extended, but he shook his head. "I'll help myself. I don't need you tugging on my arm." And he definitely didn't need another handholding episode.

Crossing her arms, she raised a brow. "Self-sufficiency never led anywhere good, unless you count Texas."

He stood. "Texas is definitely counted as good. A huge chunk of good."

Smirking, she circled behind him and brushed the dirt from his shirt. Her hands tickled the small of his back, and he sucked in a breath and straightened. Though quick and efficient, her movements roused thoughts better left latent.

"I'm serious, Luke."

He pulled away from her swiping and faced her. "When have we had a serious conversation?"

She stepped back as if slapped.

His loose cannon of a tongue had struck again. Maybe he needed to switch from reacting to thinking first. "I didn't—"

"Forget it." She waved her hand. "I know you don't take anything I say seriously. Our rapport is built on your teasing me."

"*My* teasing?" He only served back what she initiated.

She bunched her mouth in a way that returned him to her pigtail days, and in those days, that look meant her fists were about to pummel. "Should I duck?"

With an exaggerated huff, she flung her arms out before bringing them down hard against her sides.

A smart Ranger knew when to placate. "What's the serious thing on your mind?"

Mary's mouth gaped.

Yeah, he liked to be the one doing the surprising, not the other way around.

"It's nothing too serious."

"All right." He sauntered toward the door, his hands reaching near his guns out of habit whenever he left a building.

"Except I don't like you coming home just to get Grace's hopes up. Your mother's, too."

The words hit him in the back, right where a lawman hates to be hit, and he turned on her.

She advanced toward him, purpose in her even stare. "Only to ride into the sunset whenever you feel strong enough, though considering how weak you are, that might be awhile."

She didn't expect to get away with calling him weak, did she? "I was weak the first days after getting shot." He leveled his gaze at her. "I was weak when the blood was staining my shirt. Now I'm sore. Not weak."

"I'll say."

He fought for patience and tried to picture Grace, not Mary. A brother endured a sister's frustration because he loved her. "Being a Ranger is a sacrifice. For everyone. I get that."

He hadn't made his decision on a whim. He'd planned his career for years, talked about it with his father, had been upfront to his family. "My mother and Grace know what that means."

"They certainly know what it means to be left behind."

Forget being brotherly. He marched into her space and stopped inches from her. "You left your father for your music. Don't pass judgment on me for leaving my family for what I love."

"I didn't want to leave. You did. And I came back as soon as my father needed me."

Faithful Mary, ever defending others. Loyal to Pine Creek and loyal to his sister, to the point of taking Luke's actions as a personal affront. It wasn't as if he'd left her.

"God has used me to bring justice and peace into

situations that were chaotic and sometimes bloody."

"Bringing God into the conversation. How can I argue with that?" Mary tipped her head. "The honorable Luke Thomas has the Lord on his side."

"You can wager on that." He'd poured himself into prayer in order to survive the loneliness, pressure, and risks that went with the life of a Ranger. "My connection with the Lord has only deepened since becoming a Ranger."

"Someone give this guy a medal."

Someone kiss this girl silent.

"Seems about right," his brother said.

Luke jerked his gaze from Mary and spun to face his brother.

Paul was propped against the doorway of the barn, arms crossed. "Don't think I don't know what you're doing."

Luke's gaze snuck to Mary's. They were standing too close. He scooted back, casual as possible. Did Paul think he'd kissed her?

Paul offered a wry smile. "I know why you've come home."

Oh. He'd not been talking of Mary.

Luke's chest heaved with his exhale. "What, to visit my family?" His peripheral vision caught Mary adding more distance between them.

Paul pushed off the doorjamb. "To pretend to care."

His brother had a way of sinking verbal daggers with an even-toned voice.

"Having other dreams doesn't mean I don't care," Luke said. "Don't blame me for wanting more from life than you."

Paul stomped across the remaining distance between them. Standing several inches taller than Luke, he made a show of looking down. "You belittle me."

Luke drew back, aware that Mary stood awkwardly to the side. "I didn't mean for it to sound —"

"Like running a ranch and loving a wife is nothing?"

A muscle ticked on the back of Luke's neck. "It's

something." Something temporary, a goal that had its end in this world. Luke kept his eyes on the permanent, the unseen realities of truth, justice.

"Mary, girl?" Mary's father shuffled into the barn. "I'm feeling good enough to join the milking tonight. Are you ready to go?"

Mary's attention swung between Luke and Paul. "More than ready."

Luke snagged one more glance from her as she rushed toward her father. Accusation draped her eyes. What had his leaving done to her?

"It's time you stayed put." Paul stepped in front of him, cutting off his view of Mary.

"What's so hard about understanding why I do what I do?"

"Why do you do it?" Paul shot the question.

They'd had this conversation before. Too many times. "I like the adventure, and I like serving people. It's that simple."

"Nothing's simple with you." Paul yanked the pitch fork from its hook, stabbed it into the ground, and rested his elbow on the handle. "You do it because you've been running from this place since Father died."

"You can't believe that." Luke yanked the collar loose from his neck.

"Tell me why you're really here."

There was no way Luke was going to confess that his captain had issued him mandatory leave. "It was time."

"Time for what?" The fork scraped against a rock, and Paul grunted. He glanced up. "You're a grown man. Maybe it's time you find the courage to be honest. If not with me, at least with yourself."

CHAPTER SIX

Mary pulled the burnt cinnamon bread from the oven and cracked the kitchen window. Night air slipped in, cooling the heated room. The faint smell of the honeysuckle vine that crept along the back edge of the house mingled with the warm scent of the cinnamon.

Papa lumbered molasses-like into the room and sank into a chair. He'd pushed himself too hard.

"I don't like it," he said.

Running the tea towel over the lip of the mixing bowl, her gaze followed his to the blank section of the wall where her piano used to sit. Even with knickknacks, books, and oversized furniture cluttering the small house, the instrument's absence commandeered her attention.

"I miss hearing you play." Papa's short, thinning hair framed a narrow face.

"We didn't have a choice." Selling the piano to Rod's Mercantile had been like a knife to her heart. They'd done the same two other times when business was slim, and as soon as things had settled, they'd bought it back. "Rod says I can play any time. He's even given me a key." She smiled at Papa, needing him to know she could handle the adversity.

He grunted as he lifted his legs up to the footrest. "We did have a choice." He released a breath that was part sigh, part groan. "We *do* have a choice."

The choice to sell. Papa had uttered those thoughts too often this past winter as his health had declined. The strain that played around the edges of his tired eyes didn't fool her.

For all his discomfort, he was no closer to letting go of Mama's dream than she was. She saw it in the way he made it to the barn for every birth, finding strength to help, and in the way he kept up with each issue of *American Agriculturist*.

"We're struggling, not defeated," she said.

Papa's smile breeched the sheen of tears in his eyes. "That's my fighter."

He could warm her heart with the right words, calm her runaway thoughts with one look.

She settled into the cushioned chair beside Papa's. "Things will get better. They always do."

Mama's Bible sat on the three-legged side table, and Mary reached for it. Papa liked to see her reading scripture, and she liked to please him. Flipping through the thin pages, she looked at the underlining. Beside various passages, Mama had written the initials of people for whom she'd prayed. Mary knew she wouldn't see an 'M' scrawled with Mama's curlicue lettering, but her eyes betrayed reason and searched anyway.

"Mary." Papa's serious but gentle voice burrowed past her thoughts. "The Fledgling is closing."

She schooled her expression. The small mine west of town, a client for years, had slowed their operations six months ago, but she'd expected them to recover. She rose and stalked to the window. The half-moon crept over the mountains, large and yellow, seemingly close enough to chase down and grasp. "We have the lumber camp, and I hear Bridges wants to expand."

Papa joined her. "I don't like watching you bear this workload. When Mama and I set out . . ." He stopped for breath.

He and Mama had trudged over the mountains with three cows, a wagon load of possessions, and Mama's nine-year-old son, Jared. Mama had brought the vision to carry on her family's heritage as dairy farmers, and Papa had brought the hard work.

"You're able to do many tasks," Mary said, "And Jake comes by in the evenings several times a week—"

"He's twelve."

"Claire has helped, and now that Grace and Luke are back—"

"Mary."

He reached over and took her hand. His fingers shook as they tried to close around hers. "Your strength has been evident from infancy, and your love for Mama's dream couldn't be greater, but we can't keep up with the demands."

The words weren't meant to condemn, not coming from Papa, but truth was truth. Mary's vision for the dairy, her work here, wasn't enough.

Scuffling sounded beneath the open kitchen window, a distraction from the emotion thickening her throat. Peering into the darkness, Mary rescued the bread from the windowsill, lest an animal decided to get greedy. The night obscured whatever scrambled below. At least something thought the burnt bread smelled good enough to eat.

She loosened the edges from the pan. Cutting off the crust might salvage it. Her entire life had been about cutting off the bad and saving the good. Being the daughter that Papa needed her to be. Investing in her music because he'd begged her to pursue what she'd loved.

Yet she'd been guilty of the exact thing for which she condemned Luke. She'd left. Turned her back on home and the papa who'd needed her.

Mary flipped the pan over the tea towel and shook out the bread.

"Why are we holding on to this place?" Papa asked.

Had arthritis seized his memory as well as his joints?

Mary's heart burned warm as the bread in her hands. "Because this is our home. This is the Pine Creek you and Mama founded along with six other families. You were the first mayor, and she the first teacher. You built the barn and cabin from wood you hauled out of the forest, and you helped build the church. Twice."

The first church had burned down twelve years ago, the victim of a lightning strike. Papa had rallied the discouraged town and led the rebuilding. He had left his mark on this town, and she clung to her belief it had left a mark on him as well.

"You donated money to construction projects even when money was slim. You spent hours bent over Rod's roof after a wind storm—"

"I don't need you to recount my past." Papa punctuated the husky words with the scraping of his chair as he pulled it out and sat down at the table. "Are we going to eat any of that bread?"

The pounding of her heart sent warmth through her chest. She tried to quell the shaking of her hands as she cut the bread and offered Papa a piece. They had reasons to press on with the dairy, more than Papa's investment in this town. His arthritis had been better the past weeks, giving her hope that the new ointment Dr. Jennings had brought by on his last visit to Pine Creek would lead to recovery.

"We've lost a bull," Papa said. "We've lost customers, and we've added the expense of buying feed instead of growing it."

The money she'd made at the Gold Mine, though it seemed a pittance, may make the difference in them being able to afford feed for winter. She'd not risk his displeasure by bringing up the Gold Mine until harvest when they'd face the large purchase.

"You've been able to help with the milkings for three days in a row." Bread crust crumbled between her fingers, warm but dry. "Can we please not talk about selling yet?" She held her breath while Papa chewed one bite, then another. "Papa?"

His brows turned in as he stared at crumbs on his fingers. Slowly, he nodded, and her breath released with a rush.

He cleared his throat and reached for a drink of water. "I hope I've been a good father, giving you what you've wanted."

She hurried around the table and wrapped her arms about his neck. "You've been perfect." She kissed his cheek. "I forgot my shawl in the barn. I'll be right back."

"Are you sure you're not going out for one more look at the calf?"

She scrunched her nose and smiled. "And what if I am?"

He waved her on, the movement slow and not without the appearance of pain.

She shut the door and rambled down the porch steps, noting the heaviness in the air that signaled impending rain. The cloudy skies had left the night without starlight, but she didn't need any help seeing her way to the barn, a route she could complete perfectly with a blindfold.

Clattering sounded from around the side of the house. Heart reeling, she strained to hear above the rush of the Wenatchee flowing on the edge of the property. She stepped toward the sound, then changed her mind. After she claimed her shawl, she'd deal with whatever animal was on the prowl. Too many noises had interrupted the nights lately, worrying her that their raccoon friend had returned to nest under the back porch.

She crossed to the barn and flung the doors open. A hint of warmth lingered from the small stove. Pausing in darkness, she listened for anything other than the normal animal sounds, her lungs burning as she held her breath. The past weeks had brought a flurry of strange noises and misplaced items. She released her breath and proceeded toward the first stall. This was Pine Creek, not Portland, and she'd not let her time in the city diminish the sense of safety she'd always felt at home.

The rough wood splintered her fingers as she felt around the post. No shawl.

51

She ruffled Mud's side. "Did you eat my shawl, girl?"

She knelt and felt along the cold dirt. Nothing. Striding the aisle, she touched each post and railing but her hands came up empty. She gave in and lit a lantern. A faded glow, indicating low oil, spanned outward but didn't reach the edges of the barn. Salt darted from the shadows into the light, meowing. Mary jumped back. These jitters didn't suit. She'd grown up in this barn, knew it like she did her own heart.

Salt purred and rubbed against her legs. She knelt and petted the ancient barn cat who'd seen almost as many winters as Mary had. Her shawl lay beneath the table in a heap.

"Did you drag this under here?"

She tussled the fur on Salt's head before claiming her shawl and standing. A honeysuckle blossom fell to the ground, and Mary frowned. This blossom was the third she'd found since the night of Luke's return when he'd spotted one on the springhouse floor. What sort of animal would haul around sprigs of a flower? A bird?

She tossed the blossom on the front table, next to the two others, wrapped her shawl around her shoulders, and carried the lantern to the birthing area. Inside the walled stall, the calf curled against its mama.

Moisture stung the back of her eyes. Her connection to the mama she'd never known was here in this barn, sitting on the milk stool Mama had sat on as a child, living the life Mama had wanted to live. Papa had hung Mama's ribbons from the posts like memorial flags, and they offered joy to Mary, a substitute for Mama's smile, which Mary had seen only in pictures.

She blinked away her tears and returned to the entrance. After blowing out the lamp, she set it on the table. Her eyes struggled to adjust to the darkness as she stepped outside and fingered the latch on the doors.

Whether he knew it or not, Papa wasn't ready to sell. And no matter how long and lonely the days, how heavy the work load, she wasn't ready to quit either.

She'd been the reason Mama had died; she wouldn't be the reason Papa had to give up Mama's dream.

———————————— ✦ ————————————

The second to last place Luke wanted to be at eight o-clock on a Friday evening was talking business with the mayor of Pine Creek, the last place being his home. Another evening of sitting around the fireplace as Abigail read to Helen and Paul directed stone-faced glances Luke's way might drive him to insanity.

So after dining with Barrett, Claire, and Cam out at old Coffee's land where the Clarkes had settled, he'd wandered back through town, noticed Johnston working late at his office, and decided to get the meeting over with. Johnston's persistence almost made Mary look tame.

Luke stretched his legs and crossed his ankles on Johnston's purple rug that looked like it better suited a Persian palace. Faint cigar smoke lingered in the small office, and large front windows looked across to the smithy where Cam had been known to work into the evening. Tonight the wide doors were closed, and the shop stood dark.

"You've been back over a week now," Johnston said.

In Luke's experience, conversations that began with obvious statements contained a dangerous undercurrent. He'd try to stay afloat and not get dragged down by any manipulative requests.

"How's the town look to you?" Johnston asked.

Apparently they were going to play at small talk first. "Construction on the hotel looks nice."

"We haven't built something this grand since the first church." Johnston leaned back in his chair, releasing a sigh. "Still can't get over the loss of that pulpit."

Blood warmed its way through Luke's veins, and a flush crept up his neck. The eighteenth century wormy chestnut pulpit had been passed down through Johnston's family and given to the town of Pine Creek one year after its founding.

"George Whitfield preached from that pulpit."

Luke nodded, fully aware of the pedigree of reverends who'd stood behind that ornately carved chunk of wood. Johnston hadn't let the town forget, and if he knew the truth about what had happened the night of that fire, he'd not have asked Luke to sit in his office and chat.

"How long are you around?" Johnston asked.

"I should receive new orders by the end of June." As long as things were straightened out, and eight weeks should be plenty of time for that. He'd never even been reprimanded before last month's incident.

Johnston leaned forward and folded his hands on his desk. "We're involved in a predicament with the railroad. You've probably heard . . ."

Luke sat back, settling in for a long update on an issue he'd heard about enough around the table at home. Talk of Pine Creek's bid for a railroad endowment was preferable to Paul's musings about the new housing endeavor and the hands he hoped to hire on. It wasn't that Luke didn't care. He cared. More than Paul credited him for. What sat raw with Luke was the way Paul talked about things, as if Luke's absence had harmed the state of the ranch. The opposite was true. Paul didn't realize the gift of it.

"And that's where you come in."

Luke blinked and struggled to catch up with Johnston. He sensed a request behind the wide-mouthed smile of the mayor. "You're making me nervous."

Johnston laughed. "Rangers don't get nervous."

"Unsettled then."

Since Luke had walked into his home ten days ago, an invisible fist had clamped around his heart. This trip to Pine Creek throbbed with hidden intentions. God's intentions. And that seemed wilder than the untamed borders of Texas. If God's intentions were for him to stay . . .

But that couldn't be. Luke was good at what he did, loved it.

"This is the short of it." Johnston pushed back in his chair. "The marshal doesn't come through enough. We need a sheriff in town, and you're it."

So that's what this was about. What a joke. Johnston didn't know whom he was asking. The secret Luke had carried from Pine Creek made him as unfit a candidate as a derringer was for bringing in an outlaw.

"Can't help you with that." Luke stood. "Good luck."

"Don't need luck. I've got you."

Luke smothered the glare that surfaced and strode to the exit. A framed map of Chelan County hung beside the door, and next to it, a photograph of the Wenatchee River where it curved around Pine Creek in an embrace.

The rock in the corner of the photograph mocked him. He'd sat there with a pile of matches, striking, striking, striking at the beginning of what would turn into an awful summer and the reason this town wouldn't want him as sheriff.

A sheriff protected its town. Worked for its good, not burned it down.

"Lord's got a reason for bringing you back."

Luke didn't want to hear a sermon from the man who'd made an art of twisting truth to get his way.

He opened the door and gulped the fresh air as if granted an eleventh hour pardon. "That reason doesn't include a shiny star and a title."

Nodding back at Johnston, he shut the door.

Heat crawled up his spine, despite the cool air of April. He crossed the street, fists clenched at his side, Johnston's words humming in his conscience. *Lord's got a reason . . .*

Candlelight flickered through the window of Rod's Mercantile, and Luke stopped his stride. The store would be closed now, as was most everything in town. Even Cam had shut down for the night.

Luke fought against the shot of adrenaline that heightened his alertness. *You're not on duty anymore.*

A thief wouldn't risk the use of a candle. Likely, Rod was checking on something.

His senses paid no attention to his reasoning. Instead, he took inventory of his surroundings: the smell of wood smoke, the sound of faraway hoof beats, and the sight of Cam's lantern in the window above the smithy.

Veering toward the corner of Rod's building, Luke settled his hand on his weapon and searched for movement in the shadows.

A flood of music burst forth, and his heart catapulted into his throat. Even with the unfamiliar tune, he knew the artist. No one in Pine Creek played like Mary.

His fingers relaxed from his gun as he leaned against the wall on the north side of Rod's, closed his eyes, and listened. He'd noticed the Smith's piano shoved into the corner of the mercantile the other day and had understood what that meant. A downturn of business for the Smiths. It wasn't the first time Mary had sold her piano.

Mary ripped through a lively melody that drew the smile up his face and soaked his mind in memory.

One song. He'd let himself enjoy one song.

Five songs later, he sank to the ground, engrossed in her private performance. His hand brushed against a sticky blossom along the bottom of the wall. He picked it up and smelled it. Honeysuckle. Mary's favorite. He twirled the flower around his thumb and forefinger while Mary's sorrowful melody segued into a triumphant tune. Her playing yanked around his emotions, made him think of his mother's smile, his father's death, and a sunset all at the same time.

Men weren't supposed to feel those things. Men weren't supposed to sit against a cold building in the dark, tracing stars with their gazes while their ears devoured every last note played by a childhood friend.

That's why he'd never confessed to Mary all those

times when he'd worked for her father that he'd made excuses to pass the window to hear her practicing, a spunky eleven-year-old but already gifted. One afternoon when the air had been clammy, he'd leaned on the windowsill. She'd worn pigtail braids.

"You ever play Milchovic?" he'd asked.

She spun on the stool and frowned. "Never heard of him."

"Someone as studied as you has never heard of Vladimir Milchovic?"

"I play whatever I'm given. This is Pine Creek, not New York."

"Then I guess you'll need to go to New York someday."

"Never. I'm not like you. Wanting to leave as soon as possible."

She'd been ignorant of why he'd had to leave.

After she'd returned to her piece, he'd called out, "You won't regret leaving. It'll be an adventure."

Without missing a note, she'd tipped her head up and responded, "Everything's an adventure for you, Luke, the Duke of many escapades."

He stood, tossed the honeysuckle down, and stalked across the street. He passed the left turn for the schoolhouse, passed the right turn to the Smith's. At the second left, he glanced over his shoulders through the darkness. He didn't need moonlight to illuminate the church steeple in order to picture how it pointed at the sky in reverence. Despite the way that image twisted his heart, condemning, he treasured Pine Creek.

"You love it here." His whispered confession fed his soul.

Leaving had never been about the loving or lack of loving. It'd been about doing the right thing, whether the town—or his family—had understood it or not.

CHAPTER SEVEN

Seven years earlier, 1885

Mary stood on the swing, enjoying the afternoon breeze in her hair as she moved back and forth. The patchy blue sky canopied the dairy, but scattered clouds huddled atop the southern mountains, dark enough to sprout fear.

Standing in front of the swing, Grace gave the wooden seat a push, her humming light as the summer air.

Across the pasture, Luke strode from the Smith's barn and looked toward Grace. One hand on his hip, he beckoned. "Ready?"

His authoritative voice carried across the field.

"Has to get home and practice his shot." Grace continued pushing. "Cecily Reynolds says he's getting good, and the only reason she'd know is because she sits and watches him like some people watch plays or attend concerts. Can you imagine chasing after a man like that?"

"I can't imagine anyone chasing after Luke. Period."

Grace shifted her gaze from Luke and smiled up at Mary. "Really? I think he's well-admired by the young ladies of Pine Creek."

True. So why'd she say she couldn't imagine anyone chasing him?

Luke stalked their direction, his swagger a mix of confidence and impatience.

"Cecily also thinks Luke's a good singer." Grace offered another push before backing up toward Luke. "She likes to stand in front of him at church."

That wasn't to hear him but to be noticed by him. The joke was on Cecily, though. Luke's mind never swayed far from the Texas Rangers, even in church.

"He sounds like a crow."

Grace laughed. "Should I tell him you said that?"

"I'll tell him myself."

"Tell me what?" Luke reached them and adjusted his dirty hat. "Never mind." He looked at Grace. "Time to go."

Grace waved to Mary and headed toward the wagon.

Luke backed up three steps, his stare possessing some sort of challenge. He stopped at the far edge of the swing's arc. She didn't bother to analyze why a moment ago he'd seemed in a hurry and now stood as if mesmerized by the swing's lilt.

She pumped her body back and forth, her feet rooted to the wooden slat, to maintain the momentum of the swing. "If you don't hurry you'll only have time for two hours of target practice before dinner."

"You saying I need practice?"

"Easy there, boy. Your shot's fine, but how about your decision-making skills? Or your cooking? Aren't Rangers supposed to know how to cook over a fire? When do you practice those things? Or how about your ability to jump on a moving train to subdue robbers?"

He scoffed. "Storybook stuff."

The swing veered close to him, and the glint in his eyes snagged her breath. The swing moved away, a slow and wide arc, and when it moved toward him again, he lunged forward. He vaulted onto the flat seat, colliding with the swing's momentum. The commotion tore the ropes from her grip, and she cried out and grabbed for his shirt as he fought for balance and lost. He fell backward toward the ground, taking her with him. His body hit first, and she landed on top, tumbled sideways, and struggled for breath.

"What was that?" She stared skyward, breathless.

"I'm sorry." He jumped to his feet and shook out his

arms and legs. "You all right?"

The branches swayed above her in the breeze, either that or dizziness had seized her. She gazed through the leaves at the clouding sky and inhaled a shallow breath.

"Have I taken down Dairy Mary for good?"

Never. She sat up, determined to bounce to her feet like he had. She'd prove to him it took more than a foolish jump onto a swing to take her down.

"Mary!" Grace ran across the field, dress hitched in her hands.

Mary waved her off and stood on shaky legs. "Don't you know anything? You jump on the swing as it moves away from you, not toward you. Move with momentum, not against it."

She stalked in Grace's direction. For supposedly being smart, Luke could be pretty dumb.

When Grace reached her, she looped her arm through Mary's. "What was that about?"

"Your brother attacked me."

A snicker from the boy next to her drew her sidelong glance.

"What would you call it?" she asked.

"Practice for boarding a train." He walked past her to the wagon. Debris clung to his shaggy hair.

"Hey, Duke, you look like you've had a rough day."

He turned around. "And that dirt on your dress means you had a good day?"

She glared.

"Or should I say, a normal day?"

Texas could have him.

CHAPTER EIGHT

Present day

Luke patted the chest pocket on his vest and felt the crumpled letter in front of his Psalms prayer book. Quickening his pace along the bumpy path, he focused on the sun's rays skipping off the mountain tops and not on the image of Paul's detachment earlier at supper.

Growing up, Luke hadn't noticed how the mountains infringed on the sky. The open sky of Texas had spoiled him.

Gus darted in front, entering the cemetery first, nose to the ground. Luke wondered what a cemetery smelled like to a dog. Death. Decay. Other animals, probably. But there was life here, in front of Father's grave. The closest thing he felt to being home. His memories of the ranch were crammed with images of his father holding his mother's hand, building up the fire in the wood stove, sitting in his chair reading the Psalms book that Luke now carried.

Inside the cemetery, Luke closed the gate and hung his hat on a spire. Someone had trimmed the spring growth around the knee-high markers. He wove around a dozen or so before he reached his father's.

Luke pulled the sheet of paper from his pocket and stared at the familiar, faded script. He rested one hand on his gun and mouthed the words Father had written in the weeks after his wound had become infected and confined him to bed.

Only thirteen, Luke had stopped working. Suspended his life. Refused to go to school, preferring to stay by Father's bed and lasso every opportunity to talk about life, what really mattered, the Rangers. He'd shared his disgust with the news from the south. Settlers dying. Outlaws doing what they wanted because the law couldn't stop them.

Father had listened and offered commentary, probed with questions about what had gripped Luke's heart. Everything. Men seeking justice, helping the helpless, seizing those who took pleasure in harming others.

Sure, Luke had idealized the life as a dream-struck thirteen-year-old. He'd made a pastoral image out of what had turned out to be grueling, challenging, and frustrating work. It was all that and better than he could have imagined.

Mother had been at Father's side, too, wiping sweat, feeding him broth, changing the dressing on his foot. Of all the things that could bring a strong man down. An accidental shot in the foot.

Sometimes the least expected snagged a man, like Captain Finch ordering him to take a leave of absence. No matter how much Luke had pried, his captain had refused to give details. Because, of course, if a man were accused of misbehavior, he shouldn't be allowed to defend himself.

Scowling, Luke focused back on the one-page note that lacked fancy words but held everything a boy needed. A few scriptures, an *I love you*, and an appeal for Luke to stay close to the Heavenly Father. Which he had. He'd just not stayed close to Pine Creek.

Luke returned the letter to his pocket and palmed the back of his neck. His shoulder had ached so much the past week he could almost hear its groaning. Gus bounded down the slope at the edge of the fenced-in plot, circled Luke's legs, and settled at his feet.

Luke ran his hand over the top of the gravestone. He'd never been one to talk to a piece of rock as if Father were there. Father was home, in heaven where the word *home* meant more than it even would on earth, and maybe that was why this place meant life and hope to Luke. The intangible things of this world—peace, truth, justice—those were the things that lasted. The things worth pursuing.

A meadowlark released a shrill cry from the vine maple nearby, and Gus raised his head, ears attentive. Luke whistled and headed for the gate. The sun lingered level with the mountains, blinding him. He pulled his hat low and swung the gate open. Gus bounded toward the bushes and disappeared down the wrong path.

"Hey, old man." Mary greeted Gus from somewhere out of sight.

The cheery resonance of her voice coiled around Luke's gut until he wasn't sure if dread or anticipation coursed his veins.

Gus burst from the bushes and ran back to Luke. Luke rubbed behind the dog's ears. "Don't blame you." He'd run from Mary, too, if she called him old.

Mary rounded the juniper, hugging that raggedy blue shawl about her shoulders. "Fancy meeting you here."

He grinned. "It's been a long time since I've heard those words." Words they'd said to each other through the years as they'd happened upon each other visiting their loved ones' graves. "Isn't it milking time?"

She glanced sideways at him as she shuffled past and through the gate. "Soon. Care to come light the barn on fire again?"

Her jab dug deeper than she could have known. Without thought his hand traversed the inside of his upper arm where, beneath his shirt, scars testified to his foolishness.

Joining her inside, he let the gate swing closed behind him. He folded his arms, knowing what she'd do. She marched across the yard, sat in front of her mother's stone, stretched her legs out, and leaned against it as if it leaning against a chair.

He tried to tell himself the only reason his feet were taking him across the grass was because he wasn't ready to go back to the house and face Paul. His sinking down against the stone across from her, mirroring her position so that the soles of their boots touched, had nothing to do with the way she breeched his resolve to keep Pine Creek at a distance.

She closed her eyes and settled into her place against her mama's headstone. "Held by Mama."

She said it every time.

The last glow of the sun crowned her brown hair. His gaze wandered from the top of her head, past the flickering of her closed eyelids, and down curves that . . .

What was he doing looking at Dairy Mary like this?

The Mary he'd known before had been a marriage of spunk and unpredictability, and that's all he'd seen in her. This grown-up Mary threw off his instincts and made his mind spin. He looked into the bushes by the fence, reorienting his thoughts to their rightful place.

"Your family must be glad you've returned." Her statement sagged with meaning.

"Graveyard rules."

She huffed. "All I did was make a statement."

A statement meant to make him feel guilty. The graveyard had been the only place as children where they hadn't fought. Arguments had been suspended. Snide remarks held back. Shared grief had shelved the tension between them, instigating a holy time-out from the usual.

"Tell me about Portland." He kept his attention on a pair of wrens hopping along the edge of the fence.

"It's busy. Not friendly, not like Pine Creek."

"What about your studies?"

"I practiced. And practiced. Attended classes. And practiced more."

"Friends?"

"I suppose we can be friends if you make up your mind to be nice to me."

He swung his gaze toward her, keeping it above her shoulders this time. She grinned, that familiar liveliness brightening her tired eyes.

"Of course I had friends." She uncrossed her boots and

crossed them the opposite way. Her sly expression was so like the image he'd tucked away in his mind and carried to Texas. "I'm charming, aren't I?"

Oh, she could be charming all right. As charming as the crawdads he used to hunt down by the creek.

"Tell me about Texas." She plucked a violet and twirled it in her fingers.

He did the same. "Seriously?"

Her fingers stilled, and she tipped her head to the left. She never tipped it to the right. "I wouldn't have asked if I hadn't wanted to know."

True. He couldn't fault her transparency. He wished he could say the same for his own.

He fought to relax his jaw. "Sky's so big you feel like it might eat you alive when you're out under it at night. Or like it might fall on you and smother you in your sleep."

She grimaced. "That's not an attractive picture."

Not as attractive as the picture before him now.

She brushed her knuckles across her lips. "What about the work? Is it like you and Paul used to play?"

He snorted. Paul hadn't minded Luke's dreams when Father had been healthy, but after Father's accident, Luke's entire relationship with Paul had frozen. Whereas Luke had suspended his life and stayed by Father's bed, Paul had worked harder, putting in longer hours on the ranch, probably to deal with the fear of losing Father. Not that Luke ever knew the reason. Paul wasn't generous with his words.

"Luke?"

He lifted his gaze from his hands.

"Don't you love your job?" The questioning tone sounded vulnerable, as if he loving his job had a direct affect on her.

"Absolutely." And in this moment, he loved her for caring that he did. "The work's demanding. Rewarding."

"Dangerous. You know Grace and your mother hate that."

"It's more lonely than dangerous."

She arched a thin, dark brow. "You? The boy who hid in the woods to practice shooting, lonely?"

He bent one leg and rested the violet on top of his knee. "Everyone gets lonely."

Emotions played over the surface of her eyes, but he was hard-pressed to understand them. The child version of Mary had possessed a minimal ability to hide her feelings. This wasn't that Mary. He didn't like how he'd lost his ability to read her, and he didn't know what to do about it.

"Johnston Brown dropped by Rod's the other day while I was playing the piano."

Luke frowned.

"He says you're running for sheriff."

Muttering beneath his breath, he flicked the flower off his knee at Mary. It hit her in the chin.

Her eyes widened, and she bent her knee, placed a flower on it, and flicked it at him. It flew over his shoulder.

"You've been misinformed," he said.

"That's too bad. Seems like the perfect fit. You get to do your justice thing, and your mama and sister get you around."

Could she let up about his mama and his sister? "It's complicated." He flicked two more violets at her in an attempt to keep the mood light.

She ignored the flower assault. "What's complicated about it? Do you have a secret from the past?"

He locked his gaze on hers, daring her to prod further. Her eyes fastened on with equal strength, and he studied their brown depth. After a full, heavy ten seconds that threatened to smother his common sense, she blinked and looked away.

"I need to get back." He pushed to his feet. "Gus!"

Mary stood while Gus darted from behind a gravestone and circled between him and Mary. They walked in silence to the gate, and he let her exit first. They either had to reconfigure their graveyard rules to include no fused glances, or this would be their last gathering between these stones.

She turned, her hair riding the tail of a breeze, and met his eyes. "I'm glad you're back."

He tried not to let his brows slip up, but they did. The girl who'd said "about time" when he'd announced his departure was glad he was home.

"For Grace's sake," she was quick to add. "And . . ." She looked away. "Pine Creek isn't the same without you."

Laughter escaped before he could catch it. Pine Creek was better without him.

"You laugh, but you'll feel the tug eventually, and it'll pull you under so fast you'll hardly have time to breathe."

It'd already pulled him under, and he had the scars to prove it.

CHAPTER NINE

Mary sank into the tub of sudsy water. A full barn tonight had made quick work. Luke had wandered over to help, and along with Jake, the twelve-year-old who helped most evenings, the milking had taken a fraction of its usual time. So many hands had allowed her to come in early for a soak and not feel guilty for the luxury.

She closed her eyes, her prayers rising heavenward on wisps of steam. The God who'd made a way through the Red Sea could make a way for her and Papa to keep the dairy. She'd sent up pleas as numerous as the spring violets dotting the pasture.

Lord, bring customers. Lord, provide finances for full time help. Lord, cause the cows of those who'd stopped receiving Smith milk and started producing their own to die.

She cringed and curled her toes against the end of the washtub. Sarcasm didn't belong in a conversation with the Almighty.

Beyond needing God to make a way with the dairy, she needed him to strengthen Papa, to mend the relationship between Luke and his family, and as long as she were composing a list, she'd ask for him to match Grace with Cam.

The catalogue of appeals dominated her prayers. If she could set them aside and listen, she might hear the Lord's infinite wisdom. Or she might hear commands she didn't want to hear. He might ask her to do difficult things. To give up things she didn't know how to give up.

She scowled and slapped her hand across the surface of

the water. Bubbles spewed up her nose, and she sneezed them away at the same time a crash sounded. Mary sat up, sending water over the side of the tub onto her bedroom floor. The air wafting through her cracked window tingled cold against her wet skin.

"Papa?"

Her sneeze had masked the direction of the crash. Had he come inside and fallen, or had the sound come from outside?

Rushed footfalls sounded beneath her window and faded into the distance. The heavy pounding of her heart ached against her chest. Someone had been outside her window. Watching? A thin half curtain dressed the darkened window. Not the best privacy, but with their nearest neighbors ten minutes away, she'd never felt the need for greater privacy.

She ducked beneath the water, rinsing her soapy hair. The lemony scent greeted her as she emerged and stepped from the tub. Turning her back on the window, she dried quickly and dressed in her loose cotton nightgown. After toweling her hair and haphazardly running a brush through it, she snatched the lantern and marched from her room. Papa's chair sat empty, the lamp turned low. Nothing looked out of place in the front room or the kitchen, and she didn't think the crash had sounded from Papa's room across from hers.

"Papa?"

No answer.

She plucked her shawl from the hook, went out the front door, and circled back where her bedroom window and the kitchen window were. She paced the length of the small house. Nothing looked out of the ordinary. Holding the lantern close to the ledge beneath her window, she ran her finger under the one-inch crack. On the ground below lay a vine of honeysuckle.

Another honeysuckle.

This wasn't happenstance. Flowers didn't grow legs and walk. They were picked. Moved. Placed intentionally.

Leaving the blossom on the ground, she strode to the barn and pushed through the doors.

"Papa?"

"Back here."

She followed the voice to the rear, where Papa sat sharpening his knife.

"Where's Luke?"

"He and Jake left." Papa studied her, undoubtedly taking note of her wet hair and unlaced boots. "Are you all right?"

Papa had enough to worry about without adding strange noises and honeysuckle to the list. Luke or Jake could easily have made the crash.

"I'm fine," she said. "You didn't hear a crash, did you?"

"No." He eyed her a minute longer, and she feared he'd press for information, but he jutted his chin toward a chair. "Have a seat."

The invitation, put forth in his soft-spoken voice, sounded like the precursor to a long conversation. Between her wet hair and thin nightgown, she didn't want to be stuck in the chilly April air for a serious discussion. "Could we talk inside?"

He set aside his sharpening tools and followed her across the yard. She entered their home, inhaling the leftover scent of salted pork from dinner, and settled in front of the fire.

Papa eased into his chair and took a few rapid breaths that leveled into deeper, even breaths. He pulled a folded piece of paper from his shirt pocket. "I have a letter here." He didn't start reading out loud like he did when they received letters from Jared, who lived and worked with Mama's family in Seattle.

Mary separated her hair into three sections and began to braid. "From whom?"

Papa rubbed the letter between his fingers. "Last month the Crawleys went to visit family in Peshastin."

An introduction to an answer didn't bode well.

"The Crawley's family has connections with another family, the Millwoods."

Mary's suspicion grew.

"When the Crawleys found out the eldest Millwood son was interested in dairy farming, they mentioned us.

A worker. "We can find the money to pay him. I'll sell all the furniture in my room." And play extra at the Gold Mine.

Papa chuckled. "That's not necessary. The son is interested in purchasing an existing operation."

Her hands stilled on her half-finished braid. She dropped them into her lap as nausea cramped her stomach. Smith Dairy had never seemed big enough to call an operation. It was a livelihood, a home. *Their* home.

"We don't know these people," she said.

A week ago Papa had agreed to hold off on talk of selling. And now this.

She filtered through the words she wanted to release but knew she shouldn't. Statements that started with *I*.

I can't believe you're doing this to us. I can work harder. I won't leave.

"We aren't ready to say goodbye to this place." Somehow her tone sounded even, controlled.

"Marry this man, and you won't have to say goodbye." Papa's eyes shone.

How could he joke in the midst of what felt like a strike to her heart?

"Would you at least take a look?" He waved the letter in front of her.

She snatched it and skimmed the words, first an introduction from the father about his son's qualifications, and then a note from the son about his vision for a dairy, the new inventions he wanted to try. The letter resounded with clarity

71

and passion.

"I don't like it." She dropped the page in Papa's lap.

He returned it to his shirt pocket and reached for his Bible.

Mama's Bible beckoned her to pick it up and follow along, like she often did when he read in the evenings, but her hands stiffened in her lap.

Crinkling pages testified to Papa's labor to find his passage. She forced her hands not to reach and help. A man didn't want to be reminded of his weakness.

"John chapter fifteen," Papa said.

His voice grew reverent as he read about the gardener, the vine, the fruit-bearing. Mary closed her eyes, trying to keep up with Jesus' narrative, but her heart fastened on the word *abide*.

Here. She wanted to abide here, the place Mama had chosen, in the town Papa had founded. That's what abide meant: to stay put and be. To hold on and tolerate the drought or storm. Not to throw away years of investment.

It had been Mama's doggedness that had marked her and Papa's new life in Pine Creek. If she'd remained alive, these struggles wouldn't be plaguing them. Even with the closing of Fledgling Mine, Mama would find a way.

Mary shuddered a breath, aware that Papa's voice had stopped reading.

"When we hold to the true vine," he said. "We can let go of all else."

Letting go was giving up, and giving up meant disappointing Mama, and even Papa, who loved this place like Mary did, who only wanted to let go because his body had worn out. There was another way. To expand and reach further out from Pine Creek, bring in more business and hire help so Papa wouldn't feel pressured.

Papa lifted his legs one by one to the footstool. "The Crawleys are taking a trip to Peshastin next week. They've invited me to go with them, and I've accepted."

She lurched forward in her chair. The fire popped, sending a litany of sparks up the chimney that punctuated Papa's fateful announcement.

Papa smiled, demonstrating a peace she'd not seen in the past months of struggle. "This is what we've prayed for."

"Not me." Mary looked away, reached for the wet mass of hair that had soaked through the back of her nightgown, and began braiding with a fury. "My prayers are for endurance, strength, provision."

"And my prayer has been for direction, and that prayer was answered by the arrival of this letter. And a conversation with Luke."

"Luke?" Speaking his name didn't ease the shock. "What does he have to do with our dairy?"

"I trust his character."

"You trust the character of someone who chose Texas over his family?"

Papa drew back, frowning. "I trust the character of someone who has a passion for serving others."

A passion for running off and leaving others. The thought stung her conscience. *You're being too harsh on him.* "I don't trust his motivations."

"Motivations are never completely pure. Are yours?"

Mary stared at her hands.

"Luke cares about justice and has the skills of a Ranger. Can you blame him for going after what God put in his heart? That's what Mama did, and it took her from her family in Seattle."

Mama's situation had been different. Mama loved home and family, had been willing to invest in people, belong to a place. Luke might want to serve others, but he didn't want to be a part of their lives. Why else would he hide from the people who'd raised him, the town that loved him?

"So what did Luke say?"

"He encouraged me to view selling the dairy as passing on Mama's dream, not letting it die."

Mary bolted from her chair and dashed to the door. She threw on her wool-lined work coat and fumbled with the buttons.

"Mary."

"I'm going to see Grace." And she would, after she saw Luke.

The ride to the Thomas' ranch took ten minutes, plenty enough time for Papa's words about Luke to lather her into a frenzy. While she could concede that Luke had some excellent character traits, including putting himself in danger for those he didn't know, she couldn't condone his meddling in her affairs.

She tethered Holly at the paddock next to the barn. The lamps shining through the front windows invited her in. She'd come in all right, and Luke was going to need more than six shooters to defend himself.

A breeze caught the door and slammed it against the inside wall as she entered. All six family members, who were gathered in the front room, stopped their activities and stared at her.

Grace set aside her sewing, stood, and greeted her with a hug. "Mary?"

She honed her gaze at her brown-haired, strong-jawed betrayer. His legs were propped up on a footrest as if everything was fine, as if he hadn't just turned her papa against her. "Stay out of my family's business."

Abigail stood. "Time for bed, little one." She snatched Helen into her arms and tugged on Paul's sleeve.

Luke's mother shut her book and followed them out, towing Grace behind her.

"Why did you do it?" She marched around the scraps of material Grace had spread across the floor.

Beyond Luke, the fire hissed. Wood shavings heaped beneath his chair, and the slow, steady movement of his knife across the pointed stick goaded her. His calmness whittled her heart raw.

"Do what?" He didn't look up from his hands.

She sputtered for a response. "Turn my papa against me."

"Whoa. That's a strong accusation." He brushed shavings from his lap, sheathed his knife, and pushed from the chair. His six-shooters hung at his sides. "Tell me how you think I did that."

"You told him to sell the dairy."

"I encouraged him to consider the options."

She glared and stepped around him to stare into the bright center of the fire. The heat billowed against her face.

"There are two of you. The dairy is more work than you can handle, your papa can't do what he used to be able to do, and your business has dwindled."

"Papa's borne a good work load this week."

"He works half as much as you."

Wetness tickled her cheeks, and she was thankful Luke was standing behind her. "Bridges is expanding. That might bring more business. And I . . ." She didn't mean to bring the Gold Mine up.

"I know this is difficult."

The quiet words unwound her heart, and she turned and met Luke's gaze. Fire glow reflected in his eyes, along with a tenderness she'd seen directed at Grace and his mother but rarely at her.

"It's not wrong to feel sorrow over saying goodbye to something that's been part of your life." He smiled and tapped the side of her head. "But it's wrong to let that sorrow keep you from using your brain."

She huffed and stalked past him toward the stairs. She should have known his compassion would be short lived.

"It's time to let go."

Spinning around, her hands dug into her coat. "If I lose this dairy, I lose the only part of Mama I've ever known."

"It's a dairy, not a person. Won't you be relieved to be rid of the hours of work and move on to something else?"

75

"What else?" She took a step toward him. "Tell me that, Luke Thomas. What else can Papa and I do?"

He looked at the floor.

"That's right. Nothing."

She vaulted up the stairs, past the closed door of Paul and Abigail's room to Grace's room. Mary peeked through the crack at Grace who sat on her bed, hunched over a mound of satiny material.

"What's the point of wearing something so fancy?" Mary shrugged from her coat, let it fall to the rug at the foot of Grace's bed, and sank onto the old, bowed mattress.

"Because it's beautiful. Feel this." Grace held out the deep purple fabric.

Mary took a handful, laid back, and ran the smooth material over her face. "Delightful."

"Don't you want to drape yourself in it?"

"I can imagine myself on a milk stool in a dress made from this."

Grace stood and gathered the material in her arms. Mounds of fabric scraps and accoutrements piled high on a table in the corner, where Grace added the purple project. "I need a shop."

"Why don't you ask Rod if you can use the empty space above his store?"

Her blue eyes lit, but the spark faded quickly. She shrugged, picked up a brown flannel shirt, and snatched some buttons from a jar. "I'm sewing Luke some new clothes."

"How about sewing him a new personality?"

Grace chuckled. "You don't really mean that."

Rolling over on her side to face Grace, Mary smiled. "I guess not."

Grace settled against the pillow at the head of the bed, Luke's shirt in her lap. "If I didn't know better, I'd think you were as attached to him as Cecily."

"But you do know better." Time to broach the subject she'd debated sharing. "Have you had any issues with

76

animals lately?"

Grace looked up, her fingers still dancing through stitches with ease. "I take it you don't mean the cattle. Do dogs count? Brothers? A four-year-old who gets into everything?" Her needle slipped, stabbing her finger. She gasped and stuck it in her mouth.

"I've heard noises behind the house, outside my window, and around the far side of the barn in the evening when I'm milking." Mary propped her head on her elbow and curled her feet under her nightgown. "I'm afraid we have problems with raccoons again."

Grace pinched her index finger against her thumb and stuck her needle in her mouth while she reached for another button.

"I've also found four honeysuckle blossoms."

Grace's brows pinched as she finger-measured between buttonholes.

"In odd places, including right outside my window."

The needle dropped from Grace's mouth. She swung her gaze to Mary's. "You're being watched?"

"I'm not ready to say that."

"I am, and this is the first I've heard of it."

"I don't have any enemies." Not including the workers in the neighboring lumber camp and farther away in Clifton, she knew every person in this valley. None of them would spy on her.

Grace tossed the shirt aside, stood, and paced around the foot of the bed. "I'm getting Luke."

"No!" Mary sat up and kicked her leg out in front of Grace, stopping her. "I don't want to make a big deal out of this. All I wanted to know was if your family's had issues with that bear again, like last spring."

"Luke would want to know."

"There's nothing to know." Just suspicions.

He'd make more of it than necessary, embarrassing her. Or the opposite. He'd call her silly for imagining things . . .

also embarrassing her.

"Please, Grace." Mary stood and took hold of Grace's elbows, looking down at her friend, a good five inches shorter than she. With a petite waist, round hips, and soft shoulders, Grace offered a lovely image of femininity, fitting for a seamstress.

"Fine."

Mary threw her arms around Grace. "Have I mentioned that I missed you while you were in Seattle?"

"Claire did a fine job standing in for me."

Mary pushed back. Grace, jealous? "Claire forces me to behave like a sensible adult."

"You are an adult."

"But being with you is like being with family."

Grace's gaze softened, and she smiled. "Thank you."

A gust of wind tossed raindrops against the window. Grace stepped around Mary and tugged the curtains closed. "Almanac's calling for a rainy May."

Lord, let it be.

Mrs. Crawley didn't collect eggs from her coop in the rain, let alone ride thirty miles in a wagon. Anything that kept Papa away from Peshastin sounded good to Mary. "As long as it doesn't thunder." She snatched her coat from the floor and winked at Grace.

Stepping out to the stairway landing, Mary looked both ways to ensure Luke wasn't lurking, waiting for another argument.

"Don't be mad at Luke." Grace leaned against the doorjamb. "He only means to be helpful."

Good intentions didn't make up for bad advice.

"You know he can't hold back an opinion . . . kind of like you. But I still love you both."

Mary grinned. With a friend like Grace, Mary could pretend all would be fine—even without the dairy.

CHAPTER TEN

The rain licked his face and heightened the tension in his chest as Luke ducked into the plain-fronted structure that housed the mayor's office.

Johnston looked up from his seat behind the massive desk like a king on his throne. Satisfaction settled into his regal smile. "You've considered the request?"

Calling Johnston's demand a request was a generosity Luke wasn't willing to extend. Luke turned a wooden chair around and straddled it, resting his arms on the splintered back. "Four people have told me they're voting for me."

"I might have mentioned you were an eligible candidate."

"Eligible implies willing. You've been campaigning for me, even after I told you I wasn't interested."

"It's not a crime to speak kind things about someone." Johnston gestured with his hands. "And I'm not the only one spreading your qualifications. Mary is also."

Luke would deal with Mary later.

"I'm returning to Texas, as soon as . . ." His captain hadn't specified, and the undisclosed amount of time shackled him. He'd not been disloyal or turned against the Rangers. He'd merely stretched his orders as the situation had called for. Couldn't they do their investigating while he continued his job? "As soon as they need me."

"Sounds unsettled." Johnston came around the desk and stood in front of Luke. The gold chain of his pocket watch glimmered in the lamplight.

"I can't be sheriff, and I won't be sheriff. How much plainer can I say it?"

Johnston chuckled and pulled on the bottom of his vest. His salt and pepper hair offered a distinguished look, one he enhanced by wearing three-piece suits and peering down his nose at people. "Why don't we let the people speak?"

"What about letting the candidates speak?"

Johnston clapped his hands. "You admit to being a candidate. That's a start."

"Answer's no." He righted the chair and stepped toward the exit.

"Election's in a month. Your opponent is a sixty-year-old retired sheriff from Wenatchee whom no one is interested in electing."

No. His opponent was a thirty-six-year-old mayor with an uncontested will.

Tipping his hat at Johnston, Luke stepped into the street. He hopped a two-foot-wide stream and crossed to the smithy, where open doors revealed Cam in his usual position, bent over the anvil. Rain, shine, and snow made no difference to Cam.

Luke rapped hard on the door and entered.

Cam turned from the anvil, mallet poised above his head.

"Busy?" Luke asked.

"Perpetually. But that's how I like it. This is the day the Lord has made, and I will rejoice."

A preacher who pounded iron and the Word. Cam was an enigma.

"What brings you to town in the rain?" Cam asked.

"I had to set Johnston straight."

"Seems about right."

"He's trying to convince me to run for sheriff."

Cam leaned his weight on one leg and rested his mallet next to the horseshoe on the anvil. "What if you do it?"

Luke settled in one of the chairs at the opening of the

smithy, bit the end of his thumbnail, and spit it out.

"Lots of benefits to being sheriff." Cam shoved his sleeves up his arms, revealing forearm muscles whose strength mirrored the character of their owner. "One roof over your head. One town, rather than an entire region, to focus on."

One town that would hate him if they knew his secret. "I work better on my own." In a large, open area without watching, judging eyes.

Cam picked up his mallet and twirled the handle in his hand. "I get what you mean. Having the run of this place is exactly what I love." He whacked on the glowing hot horseshoe a few times. "Can you believe I still haven't met the man who bought it?"

Cam bore the mark of a true friend: knowing when to move on from a conversation.

"When did the smithy change ownership?"

Shaking his head, Cam grinned. "You have been gone a while."

The words weren't intended to condemn, not coming from Cam, but they joined the myriad comments about Luke's absence in a chorus of disapproval. Being absent wasn't a sin. He'd not broken God's greatest commandment by going to Texas. He loved the Lord his God with all his heart, soul, and strength.

What about the second commandment, loving your neighbor?

He had neighbors in Texas.

You're running.

Pursuing justice, he corrected his thoughts, which for some bizarre reason had taken on Mary's voice.

Cam grabbed a rag and wiped his forehead, leaving a streak of sweaty dirt. "Neil sold to an investor several years ago. I've received a few letters from this new owner, an S. Klein, but never a visit. He makes a profit. I do the work."

Luke stretched his legs in front and crossed his ankles.

81

"As far as I'm concerned, you might as well own it."

Cam narrowed his eyes, gave the burning metal a final smash, and set aside his anvil. "But I don't." He snagged his rag from a rusted hook and wiped his brow again. "I almost forgot. Got a letter for you from Texas."

"*You* got a letter for me?"

"Johnston granted me the role of postmaster."

Figured. Johnston handed out jobs to the residents of Pine Creek like a father assigned chores.

Cam took his time drinking from a cup of water before walking to the back and sifting through a pile of letters on his desk. "Any idea who it's from?" He returned and handed Luke the envelope with the Texas Ranger insignia.

Luke's heart pounded. "Probably new orders." An apology for the misunderstanding. A cleared name and a call home.

Cam leaned on the desk while Luke ripped open the envelope, pulled the paper out, and read. His jaw clenched, and he tried to swallow, but his tongue stuck to the top of his mouth. His eyes lost focus, blurring the words.

Not a summons, nor an apology. Not a cleared name.

Luke tore his eyes from the news and met Cam's gaze. "I'm a wanted man."

───────────◆◆◆───────────

Mary schlepped through the mud toward the barn, fatigue pulling on her every thought after a day of excessive work. Papa had woken with swollen joints, thanks to continuous rain and his attempts to milk with her the past three days. She'd worked on her own today, the hated loneliness aggravating her heart. The dairy demanded every moment of her time. Pulled her away from opportunities. Left her body drained and her mind painfully weary.

Luke's question pestered her throughout the rhythm of her day. *Wouldn't you be relieved . . .*

No. The answer was no. Not even the temptation of

free evenings or a less demanding schedule lured her to give up Mama's dream.

She took a moment to draw refreshment from the familiar odors of damp hay and fresh mud on her boots before starting in with the milking.

"Moving slow?"

Mary yelped and spun around.

Grace pushed through the doors, Claire following.

"With Jake unable to help and your papa in pain, we wanted to offer our assistance." Claire smoothed her hand down a dark striped skirt with a scalloped ruffle along the bottom. Not exactly a milking ensemble, but a simple, unassuming outfit for a city girl.

"Barrett tried to tell her she'd be a distraction, but she didn't listen," Grace said.

"You will both be wonderful, helpful distractions."

Grace busied herself, but Claire remained in the aisle, wearing uncertainty like a badge. At least she was willing to offer more assistance than a kind heart and listening ear, which had been the extent of her help during the winter months when she'd settled into a chair and talked with Mary while Mary did the work.

"Start with Mud." Mary jutted her head toward the first stall and handed Claire a bucket. "Remember how I showed you?"

Claire edged the stool near the hind legs.

"Closer," Mary said.

Claire nudged it another few inches.

"Come on, Claire. You know where it goes."

With a groan, Claire shoved the stool close and sat down gingerly.

"She's fidgety. Don't let her step in the bucket."

Claire leaned forward and grabbed a teat. Mud shifted, and Claire's hands jerked back.

Mary secured a rope around one of Mud's front legs and tethered it to a post, lifting it off the ground. "This will ensure she won't kick."

Claire's brow furrowed. "Are you sure?"

"Yes." Mary winked. " I'd let Mud kick Luke, but on you, I take pity."

"I don't get this rift between you and Luke."

Mary settled next to the neighboring cow and shone the lantern near the teats. She gritted her teeth. Redder than yesterday. "There's no rift."

Grace's laughter sounded from several stalls over.

Mary felt for lumps in the teats and udder. None. Either way, she wouldn't mix the milk in with the others' tonight.

"If it's not a rift, then what is it?" Claire asked. "Am I missing an important story?"

"You are missing years of stories," Grace called.

Mary fetched the salve. "There is no story."

"No rift and no story." Claire sighed. "And no milk here."

Mary glanced over. "Squeeze off the top and then roll your fingers downward. Open your hand and repeat."

Claire tried again, but failed. Mary rose, bent over Claire's shoulder, and milked until the flow started. Claire took over. The stream of milk slowed but continued.

"I'm going to make a dairymaid out of you yet." Mary returned to her cow.

"Luke said he came to help Saturday night, and you were gone." Grace leaned against the stall post by Mary. "Were you out courting?"

Claire swung her head around.

Grace's hazel eyes, so like her brother's, pried for information. "You can't be out courting in milkmaid clothes."

"I happen to love my clothes," Mary said.

Claire brought her bucket for Mary to peer inside. "This is all she's giving me."

The bucket was a quarter full. "Seems right. I'm drying her out to freshen. Try the other side, but untie her leg first."

Claire returned to Mud, and Grace settled across the aisle and began milking. "I finally asked Luke about Rachel."

Who? Mary forced herself to keep working.

"He's been so cranky with Paul that it's hard to catch him in a good mood." Grace's gaze flitted sideways across the aisle. "Have I mentioned Rachel?"

Never. "I don't remember."

"She's the daughter of his captain. He wrote about her in a few letters last year, and I thought he'd found someone special, but he stopped mentioning her."

Good for him, finding a Texas girl who must also love a sky that—how had Luke put it?—was so big it looked like it could eat you alive. Mary had no desire to be devoured by anything Texas, sky or other.

"Saturday night after helping your papa," Grace continued, "he seemed in a pleasant mood. Whistling. I asked him—"

"Ah!" Claire jumped from her stool. "Mud!"

Mud's hind leg rested in the pail.

Claire brushed at the milk that had splashed the bottom of her dress. "I'm sorry."

"It's not your fault." Mary removed Mud's leg, and swatted her on the hip.

"I think I'll take my chair in the corner and provide encouragement," Claire said, "which I'm far better at."

Mary smiled and paced the aisle to the back. The storage room was dark, but she didn't need light to snatch another can. She grabbed one and spun around to return but stopped at the sight of the side door standing open a foot. That was the third time in two weeks she'd found the door ajar when it should have been shut. She latched it, noting the weak connection. Perhaps the cat had pushed it open.

But the suggestion didn't satisfy. Odd things, like noises, misplaced items, and the door ajar, had been occurring lately. Her mind spanned a string of possibilities, from animals to a situation that belonged in a Grimm's fairytale.

Shoving the implausible aside, she returned and set the empty can on the cart.

Grace had moved to the next cow. "If you weren't courting, what were you doing?"

Seeing no use in keeping the secret from her best friend, Mary confessed. "I visited Clifton."

Grace jerked her head toward Mary, milk spraying across the aisle. "Why would you do that?"

"I play the piano for three hours at the Gold Mine on Saturday evenings."

Claire gasped.

Mary smirked. "You don't even know what the Gold Mine is."

"I can imagine."

"It's the hotel."

Grace returned her attention to milking, offering her sober profile to Mary. "It's the bar in a mining town, and it attracts not only hordes of miners, but area lumbermen as well."

Claire gasped again.

"It's not as bad as it sounds," Mary said.

The Gold Mine played more roles than Claire understood, and Mary's serving up classical music added reputability to the place. Mary walked past Grace and rubbed her hand over a cow's velvety ear. "Tell me what you're thinking before you frown so hard your face gets stuck."

Grace's chest rose and fell with each breath as she poured over the task of milking as if pouring over the latest fashion designs from France.

"What I do is perfectly safe. The men are a bit rowdy, but they love the music." Mary's defense didn't ease the strain on Grace's face, and if Mary were honest, didn't alleviate her own concerns. So she tried harder to convince Grace. And herself. "You don't understand. You can sew clothes for anyone, anywhere. There is no concert hall in Pine Creek."

Grace shook her head. "Rod said he did more business

one Tuesday morning than usual because you came to play on that day and customers lingered."

Rod was generous to let her play the piano anytime, but he didn't pay her to do so.

Mary knelt next to Grace. "Please don't say anything to Papa. By the end of summer, Bridges will have expanded his camp, giving us more business. This is temporary."

"You're asking me to keep quiet about too many things."

"They're small things."

Grace raised a brow, but her attempt at stern fell short. With a sigh, she nodded, and Mary hugged her.

"That goes for you, too, Claire." Mary looked across the way.

Claire propped her hands on her hips, and Mary expected an argument, but instead, Claire also nodded.

"Take Luke with you to Clifton," Grace said.

Hah! He'd spawn an overreaction the size of Texas if he found out. "I'll be fine. You can pray, if you're worried."

Grace's prayer life was rich as cream, another reason she belonged with a man like Cam. Claire shot an arrow prayer up to the Heavenly Father for her two friends.

"I'll keep quiet and pray. But only if you agree to come over and let me fit you for a new dress."

Mary groaned. "I have no money for a fancy dress."

"I didn't say you'd pay, and I didn't say fancy."

"You meant fancy."

Grace stood and brushed shoulders with Mary as she moved to the cart. "I'm sorry to be manipulative, but those are my conditions." Her sweet smile held more concern than true exploitation, despite her demand.

"Fine," Mary said. "You pray and keep mum about things, and I'll let you measure me and prick me with pins."

CHAPTER ELEVEN

Luke tugged on the lead rope of the frustrated steer. Its back legs were swallowed knee high in mud, and its front hooves pawed the slippery ground, vying for traction. The drizzle that had misted the air since sunrise transitioned into a steady, gentle rain.

"Come on." Luke dug his right foot into the ground in front of his left, leaned his weight back, and pulled the rope.

With a strangled bellow, one of the steer's back hooves made it out first, followed by the other. Luke untied the rope, granting the steer complete freedom, and gripped his burning shoulder. Now if only someone would tie a rope around Luke and tug him out of Pine Creek.

Wait. That's what his captain was trying to do. *I believe in your innocence and will continue to fight to prove it*, he'd written.

A witness, which I will not name for reasons of confidentiality, has come forward and charged you with working alongside the Fowler Trio in several robberies, including the Fort Worth Bank robbery last October that led to the death of two Rangers.

Nothing could be worse than being accused of unfaithfulness, of turning against the ideals to which he'd committed his life.

He amended the thought. Burning down a building and hiding the truth was worse. At least in the first instance, his innocence comforted him.

Luke's stomach growled, and he glanced at the filtered

sunlight attempting to push through the rain clouds. The bright spot in the sky above his head told him it was time to return to the house and endure more of Paul's well-used cold shoulder. Paul had labeled him as the one who'd abandoned the family in its time of need. And Luke had labeled Paul as the one who'd begrudged Luke his dream.

They couldn't bridge the impasse, and trying no longer seemed important.

Luke hitched the rope over his shoulder and took off toward the barn. Across the field, a rider in a vest, gun slung across his lap, made his way along the fence line toward the house. Luke's stride paused a moment before realization set in.

He tossed down the rope and ran to intercept the rider. Things were going down, but his family didn't need to see the arrest.

"Hey!" Luke waved, slowing his pace when the man turned his horse toward Luke.

"You Luke Thomas?"

The marshal star on the man's vest confirmed Luke's suspicions.

The man swung down from the chestnut roan and tipped his too-clean hat back. Slender and beardless, the youth looked like an easy takedown.

Something you are not thinking of doing.

Adding resistance to law enforcement to the false accusations wouldn't help his cause. "I suppose you're here for me."

The marshal laughed and thumbed his belt buckle. "It's not like that. Name's Lars Swensson." The blond had an accent to match his Scandinavian name. "Not yet, at least. I need a statement from you."

Air rushed out of him. "That's it?" The letter had said to expect a visit from a marshal, and in Luke's mind, that meant arrest.

"Not quite so simple. In addition to a deposition, for

which the Rangers require an official witness, I need your promise not to leave town without their permission."

Instead of jail, they'd keep him in Pine Creek.

The marshal squinted his blue eyes and smiled. "You want to find the mayor and get your statement over with, or are you going to offer me lunch first?"

Neither. Johnston wasn't going to be Luke's official witness, nor was bringing this lawman into his house for lunch an option. "Let's get the statement over with. Will the postmaster work as a witness?"

"Fine with me."

"Go on out past this pasture to the road. It'll take you in to town. I'll meet you in fifteen minutes."

"I know where to find you if you don't." Marshal Swensson offered a lopsided smile, mounted, and tipped his hat.

The marshal's pen poised above the paper, waiting for Luke's response.

Luke pulled his collar away from his neck. "I don't have the money."

The deathbed confession of Wiley Fowler, oldest in the trio, had condemned Luke.

"Did you ever see the money from the March hold up?" Swensson asked, reading off a list of questions.

"Not for that hold up. A month earlier the trio held up the Mills Point bank, and I came across them in their camp that night. I saw the money then."

The blond bangs of Marshal Swensson shook as he scrawled Luke's answer with a quick hand. "Why didn't you move in then for the arrest?"

"I was under orders not to, and I didn't find out until later that the money I'd seen was from the Mills Point hold up."

"But you did move in after the Billerton robbery?"

The night he'd been shot. "Yes."

"Without jurisdiction?"

A Ranger's jurisdiction was left up to his discretion. "I always have jurisdiction."

Marshal Swensson finished scrawling and peered at his notes. "But you were commanded not to act, is that correct?"

"I was advised against acting."

"Why?"

"The Rangers suspected they hadn't discovered all of the Fowlers connections yet."

"But you acted."

"I saw an opportunity." When a man worked an area by himself, he did what needed to be done when the time presented itself. That rarely required bending the rules. But sometimes it did.

"This is what's going to happen." Marshal Swensson packed up his writing supplies and the ten pages of deposition from Cam's desk.

Luke swigged the warm water Cam had given him two hours ago when they'd started.

Marshal Swensson stood. "After all the depositions are collected, the judicial committee will review them and make a decision. You're to remain in Pine Creek should we need to contact you further."

In other words, should they need to haul him to jail.

The marshal dropped the papers into his saddle bag and held out his hand. "Thank you for your cooperation. You made my job easy."

"My pleasure." He'd put forth any effort to give truth the edge over whomever had shifted blame to him.

Because that's definitely what had happened. Someone had given false testimony. The Rangers would not have suspended one of their own and moved forward with an investigation solely on the testimony of an outlaw, Wiley Fowler, who'd said Luke had the money.

So who had lied? Another Ranger? A city official,

politician, lawman?

"If you need anything, I'll be stationed in Clifton for the summer."

"Thank you." Luke nodded. "I have one question."

Swensson turned at the door, his youthful expression humble. "If I can answer."

"I want to know who implicated me. Who's this witness the Rangers have speaking against me?"

The rain had eased into a mist. Swensson shifted his feet. "I'm not entirely sure. At least, I don't have a name."

Which meant Swensson knew something but wasn't allowed to tell.

Luke leaned against the doorjamb and watched Marshal Swensson stride toward the livery to retrieve his mount. He shoved his sleeves above his elbows. Even with a cloudy afternoon, the fire having burned low, and the doors open, the smithy boasted sweltering air. "I'm sorry I wasted two hours of your time."

"Not anything about these two hours has been wasted." Dried sweat marked a 'u' shape across Cam's chest. "Now I know all your secrets."

Luke snorted. "This is just the beginning."

"What else are you hiding besides accusations of bank robbery and failure to obey orders? Murder charges?"

A long time ago, Luke had killed a part of himself, but . . . "Nothing like that."

"Childhood stuff?"

Cam wasn't Pine Creek's pulpit supply merely for his Biblical knowledge and preaching skills. He had an ability to hammer into the spiritual side of people like he hammered iron.

Cam pulled out a tin of biscuits and offered one to Luke. "Courtesy of Mrs. Lunsford."

Luke ate one in three bites. "When are you going to learn to cook for yourself?"

"No need. I have every widow and able bodied wife

taking pity on me. Preacher's benefits, I suppose."

"You know you only fill the pulpit three-quarters of the time, right? Doesn't old Newton still come once a month?"

"Yep."

Johnston strutted down the boardwalk toward the smithy, and Luke turned from his position against the open doors, but not before the mayor's attention caught him.

"Election's getting closer." Johnston stepped one foot inside the smithy, holding his arms close to his side and scanning the filth with a grimace on his face.

"So it is," Luke said.

Johnston didn't seem put off by Luke's less than enthusiastic response. "Exciting things are happening in town. A man of your character and reputation would add more value than I know how to express."

"Try." Luke smiled, calling Johnston out on his ambiguous compliment.

Brushing imaginary dust off his suit coat, Johnston pulled back his shoulders. "The Crawleys said you've been helping them with property rights, and I've seen you giving gun safety lessons to several youth."

Luke shoved his hands in his pockets. "Isn't Cam qualified for sheriff?"

Johnston frowned. "His shot's not half what yours is, and besides, he's got other things to do. Business will increase if we get that railroad endowment." The mayor scanned the cramped shop. "You should think of expanding."

Cam wiped his hand along the back of his mouth, ridding the crumbs. "It'd be easier to do if I owned the place."

"The owner hasn't showed. Isn't even from the area. How's he supposed to know what Pine Creek needs?" Johnston smoothed the front of his suit coat. "We who are here know what's necessary. Go ahead and knock out that side wall. You've got my support."

Luke smiled at Cam behind Johnston's back but sobered his expression when the mayor turned.

"We've got to get you into office as soon as possible," Johnston said. "Things are falling into place for our bid for the railroad, and having a sheriff is essential."

"I'm not running." Luke took another biscuit, sank into a chair, and let the moist goodness distract him from Johnston's glare.

"Luke—"

"This isn't my home anymore."

Huffing, the mayor stalked away.

Luke wiped his hands over his face. "Guess we both have our list of complications. Mine are worse."

"How do you figure?" Cam asked.

"I'm wanted."

"For deposition, not jail. If I start knocking out walls and frustrate my boss, I might lose my livelihood."

Luke smiled. "Did I mention the Rangers are hiring?"

The milk cart crept toward the lumber camp, the crunching beneath the wheels mingling with Mary's humming. The rattling bottles in the back added to the chorus, as did the clattering of her teeth. She tugged her coat tighter, warding off the drizzle and damp, spring air.

Rain had fallen for most of two weeks, rendering the roads a muddy mess. The skies had cleared in time for a beautiful sunset yesterday and ushered in overnight freezing temperatures that had frostbitten her garden seedlings.

All that seemed of little consequence because Papa had delayed his trip to the Millwood's.

The route narrowed and veered into a canyon as she crossed from Smith land to Bridges land. He'd built the main part of his camp where the canyon opened into a plateau blanketed with pine trees. A log chute sloped down the mountainside to the steam-powered mill situated along the Wenatchee. He'd set up his place for a bright future, meaning if she and Papa could hold on, Bridges could provide more opportunities for business.

Her horse, Holly, rounded the bend into the camp where midmorning quiet stretched over the cabins. Mary pulled up to Shanty's tent and stepped from the cart.

Her knock on the opened door roused a dog from its place in front of the hearth.

Shanty sauntered from another room, a mixing bowl propped on her rounded hip. "Good to see you, child. You got milk?"

"Plenty. Would you like one can as usual? I have more if you need it."

"One will do, honey. Set it here." She tipped her head toward the entrance. "I got to check my bread."

The black woman disappeared. Mary let down the back of the cart, unhooked the can from its anchored place on the side, and rolled it down the makeshift ramp. Bending her knees, she lifted the milk from the rollers to the ground next to the door.

"You leave it there." Shanty came back in the room wearing a streak of flour from her hairline to her chin. "I'll have one of the boys move it." She looked Mary up and down, a frown deepening. "You cold, child?"

"My hands and face."

Shanty waved a hand over her shoulder and led Mary into the next room, where several ovens lined a wall. Wood smoke enhanced the spicy scent of lunch.

"Drink this." Shanty shoved a mug of steaming liquid into her hands. Small flecks of green floated about.

"What is it?"

Shanty laughed. "It be broth and herbs. You heard of broth?"

Mary sipped the salty brew. Her cooking skills had fallen prey to the demands of the dairy. They subsisted on eggs, seasonal vegetables, fried chicken, and if Papa hunted, smoked venison. A wearisome diet. Her broth consisted of throwing chicken bones into a pot of simmering water, a simple and rushed concoction compared to Shanty's, which had probably cooked three days with onions, celery, and herbs.

"Take it with you. I know you can't stay."

"Thank you."

Shanty walked Mary to the door. "Tell Luke next time you see him that I want him to come back and visit some more."

Luke had visited Shanty? The widowed Mrs. Lunsford had spoken of Luke's visits as well. Seemed he'd made rounds like a preacher.

"I can't get enough of them stories he tells."

Stories, indeed. Exaggerations, likely.

"Now why you be doing that?" Shanty placed a hand on her hip, silent laughter shaking her bosom.

"What did I do?"

"You be rolling your eyes when I mention Luke. Shanty knows what that means."

Mary caught herself from rolling her eyes again and retreated through the door.

Shanty's laugh followed her into the cool sunshine. "We'll talk about Luke next time."

Next week she'd send Jake, though that wouldn't work because he had school. She'd send Luke, and Shanty could have her stories.

She waved to Shanty, climbed into the cart, and turned the horse toward home. If she continued on past Bridges land, she'd eventually get to Clifton. The gatherings had become larger and noisier with each Saturday as men had grown accustomed to the music and loose with their manners.

Unfortunately, the pay had not grown, unless she counted the satisfaction she experienced when she played for others. Too many days, the dairy locked her away with its demands.

But she wasn't going to allow those thoughts voice again.

Mary blew out a breath, and a faint cloud dispersed. Chilly, but not frigid. At the bottom of the hill, lumberjacks unloaded equipment from two wagons.

Matthew tossed a jump board onto the ground and hopped over the side of the wagon.

"Matthew."

The tall man jerked his head in her direction and waved. He jogged across the stump-filled meadow looking handsome in his red and black checkered coat and short pants. The crisp sun brought a pale hue to his blue eyes, and a shy grin lit his narrow face.

Mary stared beyond him at the grove of aspen. "Are you going to harvest these?"

"We *are* lumberjacks. It's what we do." He leaned his arms on the edge of her cart, his eyes level with hers.

The Bridges specialized in pine and hemlock. "They're beautiful trees. Do you have to cut them?"

"Trees are reproducible. There's enough to go around. We have a large order for aspen from a furniture maker in Wenatchee." Matthew looked over his shoulder at his team. "I'm training some new jacks today."

The men looked in her direction, their smirks matching the size of their equipment. Men and their leering.

Matthew followed her gaze, and his expression hardened. "Back to work."

His commanding tone drew her respect.

He returned his attention to her, and a broad-shouldered youth that hardly looked old enough to be finished with a basic education winked at her.

She glared his direction before focusing on Matthew. "You've done well for yourself." She liked seeing the quiet, steady boy she'd known maturing into a leader.

"Daaaiirrry Maaarrry."

Those drawn out words. That voice. She cringed as Davis Keller punched his way from the brush and joined the group of men.

"Am I glad to see you," he said.

"Same to you, Davis." Mary grinned, but the sentiment didn't reach her heart. Some childhood friends had worn out their welcome before the passing of adolescence.

Matthew's eyes threw daggers at Davis. "You're late."

Davis shrugged. "My apologies, sir."

He jumped into the cart and wedged between Mary and the side. Putting his arm around Mary's shoulders, he settled in as if for an afternoon drive.

Matthew's stance went rigid, and he looked like he might rip Davis from the wagon with one hand and throw him over with the rest of the men.

"Can you believe I have to call this man 'sir' now that he's my boss?" Davis grinned.

Attempting to be subtle, Mary scooted as close to the opposite side of the constricted space as she could. Davis had been trouble from the time he'd snuck his mother's medicinal whiskey to school. Forget subtle. She pressed into the corner of the seat and made no effort to hide her desire for space. Not that she need fear offending Davis, whose oblivion to the feelings of others mirrored that of a rock's.

"All right. Get your equipment sorted." Matthew snatched Davis's elbow and pulled. "Now."

"Sure thing." He shook his elbow free. "Don't lose your patience, boss." He bounded to the ground and moseyed toward the men.

Matthew's shoulders relaxed, but his narrowed eyes eagled Davis until he reached the team.

Spreading her skirts, Mary settled back in the middle of her seat.

"They're not as bad as they come off," Matthew said.

A belch sounded from the midst of the dozen jacks.

"Then again . . . I'd like to move to the business side of operations someday. Seems more suited to family life."

Her eyes softened as Matthew relaxed again to his old self. "You'd rather be inside when you could be out, breathing fresh air, using your body to earn a living?"

His lopsided smile sent a tremor through her heart.

"Spoken like a dairy farmer. Where's my pianist?"

"Missing her piano. But there's nothing to do about that." The sooner she accepted the fact that money would be the thorn in the side of the dairy, the sooner she could grasp contentment.

"There is something you can do." The skin around his eyes tightened, and he focused on his shifting feet, as if nervous. "My father's got vision—"

"No." Enough with this idea.

"Hear me out." Matthew folded his hands on top of the cart. "Have you ever known him to be unfair?"

Ambitious, but not unfair. "No."

"Father's bought ten more oxen to transport boards from the mill into Wenatchee. He and Johnston have been working together to get the railroad through here, which would—"

"Again with the railroad? Why can't the town put that to rest? It's not going to work. We don't have the amenities they desire, and they're coming west too quickly for us to fix that."

"Which is why—"

"If they were still interested in Pine Creek, we'd have heard by now. It's been a year since the delegation's visit. Is it so hard to let go of something that is obviously not going to happen? Not that I wouldn't be glad for more business for the dairy."

Matthew's mouth slackened, and his brows angled in.

"What did I say?"

The criticism disappeared, and he smiled, a true and real Matthew smile that softened his angular face. "You're interrupting me as if I'm Luke."

What did Luke have to do with anything? "Luke has no desire to tangle with the railroad, or anything else unless guns, adventure, or justice is involved."

"Or you." Matthew ripped his hat from his head and shuffled his fingers though his hair.

Claire. Shanty. Now Matthew. Through the years, her name had been linked with Luke's far too frequently, and it was becoming downright ridiculous. Either she was terribly blind, or . . . She couldn't think of an *or*. But she wasn't blind. She saw Luke's lackadaisical attitude toward Pine Creek, and toward her.

Matthew pushed back from the cart. "I need to get back to my men. For now, keep in mind that my father's interest in buying your land doesn't mean you'd have to close the dairy."

Her gaze sought his.

"He understands your family's value here, and he doesn't need a dairy. If you sell to him, he'll let you continue on with a small rent that's less than your loan."

She jumped from the wagon and gripped Matthew by the arms. "Are you being honest with me?"

Matthew dipped his chin. "Why wouldn't I be?"

"Because this is too good." Her smile stretched so broad it hurt her face. "You don't know how much I needed this news today after what Luke did this week."

Matthew frowned.

"Thank you." She stood on tiptoes and kissed his bearded cheek. "I'm going to talk with Papa."

She climbed in the wagon, and Matthew patted Holly on the rump. The cart jerked into motion. Glancing over her shoulder, she followed Matthew's progress back to his workers. The one who'd winked offered a wave, and she straightened and faced forward.

God had sent rain. He'd delayed Papa so that she could run into Matthew today. Tonight, she'd lock herself in Rod's and play out a litany of thanksgiving. Finally. The answer that would satisfy both hers and Papa's needs.

Chapter Twelve

Luke shoved his hands in his pockets and strolled down the drive from Barrett's and Claire's. The shadowed ridgeline stood dark against the deep blue sky of a starry night. Between the food and the company, he'd been able to deflect his thoughts from Texas. For a short time.

Moonlight shone the way past the sign that marked the entrance to the land which Luke had roamed with Barrett and Cam as a youth. Alert to the sounds around him, Luke let the fresh air soothe the stale thoughts that returned.

He was wanted. Not for arrest, but a guilty verdict would change that.

A week had passed since he'd given his statement. They'd compare it with other statements and make a decision regarding his loyalty. Since when did someone else get to decide where he'd cast his loyalty? He'd directed it at the Rangers, and they'd returned the favor by questioning it.

The three-quarter moon reflected off windows as Luke made his way through town. The near-finished hotel sat dark. A month from now, lights would wink from behind closed shades and good smells would drift into the street and invite in the hungry, the lonely, and the downtrodden.

Him.

He passed the mayor's office and the empty building adjoining it. If Grace had her way, it'd become a dress shop. If Johnston had his way, it'd house a lawyer.

And after the empty office, the empty jail. Up until now Pine Creek hadn't needed more than the presence of a marshal. Johnston had been intimidating enough.

Luke rubbed the swelling in his shoulder. Since one of the Smith's jerseys had slammed him into the stall post five days ago, bruising his wound, the throbbing had increased from periodic to constant.

Faint music rose above the crunch of his footsteps. He strode past the forge, across the alleyway, and stopped at the corner of Rod's. He leaned against the building, letting the strain of his suspension from the Rangers rest on the beauty of Mary's music. She drove those keys with the intensity that Paul drove the cattle.

Such beautiful music from a person with more barbs than a brier bush.

Why do you do that?

His breath hitched. He'd developed a routine of thinking about Mary as the fiery troublemaker she'd been as a child, but that wasn't fair to her—nor to his deeper, more impartial perspective. She was spontaneous and had a thirst for fun and a desire to be with the people she loved. Her commitment to her father and mother's dream was admirable. Her work ethic surpassed that of some of his Ranger friends. And her loyalty to Grace had offered him comfort when he'd thought of his family far away, even when he'd known that Grace and Mary were separated by their studies.

He sank to the ground, extended his legs, and leaned against the building. His hand brushed something soft and flowerlike. He picked up the sticky blossom and held it to the moonlight, but he knew by its smell what it was. Honeysuckle. He tossed it into the street, crossed his arms, and closed his eyes to listen to Mary's playing.

A dog barked somewhere across the street, and he opened his eyes. A shadow hugged the southern wall of the hotel and slipped around the side. Luke sat forward and stared into the darkness. Mary's playing blocked any sound of footsteps. H rose to his feet, hands reaching for the comfort of his guns.

Mary's playing continued, a fast-paced — *allegretto* — movement he didn't recognize.

Leaving his position against the building, he focused his attention where he'd seen the shadow disappear and crossed the road toward the hotel construction. Intuition quickened his pace. He jogged into the darkness beyond the site, his right hand firm on his weapon.

A faint trace of alcohol rode the air. The landscape turned hilly and shrubs and trees thickened. He stopped his jog and strained to catch a noise. Nothing. How much would he push this pursuit to satisfy his curiosity? Wasn't a crime to be in town after dark.

A twig snapped ahead of him, renewing his urge to hunt. He strode forward, debated calling out and demanding who was there. He smelled alcohol again and set into a jog. Ducking beneath a swag of evergreen, he rounded a pine tree. A branch speared his shoulder, and he cried out, gripping the searing pain. He slouched against a trunk, the search off. And what had possessed him anyway? No one had been in danger. He'd had no evidence of trouble afoot, only an intuition. Acting on intuition was what had gotten him in trouble with the Rangers.

He turned back, breathing through clenched teeth. Danger or not, someone had been lurking. Watching, perhaps. Vandalizing, more likely. He had two choices. Visit Johnston and offer a warning about suspicious activity and give Johnston an opportunity to make a case for him as sheriff. Or brush off his instincts.

Rotten options, both of them.

He crossed the quiet street toward Rod's. The music had stopped, and the store front, which before had been dimly lit by a single candle, was now dark. He made his way south out of town, aware that ahead of him, Mary was probably walking home. In the dark. The same dark that concealed the man he'd just pursued.

You're overreacting, looking for adventure where there is

none.

At the fork where his road veered from Mary's, he paused, considered following.

It's not necessary. The pursuit happened on the other end of town.

Ignoring the hunch, he headed toward home.

How could a place such as Pine Creek, or a chunk of land and a house such as the Thomas homestead, suffocate him and attract him at the same time?

When he reached the two-story farmhouse, the glow of a single lamp in the front window welcomed him, his mother's doing. Quiet enveloped him as he entered and hung his coat. He blew out the lamp and took the stairs, mindful to avoid the steps with creaks loud enough to wake Helen. She'd moved to a cot in the corner of Paul and Abigail's room when Luke had returned and taken over his old room where she'd been sleeping.

They'd made space for him, and he'd been too selfishly absorbed in his issues to thank them. The realization stung, shamed him.

At the top of the stairs, the sound of Paul and Abigail's muted voices snuck through their cracked bedroom door. Luke peered through the narrow opening. Candlelight flickered on the walls, illuminating Paul on his side next to Abigail, stroking hair away from her face. Their whispers conveyed an intimacy that stirred Luke's imagination. Made him wonder if contentment felt as good as it looked.

He'd sacrificed a chance at a simple life when he'd chased after the Rangers. And it'd been worth it, despite the heart pains that growled each time Paul spoke to Abigail with tenderness or hoisted Helen into his arms.

Abigail's delicate laughter sounded, and Luke looked away, stepped toward his room. A floorboard screamed his presence, and Gus wandered out from Luke's room.

"Luke?"

Paul always knew when he came home. Even if none of

the stairs creaked, Paul heard and called out.

"It's me."

Gus circled his legs and returned to his rug at the foot of Luke's bed. Moonlight cast a soft shadow of the maple against his wall. Luke unbuckled his guns and set them atop his dresser.

A knock sounded at his door, soft and unlike Paul's. He toed his boot off and flung it aside. "Come in."

Grace slipped inside and shut the door behind her. Wide, sober eyes met his. "Did Mary say something to you?"

The answer to *Did Mary say something?* was continuously yes, though Grace seemed to have something particular in mind.

"I was at Barrett's house. I haven't seen her."

Grace fisted her hands and pulled her lips taut.

"What was she supposed to say to me?"

With her light brown hair hanging in a braid over her shoulder, Grace looked like the vulnerable child he remembered defending from Davis's incessant teasing.

She sighed. "Nothing."

Before he could argue, she slipped back through the door.

***

The sun was a breath away from cresting the mountains when Luke threw on a pair of trousers and stumbled down the stairs and into the kitchen. The smell of bacon had pulled his hide from deep sleep.

"Grace, you know how to get a man to face the day."

His sister stirred breakfast on the stove, her eyes sparkling. "A real man's faced the day by now."

He grabbed the coffeepot and poured, but the smattering of drips filled less than an inch.

Grace kissed him on the cheek. "You should have been up for the first round of chores."

He snagged a piece of bacon from the drip cloth. "You

taking lessons from Mary on how to pester a guy?"

"I'm sure I could never hope to accomplish the level of pestering she's reached with you."

He sat at the table while Grace stepped outside and yelled for Paul. She'd spent the last two mornings helping Mary. He'd helped three evenings the previous week. No way could Mary maintain the frenzied pace of five hours of daily milking, an hour and a half of deliveries, and normal household chores of cooking, cleaning, and laundry. Not to mention gardening, upkeep of facilities, stall mucking . . . And he knew she snuck to Rod's for at least thirty minutes a day to play the piano, if rumors could be trusted.

Grace yelled Paul's name again, stretching it out into the morning stillness.

His mother entered, a tattered apron tied around her middle. "You'd think after all these years we'd have bought a bell."

Footsteps pounded, and Paul pushed through the door, followed by Abigail and Helen. He tossed his hat on a hook, and thrust his hands in the basin of water. With one quick glare, Paul sent Luke's mood skidding.

The lines around his mother's eyes tightened as she glanced between them.

Options were slim. Eat in silence, pretend Paul wasn't upset, and submit to his leadership for the day's work. Or confront him.

Luke wasn't the silent type, or a pretender. "I don't think oversleeping deserves a look like that."

His mother thrust a hand over the table. "Blessing first, then . . ."

Then fighting.

Grace delivered the final dish, took her seat, and offered a prayer that sounded like a thankful plea for peace.

Luke waited a moment after the *amen* before looking at Paul — who was already looking at him with the vengeance of an army.

"I overslept." Last night he'd stared at his ceiling, wishing for a starry sky above to help shut off the thoughts that trapped him. Thoughts like what Grace had meant about Mary speaking to him and why he even cared enough what Mary was going to say to lose sleep over it. Eventually, he'd opened his window and sat on the edge of the bench, thinking about Paul with his arms around Abigail, the deposition he'd given, and why his shoulder hurt so much. And when his thoughts circled back to Mary, he could have howled at the moon. Her loudmouth seemed even louder in his thoughts than it did in person.

"Abigail and Helen slept longer than usual, and they still made it to chores, and in Abigail's condition, that's saying something."

Luke swallowed a growl and glanced at Abigail's swollen belly. "What's it saying?" He dared Paul to call him lazy.

Paul took a heaping spoonful of eggs without his gaze wavering from Luke's. "You were out late."

"I'm not ten. Would you like a full account of where I was?"

"Please tell me it wasn't Cecily's."

Grace laughed, but when she caught Paul's serious expression, her laugh cut off. She swung her eyes back to his. "Luke?"

He smirked. "I don't know where that line of thinking came from. I was with Barrett, Claire, and Cam."

"Cecily likes you," Paul said.

"Good and fine."

"She's changed."

"Good and fine." Luke shoved a bite of potatoes into his mouth.

"Please, not Cecily." Grace furrowed her brow. "She's so pretentious."

He nearly choked on his potatoes.

"Grace." His mother frowned.

107

"Did you ever answer any of her letters?" Paul asked.

Grace groaned and tipped her head back. "She wrote letters?"

She'd written a letter. Short and to the point, apologizing for her flirtatious behavior when they'd been younger. He'd answered it, because an honest confession deserved a pardon.

"Look." He pushed the eggs and potatoes together on his plate. "I'm not here to court anyone. My time is short. It's just a visit."

Paul shoved back his chair and stood. "Let me get this straight. You think that by showing up here and staying the summer, you'll have paid your dues and we'll be satisfied?"

As if family membership was contingent on what a person contributed. "I thought this was a family, not some association."

Paul cringed.

"What do I owe this family that I haven't given?" The question was out before Luke considered the consequences of asking it. He rushed, not giving Paul a chance to spout off a list. "You have a wife and a family. That was your dream, and I'm happy for you." He stood, matching Paul's stance. "I wanted to be a Ranger. That was my dream. I don't see how me pursuing my dream translates into me not caring for my family. It's possible to love from a distance, you know."

"No. We wouldn't know. Because when you're at a distance, we have no way of knowing that you love us."

Luke stepped back, tipping his chair over. It slammed against the floor. "I write letters."

"Love is more than letters. It's sweat and blood and presence."

Abigail placed her hand on Paul's forearm. He shook it off.

Grace and his mother fixated on their plates. And Helen, bless her four-year-old heart, appeared fascinated by the biscuit in her hand.

Luke turned to his mother. "Do you wish to condemn me, too?"

She tossed her napkin on the table and stood, tears moistening her eyes. "No. Not at all." She wrapped her arms around him. "I won't pretend it's not difficult having a son across the country and knowing years might go by without seeing him." Her voice trembled. "But I'm happy for you."

He saw through her effort to offer support.

"I don't want you to fight." His mother looked between him and Paul. "You're home for as long as you can be." She directed her attention to Paul. "And we'll accept that for the blessing it is."

Luke stomped through the field, Paul's dog dancing in his footsteps and dodging in front of him. The collie had no manners, rushing at will around the grazing cattle. The bag Luke had swung over his shoulder bounced against his back as he pushed around muddy areas toward the cattle clustered in the corner of the pasture.

Paul found fault with everything, even Luke's desire to walk and not ride his horse. A man had two feet for a reason, and Luke was in the near pasture, not the upper pasture, not the south pasture, not the river pasture.

He dropped his bag near the fence and pulled out the ointment that was supposed to keep ticks off cattle. Paul had said to rub a line down each steer's back. Yeah, because cattle enjoyed being petted like dogs.

Leaning against the fence, he tossed the medicine on the ground and reached into his pocket. He'd snatched a book of matches from the shelf on his way out the door. They'd caught his attention, or maybe he'd sought them out. Old habits he'd thought were dead had resurrected since his return.

He ripped out a match and struck it. The flame gave a whispered hiss and began its descent down the stick. He fixed his eyes on the steady burn, but rather than calm him as it used to, his chest tightened.

Rustling sounded behind him, and he turned to see Mary emerge from the woods, towing a cow behind her. Luke dropped the match and stamped it out, praying she hadn't noticed.

Her dress swished around her ankles as she approached the fence. "How are the wounds?"

"Fine." He wasn't an invalid. "Who's this?"

Mary leaned on the fence. "Gretto."

"What type of name is Gretto?"

"Don't you do detective work, Ranger? Figure out the mystery." She wrapped the lead rope around the fence, climbed the slats, jumped over, and landed in manure. Wrinkling her nose, she wiped her feet against a post.

Mary was one mystery he'd never crack. The way she didn't fuss at things like manure or calluses, yet cried at the faintest roll of thunder.

Sun broke through the mist behind her. "Why must you smile at me like—"

"Like I'm trying to figure out the mystery of you?"

She curled her lips. "You're the enigma."

"That's high praise." He reached around her to pet Gretto.

Mary shrank from his nearness.

"I can be slow on mysteries when they have to do with you. Why don't you just explain her name."

She leaned against the fence. "Gretto made such a quick entrance into the world that I named her Allegretto, which is an Italian musical term for a fast tempo. I call her Gretto because it's shorter and easier."

He nodded. "Did Paul buy her, or did you just bring her over to play with the cattle?"

She grinned. "The latter."

He frowned.

"It's breeding time."

What a numskull he was.

"Don't blush, Luke Thomas. It doesn't befit a lawman."

He ducked his head under the pretense of shoving the ointment back into his bag. "Your bull's in our field?"

"Next one over. The fence in the field we use for him is broken."

He'd be fixing it tomorrow.

She hopped back over the fence and snatched the lead rope. Luke led the way down the fence line past the grove of junipers.

"You know when to bring her back to me?" Mary asked.

"I grew up on a ranch, remember?"

"It's been a while."

And she'd not let him forget.

A red winged blackbird swooped in front of them on its flight to the marsh by the creek. Luke had enough heat in his face to justify a dip in those waters. He'd best change the subject before she launched into a lecture on breeding cattle. Proper or not, she'd do it, if merely to tease him.

He slipped out one gate and opened another, leading the way into the next pasture where the Smith's bull grazed. Mary untied Gretto, and the cow ambled through the opening. Luke swung the gate closed and avoided Mary's gaze as he walked back toward the cattle.

"Paul's generous to let us use the pasture. I know that's not without cost to him and your ranch."

"He's got a big heart." A heart that stayed hidden to most but apparently not to Mary.

"This from one brother who doesn't get along with the other?"

He looked over at her. Her eyes possessed that prodding openness that made him uncomfortable yet fascinated him.

"It's not that we don't get along."

She laughed. "Is what you two do what getting along

111

looks like in Texas?"

Mary talked about things *in Texas*, as if Luke had chosen a life in China. "Why don't you come to Texas yourself to see what life *in Texas* is like?" Not that he was inviting her to follow him back. Mary in Texas . . . the thought both intrigued him and made him want to roll his eyes.

They'd returned to the fence Mary had hopped, and she flung Gretto's rope over it. A frown passed over her expression, and he followed her gaze to the ground.

The match.

She was right to be perplexed about the match's place in the field.

He toed it into the dirt and snatched his bag off the ground. Rummaging through the contents, he scowled.

"Looking for this?" Mary held up the medicine he'd pitched on the ground earlier. She tossed it to him a little hard.

"Easy." He tucked the tin tube into the bag and stalked around to the edge of the group of cattle.

A tug on the bag from behind turned him around.

"Let me," Mary said, taking the bag from him.

He moved to the first steer and she handed him the ointment. Apparently, she felt he'd been gone so long he needed help with ranch work.

"Does Texas have mountains like this?"

His gaze jerked up at the sound of her quiet, wistful voice.

"Are the colors vivid enough to hurt your eyes? Is the air fresh enough to eat?"

"How do you eat air?" He ignored the sparkle in her eyes. "Texas is huge and diverse. Where I am, hills roll across the land. The underbrush is dry. Sage, juniper, and such, except in spring when green overtakes brown for a couple months and bluebonnets carpet every square foot. It's quite beautiful."

She held the bag open while he picked out the wire cutters and snipped off a short section.

"As beautiful as here?"

She was setting a trap, and for whatever reason, he didn't mind getting caught. He twined the wire round the end of the steer's tail, marking that it'd been treated. "Nope. You satisfied?"

Silence. He looked over.

Dark wisps of hair blew into her face. "Are you satisfied in Texas knowing that your family is struggling?"

"What do you mean by struggling? The ranch is doing quite well. If you mean they miss me, you're right, and I'm sorry for that, but I'm content to do what I'm supposed to be doing."

They worked side-by-side, weaving through the cattle, smearing and marking. Mary chatted about her father's health, her attempt to teach Claire how to behead a chicken, and Grace's dreams to open a sewing shop, something he still believed was a useless endeavor, but what did he know about women's need for clothing?

They'd circled back to the fence by the time the conversation lulled.

"I helped milk Saturday night, and you were nowhere to be seen," he said.

She stared across the field, stoic.

"I get it. Private matters." Resting his arms on the back of a steer, he studied her.

Stiff-shouldered and tight-lipped, she looked as if she wanted to argue but had committed to keep her mouth shut.

For all he knew, she'd needed a night away from the cows. He couldn't do what she did day after day without a bit of insanity stealing in. Then again, a young, beautiful woman like her . . . he supposed any number of men wanted her attention.

Maybe one had it.

Nah. She'd not have been able to keep quiet about something like that. He'd have known that first night in the barn.

She brought her eyes to his briefly, then looked away. "I'm not courting, and I know you don't think that's possible anyway."

He laughed and shoved his hat up his brow. "If anyone wants to court you, bless him. He's got my vote for bravest knight."

A hint of a smile lifted her lips. She'd taken it as a compliment. "How about you?"

His eyes widened. Was she asking if he were brave enough to court her?

"I heard something about the daughter of your captain."

Thanks, Grace.

"What do you want to know?"he asked.

She backed up against the fence and hoisted herself up to sit on the top railing. Swinging her legs back and forth, she shrugged, but he saw through the feigned indifference. Her eyes were too alert.

"She's young, sweet like Grace, a portrait artist, and isn't interested in me."

Mary raised a brow. "She turned you down?"

"Hard to believe, huh?"

Another shrug, this time with an accompanying smile. "I wouldn't sound so confident if I were you."

He had the urge to push her backward. She might have more curves than five years ago, but the playfulness she'd had as a child hadn't changed.

"Guess who's back in town?" she asked.

He rubbed the ointment on the last steer of the group, frowning at a small growth near the shoulder. He'd have to remember to tell Paul later. "Preston?"

"Davis. He's working with Matthew."

Luke ducked his head to hide his scowl. Davis had stirred up trouble in three towns before moving to Wenatchee a year ago, or so Grace had heard.

"Don't you find it interesting that Barrett, Grace, Davis,

and you have all returned in the last year?"

A coincidence, since his return hadn't been on his agenda.

"Pine Creek haunts people," she said. "Draws them back by the suspenders when they least suspect it."

The town had haunted him, all right, but he wasn't going to take her bait and confess what had brought him home. Let's see how she liked to be preached at. "I had a good talk with your father Saturday."

Her legs stopped their pendulum movement. "Plotting against me again?"

He wiped his hands on his pants, the frustrated voice of Randall Smith strong in his mind. "He's in a hard place, wanting to please you but trying to do the right thing." No one wanted to watch his daughter do half his work. "You need to consider the Millwoods."

Mary clamped her mouth shut.

"A man doesn't like to feel helpless."

"How would you know?" Her hands gripped the railing on either side of her.

"Contrary to what you think, I've felt helpless."

"When? Right before you got shot?"

She had no idea, even if she thought she did. "No. The summer my father died." Every minute he spent in Pine Creek, the memory of that summer fringed his thoughts. Texas sheltered him. Maybe the memory haunted him every now and then under a cloudless night sky, but most days he didn't have time for the past to invade the present.

He strode over until he stood so close, her knees pressed into his stomach. "Your father's health is unpredictable. Business has gone down, and you can't afford to hire the help you need."

Her lips pressed together, then released.

"It's just a place," he said. "Let it go."

Her eyes skirted around, passing over him, meeting his, darting to the field, circling back to his. Soft, warm breath released from her half-opened mouth. He was about to get an earful.

"What would you know about what is best for me and my family?" Her voice was hushed.

He wasn't fooled. She was seething and barely restraining herself.

Her eyes narrowed. "What have you been doing the past five years?"

Saving lives. Arresting gunmen. Transporting murderers. Protecting citizens. Things best left undeclared at the moment, given the muscle that twitched near her temple.

"Ignoring the past. That's what." She poked his chest.

He tightened his jaw.

"More than that. Ignoring the present because you couldn't face the past. I live the past every day I go to the barn and see my Mama's ribbons, but you won't even admit that you have a past."

His ears ached from clenching his jaw so tight. "You want to know what kind of past I have?" A dishonest, shameful past. His nose stung, and fire burned behind his eyes.

"I'm waiting."

He shook his head.

"That's right. You don't want to say, because while you ignored the loss of your father, I faced the loss of my mother."

"The two aren't even comparable." He cleared his throat, surprised at the tightness that had grabbed his voice. "I knew my father."

She gasped. "And because I didn't know my mother, I don't mourn her as much?"

Yes, exactly. For years his father had invested in his life. Mary had nothing but ribbons and stories—sad, for sure, but how hard could it be to mourn someone you never knew?

She shoved her finger into his chest again. "Admit that's what you're thinking."

"Don't take it personally. It's not an issue of mourning more or less. It's different."

She ripped her eyes from his.

"All your father's asking is that you meet and consider a family that might adopt your mama's dream. Are you going to think of him or yourself?"

Her brown eyes turned back, narrowed in on his, and he felt the squeeze reach into his chest.

"I could ask you the same thing, but I don't need to. You already answered that you'd rather think of yourself when you ran away five years ago."

Ridiculous. He'd had enough of all these accusations. Paul. Mary. Even his mother in her subtle way, had questioned him. He nudged Mary's shoulders.

She wavered, thrust her arms to the side, and toppled backward.

He lunged for her but got a boot in his face. Her hands reached behind her to break her fall. Jumping the fence, he kicked himself for treating Mary like he would have Barrett or Cam. He knelt beside her and reached for her shoulders as she pushed to a sitting position.

Her jersey-sized scowl prompted his repentance, and almost his smile, but discretion argued against that. "I'm sorry."

She looked at her hands, dirty from colliding with the earth moments before the rest of her body. "Do you have any idea how valuable these hands are? What if I'd broken my wrist?"

"I didn't think you'd fall." That should be a compliment, that he'd expected her to right herself from a nudge.

"These are my milking hands. My piano hands." Mud pasted on her palms. She flashed a smile, his only warning, grabbed his face in her hands, and rubbed.

He'd deserved that. He stood and brushed off his trousers.

"Aren't you going to offer me your hand like a gentleman? After all, you keep telling me that Rangers aren't a law unto themselves like I prefer to believe."

He shot out his hand, needing no further goading. "What does it take to get you to be quiet?"

"A little respect wouldn't hurt."

Neither would a kiss.

No. A kiss—rather its repercussions—would kill.

She closed her slimy fingers around his. Her grasp contained all the strength he'd expect from a girl who worked with her hands. As soon as she steadied herself, he released the hand that felt like it'd been around his throat, not his fingers.

He stalked back to his bag and picked it up. "I'll bring what's-her-name back in a few days." He waved over his shoulder and didn't wait for a response. After crossing half the field, he dared to look back. Mary stood at the fence, elbows propped on the railing, staring after him.

Mary'd been trouble since the day she'd thrown his shoes into the creek as a goofy seven-year-old. Trouble that resulted in wet shoes was a nuisance. But trouble of the heart, the kind she'd dished today, was trouble worth avoiding.

CHAPTER THIRTEEN

Five years earlier, 1887

Luke snuck out the back of the silent house two minutes before eleven, ignoring the whisper of his conscience. He wasn't doing anything wrong. Just having a little fun. A farewell party, the boys had said. At nineteen, he'd finally broken from Paul's expectations and would be leaving for Texas in a few days.

Barrett and Cam had started a tradition of midnight cookouts on the Thomas-Smith property border the summer Luke's father had died. Luke supposed the boys had wanted to cheer him up. Instead, he'd gained a fascination with fire and began sneaking off with matchsticks. When a boy felt nothing but emptiness inside, he sought sensation elsewhere — in his case, the burn of a match.

His boots crunched on the rocky path as he cut off into the woods. The full moon spilled light through the trees, and the warm April air testified to the mild winter they'd had. He touched his shirt pocket, reassuring himself that Father's booklet of Psalms was where it was supposed to be. And soon he'd have a badge that read *Texas Rangers*.

After a ten minute walk he arrived at the northeast corner of the Smith's land where a small basin tucked between a couple hillsides. The group had shifted from its early days. Barrett had left to finish his studies. Cam was spending a year in Seattle apprenticing with a blacksmith. Luke had watched them go after their dreams while he'd bowed before the request of his mother and brother to stay. No more.

He broke through the tree line into the meadow and spotted Quinn and Preston throwing logs on the already large fire. Flames licked the blackness, smoke billowed heavenward, and Matthew's harmonica music did a duet with the popping of the fire. A sense of contentment settled over him.

"Hey, you get lost or something?" Davis came from the far side of the fire and slugged him on the shoulder. The first time they'd met, Davis had gotten lost. They'd had to search the dark woods for him. Ever since, it'd been Davis's joke — on others.

"Funny." Luke settled next to Matthew on a fallen tree.

Preston squatted on the opposite side of the fire, always the one poking about with a stick. "I thought you must have stopped by to serenade Dairy Mary Quite Contrary."

Quinn laughed. "Yeah, right. He'd get four notes in, and she'd be throwing tin cans out the window at him."

True. Mary was like a rattler, poised to strike without warning. Unprovoked. All right, maybe not entirely unprovoked. She was so opposite Luke's sister that he enjoyed picking on her.

"You said your goodbyes yet?" Preston asked.

"Some. I stopped at Mrs. Lunsford's, and she gave me a list of her favorite Bible verses. Does that count?"

Preston smiled. "I meant with Mary."

"No need."

Quinn sank to the ground and pulled out a bottle. He uncorked the top and took a swig then passed it to Matthew, who also took a swig.

Luke frowned, turning his head away from the smell. "What's this?"

Davis pulled out his own bottle. "Come on, Duke. It's a proper send off." He held the bottle out to Luke.

"No, thanks." He'd never seen his friends drink, and while he could imagine Davis and Quinn experimenting with the bottle, he'd never pictured Matthew as the type to drink.

"We're adults now," Davis said. "Hard working, wage earning, responsible adults."

Debatable. Davis had worked at the Fledgling the past year, and the rumors about his behavior weren't pretty.

Matthew resumed playing his harmonica while Quinn, Davis, and Preston discussed the positives and negatives of every eligible girl in the county. Emphasis on the negatives. Preston's months of working with Matthew at the lumber mill must have turned his manners to sawdust.

"Now Cecily. There's a woman." Quinn whistled low and hiccupped.

"A woman you don't stand a chance with." Davis stopped pacing and took a seat on a stump. "Luke could have her with one charming smile."

Quinn laughed. "And a few compliments. Cecily's always got to have something nice said about her."

"And you're always obliging." Preston shoved his bottle in his pocket.

Luke stood, brushing off his pants. The past year had worked callousness into his friends, and their lewd comments had increased as their church attendance had decreased. Gone were the days when the fun of the bonfire was being out in the woods in the middle of the night without their parents knowing. If this evening were an example of adulthood, he'd be happy to remain a youth.

"Cecily's changed since her sister's death," Luke said. He wouldn't stand for tarnishing a reputation. "She's lost her self-centeredness."

Davis jumped from his seat and began to pace again. "How would you know, Duke?"

"Oh, he knows." Preston grinned. "Cecily's never been selfish round Luke. She'd give him—"

"Enough." Luke held his hands up, the charm of the bonfire gone. "I got to go."

He strode from the clearing, chased by grumbles from his friends. Twenty feet down the path and out of the circle of light, he stopped, ran his hands through his hair, and tipped his head back to peer at the sky. A million stars poked through the black of night. He'd be staring at this sight more and more if he made it as a Ranger. And he would make it. He'd been planning for it since his twelfth birthday when his father had bought him his first pair of six shooters.

Laughter and whoops sounded from the direction of the bonfire.

"Daaaiiiiry Maaaarrrry." Davis's voice slurred through the night. "That you hidin' behind that rock?"

Matthew's harmonica faded.

Luke honed his ears toward the conversation.

"So it's true."

Yep, Mary's voice. Luke groaned.

"I can't believe you boys have been sneaking onto our land all these years. You can't light up your own woods?"

"Nothing to worry about, Mary."

Matthew's voice.

"I'm surprised you're here, Matthew," Mary said. "I thought better of you."

Mary had never hidden her admiration for Matthew, *a true gentleman*, she'd said. Well, that *true gentleman* had drunk too much tonight, though Mary hadn't seemed to notice.

Luke retraced his steps to the clearing but stopped shy of entering. Mary was capable of handling mischief. Maybe, instead of digging her hole deeper, she'd dig herself out.

Davis paced around Mary. "Don't pretend you never knew our secret. I'm sure Luke whispered it in your ear along with all those sweet nothings."

Not good. If anything would goad Mary, it'd be comments like that. Comments that tied her to him—the boy she'd deemed *unmarryable*.

Mary jutted her chin forward. "Take out the sweet and you've got yourself the truth. Nothing."

That's right. She was Grace's friend. He'd hardly interacted with her.

Except for that one afternoon during the thunderstorm.

And the disaster when he'd attempted to rescue her kitten.

And when she'd trailed him to his shooting spot and challenged him to a competition — which had been no competition at all.

Fine. They'd interacted a fair amount. That was life in a small community.

"Put this thing out and scram." Mary's demand didn't discourage Davis's swarming about her.

Matthew stood, swayed, and shoved his harmonica in his pocket. Luke's body tensed, leaned forward, but he hesitated charging in, resisted the energy building within him. *Handle this, Mary.* He wanted to step from the shadows, take Mary home, tell her to stop intruding. But that show of concern would confirm their unfounded teasing about him and Mary.

The only thing between Mary and him was his sister.

Preston marched up to her. The shortest and stockiest of the group, he stood eye to eye with her. Her hands rested on her hips, and Luke could imagine the sizzling expression in her gaze.

"Aw, lighten up, Dairy Mary." Preston leaned toward her.

She jerked back.

The boys wouldn't hurt her. Would they? Luke had no choice. Growling beneath his breath, he stepped from the woods. "Break it up."

Attention snapped to him, but instead of moving from Mary, the boys laughed and held their positions.

"I knew it." Quinn chuckled too loud.

"The knight has returned." Davis marched up to Mary and looped his arm through hers. "My lady, I'll save you."

Luke shoved his way into the huddle and took Mary's arm from Davis. Her fingers dug into his upper arm.

Don't let them get rough.

123

The prayer slipped through his mind, a deviation from the typical, short pleads he directed at God regarding getting him out of Pine Creek and south to Texas.

Davis grabbed Mary's other arm. "Why don't we ask the lady who she wants to escort her home?"

Luke's glare burned the back of his eyes. "Why don't you let go? Now."

Davis shrugged. "The more's the *Mary*-er, right?"

"Wrong." Luke pulled Mary's arm from Davis's drunken, loose grasp and put her behind him. He lowered his voice. "Don't make trouble, Davis."

Davis's eyes glossed, his lips churned into a scowl, and he nodded. "Shoot, Luke. You have to spoil everything." He stepped back.

Behind him, Mary released a breath. Relief? As if the girl who pushed around one-thousand-pound cows had been scared. After another long glare at his friends, he spun about, snatched Mary's arm, and walked her into the woods. No sounds followed from behind. He kept his stride long, half dragging her down the path toward her home. Pain shot through his jaw as he clenched his teeth.

She stumbled and dug her fingers into his arm, but he kept going, and she regained her footing. They climbed a short knoll and entered a field. Across the open space, bathed in moonlight, the Smith homestead nestled in the bend of the river. The sound of the current grew louder as they neared the barn.

He halted in front of the two-story structure and turned to face her, releasing her arm.

She huffed. "I know. Save yourself the breath."

No, he wouldn't. He had breath to waste. "Why?" He didn't care how she'd found out about the bonfires. He wanted to know what possessed her to go all Texas Ranger on a rowdy group of men.

"Because it's not right that they're threatening my land with fire."

"Why didn't you tell your father?"

Her eyes narrowed. "He doesn't need something else to worry about."

Luke blew out a breath. "You could have told someone. Brought someone with you. Why confront men who've been drinking?"

Her eyes widened.

"You didn't know they were drunk?"

She straightened and stepped into his space. On tiptoes, with her head tilted up, her face was inches from his. "They aren't strangers. I've known them forever. Besides, drunk or not, they shouldn't have been where they were." She raised a brow, and he noted the womanly quality that had begun to steal over her young face.

She sniffed near his mouth.

He jerked back. "I don't drink."

"Wouldn't put it past you."

He bit the inside of his cheek and struggled to hold back the thunder that pulsed in his chest. She couldn't be serious.

She sniffed him again and winked. "A woman can never be too sure."

"I can't believe this." He stepped back, her jest pulling the fight from him. Until he pictured her next to that bonfire, his friends surrounding her.

The fight bounded back. "Listen here." He reclaimed his position in her face and gripped her upper arms.

She tilted her head, meeting his gaze with nothing less than the tenacity he expected from her.

"I'm leaving, and—"

"About time."

His gaze roamed her narrowed eyes, that tightened jaw, and those lips, pale in the moonlight—taut as his fishing line when he hooked a big one. His mouth moved toward hers.

What are you doing?

He drew his head back and shrugged off the lapse of sanity. "I can't keep an eye on you — and Grace — anymore."

Her gaze flitted to the side. "Doesn't matter. The only thing you've ever been able to keep your eyes on is that target of yours."

It'd paid off. He'd have one of the best shots of the recruits. Or so he hoped. But that wasn't the point right now. The point stood before him, glaring, making his gut feel more coiled than a mess of vines. Saying goodbye to Dairy Mary shouldn't be this difficult.

Was that what this was about? Saying goodbye? He didn't do goodbyes.

But he did lectures. "I can't have you getting Grace in trouble. In several years she'll be off to an apprenticeship somewhere, and I don't want you doing anything crazy like convincing her to stay here."

Mary scoffed. "Staying isn't crazy. Leaving is. Which makes you the madman."

"You've got to be one of the most . . ." His thoughts jumbled, stuck on what had nearly happened a moment ago. He had *not* been about to kiss Dairy Mary. Exhaustion had dulled his keen sense.

"Call me stupid and get it over with."

He snapped his thoughts back to Trouble. "Fine."

She picked fights with him as if it were as crucial to life as eating. Confronting drunks *was* stupid, as was this unexpected melancholy over saying goodbye to his younger sister's friend. "You're stupid."

Her mouth crumbled.

He released her arms and rolled his eyes. "You're not stupid, all right?"

She took off toward her house.

Say goodbye. "Mary."

She stopped and spun. Moonlight caught the expectancy in her expression.

Goodbye wouldn't come. It hitched somewhere with

126

his breath. "Grace delivered her first calf solo tonight. Did a great job. I'm sure you'll hear about it in church tomorrow."

She nodded.

"'Night, Contrary."

He watched her walk into the house, the usual confident step hindered. She deserved a goodbye blessing, a well-wishing on her future. But the unfinished business he had in this town walled him off from goodbyes. It didn't matter that Mary had no idea about that night six years ago. He knew. He had the scars to help him remember.

He didn't have closure with Mary or with Pine Creek, and there wasn't enough bravery in the entire Rangers to bring it about.

Coward. He'd not make it in Texas if he were going to be as yellow as this. Some things in life took more courage than facing bullets.

CHAPTER FOURTEEN

Present day

Mary drowned out the conversation and let her fingers loose on the piano keys. She should be mucking stalls with Papa, who'd insisted he felt strong enough to work today, but she'd stopped at Rod's on a whim. Dairy demands couldn't keep her from a few minutes of playing. Or a half hour. Sometimes an hour. And last Wednesday, three hours.

She yawned, and her fingers stumbled through a modulation. She'd been up through the night, delivering a calf, a doozy of an experience that had required Papa and her to rope hooves.

The door slammed, and she jumped. Midday playing had its disadvantages. With the piano tucked against the side wall, she could forget the eight aisles of merchandise and constant mulling about of folks. Until the door slammed, or someone bumped her from behind, or a child knocked over a display of books. And every so often she had a creepy sensation that someone had stopped to watch over her shoulder.

A musician loved an audience, but she also loved the privacy and space to work on new pieces and to enjoy, unhindered, the emotions of her music.

"What do you think of this?"

Grace thrust a flash of material in front of her face.

Mary stopped playing and leaned away from the sampling.

"Do you like the color?" Grace had pinned her light

brown hair up in a fashion reminiscent of Claire.

Mary wrinkled her nose. "I don't even know what to call it. Putrid?"

Grace offered an amused look and fingered the lace on her collar.

"It looks like Mud got into my garden, ate all my spinach, and—"

"All right. You don't like the green."

"Oh. Is that what this is supposed to be?" Mary slid off the stool and stretched her hips back and forth.

Grace held out another piece of fabric. "What about this?"

Slightly less undesirable, but no good. "It looks like stale bread mold."

"You're impossible, which reminds me." Grace leaned close. "Any more honeysuckles?"

"One." Mary wandered to the fabric section, seeking to distract Grace, and selected a blue bolt. "I like this."

"It's dark and dreary. It'll do nothing for your complexion."

"That sounds like a word Claire would use. I'm sure she would love a new dress."

"I've chosen to showcase my work on you, not her."

Cecily's laughter sounded from the counter at the back. Mary peeked at the beauty behind the counter and then noticed the specimen in front. "Seems your brother is enjoying his time away from Texas."

"Focus on the task at hand," Grace said.

Cecily's laugh rang out again as Mary reached for another bolt. "I like this."

"White will show too much dirt."

"Make me a blouse, then, instead of a dress."

Grace bundled the white, original putrid, and a soft lavender in her arms. "Tell Luke. Please."

"Tell him he should put his hat in the ring for sheriff? I've been campaigning for him."

"You know what I mean."

The honeysuckles. "He has enough to think about."

Grace headed for the counter. "He's got nothing to think about. He's on medical leave."

Behind his disturbed eyes, she was certain Luke churned plenty of thoughts. On leave or not, that man had things to think about.

Mary returned to the piano stool.

Mrs. Crawley maneuvered her stout figure around the end of the shelving and leaned close to Mary. With a glance over her shoulder, Mrs. Crawley whispered, "I don't understand. Is Luke running for sheriff, or not?"

"He doesn't understand, either."

Mrs. Crawley straightened and swatted her on the shoulder. "You two are more fun than the otters down at the river."

The glimmer in Mrs. Crawley's eyes sucked the words from Mary. Speechless was an unfamiliar feeling.

"He's young, but I'm thinking he makes a better candidate than the old man from . . ." she frowned.

"Wenatchee."

"That's it. Luke's got an air of responsibility about him, and we did watch him grow from a freckled boy into quite the handsome man. Are you endorsing him?"

Luke had never had freckles.

Mary straightened and cleared her throat to regain Mrs. Crawley's attention which had wandered to the back counter. "Luke has a passion for justice, can be trusted" — at least with matters the law — "and I fully endorse him for sheriff."

Mrs. Crawley's smile shrunk her eyes to slits. "You've been helpful, dear." She patted Mary's back and sauntered away.

Mary started up a gloomy Beethoven piece. Beyond the melancholic minor tones, other noises vied for her attention: the tinkling of nails, the opening and shutting of the food bins, a fussing child, Grace's voice, kind and encouraging.

Humming by her ear.

She jerked around.

Luke grinned. "Is that 'gretto?"

"No."

Luke had his six shooters on, as usual, but his trousers were free of dirt. "Your cow's safe at home again."

"Thank you." She stood and brushed her hands down her skirt. A souvenir from the morning's chores garnished the front of the worn and simple material. She'd never minded the work or the effects of the work on her wardrobe, but a new dress with Grace's flourishes appealed to her feminine side, which she neglected too often.

She looked at Cecily, who was helping someone at the counter. With her golden hair and blue eyes, she'd been the epitome of beauty among the youth of Pine Creek. Nothing had changed externally about Cecily, and her swing from selfish to altruistic had filled in the missing depth of her beauty.

Luke stepped in front of Mary, blocking her view. "Are you done playing? I was just beginning to listen."

"Wipe that pretend pout off your face. If you'd not been so enraptured by your conversation with Cecily, you could have been listening longer."

Luke laughed. "Do you always say exactly what you're thinking?"

"Isn't it refreshing?"

"Not always. Biting one's tongue can be a virtue, too."

"Maybe it can be *someone's* virtue, but not *my* virtue."

Mary stalked to the front of the store and pushed through the doors. They slammed behind her. Crossing the road, she angled toward the school. Someone yelled Luke's name. He must have followed. She looked over her shoulder to find him five feet behind, waving at a woman down the street.

"An admirer?" she asked as he caught up to her.

"A widow with four children; she's new to the area. I

131

taught the two boys how to shoot yesterday."

"But not the girls?"

Luke frowned. "You're ornery today, and that's saying something."

She stopped and faced him, hands on her hips. She opened her mouth, and then shut it, pleased at herself for grabbing hold of *someone's* virtue and not snapping back. Considering Luke's raised brow and smile, he shared her pleasure. She'd determined to get to the bottom of Luke's heart, that turbulence she'd glimpsed while in his pasture. A wild mouth wouldn't lead her to his secrets.

"Were the boys any good?" she asked.

"Not bad, and when I'm done with them, perfect."

A smile vied for her lips, but she fought it. Beyond the arrogance of his statement lurked deep confidence. He wasn't boasting in order to make himself look good. On the contrary, he took his talent seriously, which is what would make him a good sheriff. Others took him seriously. *She* took him seriously, despite the way her words ran amuck around him.

His eyes reflected the sun, and she forced herself not to shrink from the warmth in them. She wasn't prepared for the admiration she saw. "You might make it perfect, if you're around long enough." She started walking again. Safety rested in the familiar, and between them, that meant banter, not admiration.

Luke's quiet footfalls trailed her as she paced toward the schoolhouse, where children bounded out the doors and down the steps. She'd ignore him, and he'd get the idea that she wanted to speak with Claire alone.

At the foot of the stairs, Mary stood to the side, letting the children descend. Luke's presence loomed large behind her. Ignoring him had never worked.

"You know you'd make a great sheriff," she said, not taking her eyes from the children. "You reach out to help people, like that widow, and Grace said you've helped Mrs. Lunsford with property laws."

"Mary."

"You're a natural peace keeper." She grinned, not that he could see from behind her. "Except with me." When most of the children had exited, she took the steps. "And this town adores you."

"They shouldn't."

"I don't know why you'd say such a thing. I can tell you care, even though you have a secret."

At the top of the steps she whirled. Unprepared for how close he was, she put her arm out to keep him from running into her. He grasped her waist and tightened when she swayed back.

"What's your secret?"

His eyes shifted. "You wouldn't believe it if I told you. Things happen, and time moves on."

"Memories don't budge. They camp out. You should know something about camping out." Her fingers poked his shoulder. "Are you still wearing a bandage?"

He shoved his hat back from his eyes. "A thin wrap. The wound started seeping."

She ran her finger over the edge of the bandage and down the outside of his arm. He shivered.

"Grace said three shots."

"A Trinitarian wound." His voice was husky.

Her smile faltered. "I'm sorry. Have I said that yet?"

"Not sure I've ever heard you say that about anything."

She stared at Grace's brother. That's how she'd seen him. Restless, unwilling to back down, fighter for truth. Good things, overall. And how did he see her? Unapologetic and loud-mouthed.

"You all right?" he asked. "You're not going to faint on me, are you? Most people don't feel woozy unless I recount the story." His voice softened. "Mention the blood, the sound of my head smacking a rock, the bile that stung my throat when—"

Mary slapped a hand over his mouth. The warmth of

133

his lips tickled her palm, and she jerked her hand back to her side.

Two more children burst from the door behind them.

Mary stepped aside as they pushed down the steps. "I need to speak with Claire. Alone."

"Planning something?"

She needed to borrow a dress for Clifton tomorrow, so yes, she was planning, but no, she wouldn't tell. "Are you busy tomorrow evening?"

Luke's eyes widened with something akin to expectancy.

"Jake will be helping my father milk. Would you mind joining?"

Looking away, he fiddled with his hat. "You going missing again?"

"Papa lets me have Saturday evenings off."

He grinned and pushed past her into the schoolhouse. "I don't think I deserve any more lectures on not being around for my family when you get to disappear and not tell anyone where you're going."

She stomped the dust from her feet before entering. "People know where I am." Grace. Claire. Matthew. The people listening to her piano playing.

Claire had pushed the desks to the outside of the classroom and situated them like a horseshoe, open to the front. Curtains hung in the windows, and vases of flowers brightened the windowsills on each side of room. Claire had made this schoolhouse like a second home for the children.

Claire finished writing something and rose from her desk at the front. "Luke, are you still able to come next Monday?"

"He didn't learn much the first time he came to school." Mary slipped through the opening in the back row of table and chairs and marched to the front. She hugged her friend. "You're kind to try again with him. I suggest using a switch when he gets out of line."

134

Luke rested his weight on one leg, hat in hand. "At least I didn't spend my entire lunch time throwing pine cones out of trees at the boys."

Claire laughed. "I thought I sent the children home, but I guess not. I could hear you two bantering before you even entered the schoolhouse."

"As if you and Barrett never bantered." Mary leaned against Claire's desk and grinned at her.

Claire's blue eyes were bright, yielding something like amusement. Mary swung her attention to Luke. He wore a scowl that threatened to darken the well-lit room. His prerogative to be grumpy, she supposed.

"Will Monday after lunch work?" Claire asked Luke. "I don't want to take you from the ranch."

"That'll be fine." He tipped his chin at Claire, barely glanced at Mary, and walked out.

Claire spun to face her, dress fanning out, eyes wide.

Mary picked up the pile of cleaned slates from Claire's desk. "What did I say?"

Laughter burst from Claire. "And you say there's no rift? No story?"

Gritting her teeth, Mary hauled the slates to the back of the room, where she set them on the bookshelf.

"I've never been more entertained than the past weeks of watching you and Luke interact."

Mary brushed the chalk dust from her hands and tucked a strand of hair behind her ear.

"You're doing better than usual at holding your tongue." Claire loaded her arms with books and joined Mary at the back of the classroom. "You know the reason Barrett and I bantered, don't you?"

Mary's jaw went slack. She'd connected her and Luke's bantering to Claire and Barrett's, a sign of their attraction to each other. She groaned. "What Luke and I do is different. It's what we've always done. You don't think Luke thought—"

"I have no idea what he thought, except that he left in a

hurry wearing a glower that I can't even imitate, and you know the children used to call me Glare Montgomery."

They stepped outside, and Mary waited while Claire locked the school. "Well, there's no use bemoaning my stupid mouth. What's said is said."

Claire issued a look that warned of a forthcoming lecture, not something Mary had the energy to withstand.

She descended the steps, squaring her shoulders. "School is out, Claire. No need for a lecture."

"Fine." Claire's single word held a hint of humor. She loaded her books into her saddle bags, untied her horse, and pulled her behind as they walked toward town. "What brings you to the schoolhouse, other than Luke?"

"Luke had nothing to do with it. I need to borrow a dress, preferably one of your looser ones that will fit my . . ."

"Curvier figure?"

"That's the polite way to put it." Hefty, rotund, those might be the less complimentary descriptions.

"You're not overweight, you know. On the contrary, you have a lovely figure."

"Thank you for your generous praise."

"My violet ensemble will work." Claire waved to a passing wagon. "But tell me, are the cows complaining about your wardrobe? Or are we back to Luke?"

Luke had left the schoolhouse. He'd left Grace, his family, and Pine Creek. He'd left many things, including, evidently, an impression on Claire. But he'd not left this conversation.

"Luke is an extension of Grace, who has been my dearest friend since we were three. I love Grace, so I put up with Luke, and you have no idea the putting up that's gone on the past seventeen years."

Claire lost the fight for a serious expression, the mirth tugging on her face unmistakable.

"My earliest memory is of Luke taking my cookie. Grace and I were sitting at the table in the Thomases' kitchen.

He took the cookie right off my plate."

"And you've loved him ever since."

Mary about choked on her breath. "Ha! I once called him the last boy I'd ever marry."

"My, that is serious."

"Stop with the mockery." Claire had no idea how serious. "More so, I called him unmarryable."

Smiling, Claire shook her head. "That's not a word."

"That's Luke for you. No existing words are adequate to describe him."

Claire laughed and took Mary's arm, a demonstrative move that showed how marriage had changed her and loosened up the anxiety she'd brought with her to Pine Creek nine months ago.

"How can I protect your sweet, genteel heart from a threat like Luke?"

"Be assured, no protection is necessary." He was no threat on her heart, despite the affection she felt for him. There. She'd labeled the thought and could move beyond it.

"I shouldn't tease." Claire squeezed her arm. "I'm sorry to hear he's been a tremendous disturbance in your life. In the weeks I've known him, he's seemed passionate, humorous, intelligent, a little moody—"

Absolutely.

"Devoted."

Mary scoffed, tugging Claire to a stop. "Devoted to what? Not his family. He's been back a month and is as restless as before he left."

Fondness showed through Claire's eyes. "Maybe what seems like restlessness is passion for his job. He misses it."

"He misses his job, but he can't miss his family?"

"You're awfully defensive on behalf of his family. He's not sinned against you, yet you act as if he has."

The pointed words snagged Mary's heart. To lessen their blow, she shrugged.

"Are you upset he hasn't missed you?"

A strangled laugh rose up in her. "I was happy to say goodbye. A man like that is never satisfied until he tromps off to attempt his own glorified adventure. Life is a game to him. It's about getting what he wants even at the expense of turning his back on family and friends. I haven't figured out what prompted him to come home, but I'll tell you it wasn't by his own choice."

Mary swallowed back the rush of heat to her mouth, the outburst having woken years of frustration.

"Mary." A frown hardened Claire's face. "Do you hear yourself?"

Mary slid her gaze from Claire's intense searching.

"I've never heard words like that from you. Luke is not only your brother in the Lord but a lifelong friend, whether you admit it or not."

"I . . ." Luke had more character than anyone she'd met, yet she'd slandered him to Claire. She stalked away.

"Come back here, friend." Somehow Claire managed a tender but stern tone. "You might be able to walk away from me, but you can't run from whatever is happening in that heart of yours. It'll stalk you until God's Spirit has his way."

Stalk. Not a word Mary wanted to hear given the noises and the honeysuckle blossoms. Her spine tingled as she slowed and let Claire catch up.

Claire took her arm again, and they passed the mercantile. Mary glanced inside. Helen plucked at the piano keys, Abigail standing behind her, instructing. Ashamed at the surge of jealousy, Mary turned away. The piano wasn't hers anymore, even if she'd been invited to play it whenever she wanted. Someday, it'd sell, and she needed to prepare herself for that reality.

"Just because he left home to pursue something he cares about doesn't mean he hates his family."

Claire's persistence taxed her.

"I left my home," Claire said. "Do you think ill of me?"

Mary swung to face Claire. "Of course not. But I know

how his family has missed him."

"And you? How you've missed him?"

Again with the talk of missing. Mary poked Claire. "Marriage has made you silly."

"Yes, well. It's made me many things."

A slam from the smithy distracted Mary, and she looked sideways into the shop. Cam hammered, focused on his work.

"Happy, content . . ." Claire's voice trailed. She cleared her throat.

Mary returned her attention to Claire whose, hands rested on her belly. Mary's eyes flew wide as they returned to meet Claire's. She squealed and threw herself into Claire's arms.

"When? How long?" Mary pushed away and stared at Claire's midsection. Still flat. "How do you feel?" She pressed her hand against Claire's wool skirt. "Let me deliver. Please. A baby is easier than a calf."

"I'll consider."

Mary gasped. "Really?"

"As long as you consider what gets you riled about Luke."

A nasty tradeoff. Because if she looked too intently at what riled her about Luke, she might confirm her hunch: her reaction to Luke's leaving had less to do with how it'd affected his family and more to do with how it'd wounded her.

CHAPTER FIFTEEN

Mary burst through the doors of the Gold Mine. She'd had to push Holly at a faster pace after being delayed by Luke's early arrival and subsequent grumbling. Word of her campaigning had found its way back to him. He'd not appreciated her speaking well of his character in relation to the election. Most men would have been grateful to receive such positive endorsements. Luke wasn't most men — in so many ways.

"I was about to come for you." Rhett crossed his arms and leered.

Jutting out her chin, she ignored him and pushed through the overcrowded room. They'd set the piano in a different place tonight, away from the door and toward the corner where the stairs were situated.

Simon patted her shoulder with a shaky hand. "Place is a little rough tonight. Might not want to stay as long." He tipped his head toward a table of men she didn't recognize.

"Thank you for the warning, but things will be fine."

The crowd had grown more difficult by the weeks, but hadn't crossed the boundaries she'd set. Yet.

Matthew waved at her, and she caught her frown before it blossomed. She understood him coming to hear her once. Twice. But every week? A man like him looked out of place in the Gold Mine, same as one of the others would appear out of place in church among the suit-wearing tradesman of Pine Creek. Matthew ducked his head and listened as the youth next to him gestured toward her.

Matthew glared at the boy and sat back in his chair.

Mary took her seat and began with a new Mozart piece. One minute into it, her mistakes reprimanded her choice. She'd not practiced it enough. What would they know if she stopped in the middle? She transitioned into a Beethoven selection she could play in her sleep. The noise level extended beyond normal, and for some reason, Matthew's presence nagged her. Her fingers slipped through a passage, and her heart skipped faster.

Settle down.

Someone tripped and knocked against her back. Her fingers stumbled again.

"Come on, girl." Rhett leaned on the back of the piano. "You can play better."

Time to take control. She stopped mid-song and stood. "I don't come here to be gawked at or treated rudely. I come here to educate you on the beauty of music."

"We don't need no education, but we could use some of your beauty," came a voice from near the door.

Muffled laughter spilled into silence. The restrained grins on some of the men mocked her attempt to subside their rowdiness. This was no Portland recital hall, much as she wanted to pretend it to be.

"Listen to the missy." Sarah Jane slapped her rag against the counter. "If you want your drinks, you're gonna show some respect."

They straightened in their seats and turned their glances from her to their laps or half-empty glasses. Rhett backed from the piano and headed toward the bar.

God, what am I doing here?

Until tonight, she'd not felt intimidated by the men, at least not most of them. She glared at Rhett's retreating back. Until tonight, she'd relished the opportunity to perform. Until tonight, she'd considered the money worth the unconventional environment. Miners and lumberjacks were people, too, capable of mercy and decency the same as the rest of humanity.

Then again, along with mercy and decency, humanity's capacity to misdirect desire reached deep. Until tonight, she'd overlooked that.

Call it what it is: Sin.

Perhaps she should take a few weeks off, reconsider this engagement.

Settling back on the bench, her fingers caressed the keys. A simple Bach two-part invention focused her back to the music, and an hour later, when she stood and bowed, the attention and respect they exhibited pleased her.

She stretched her fingers, crossing to Sarah Jane, whose stern eye had likely roamed the room and speared a few men during Mary's performance.

"Thank you," Mary said.

"They don't mean any harm. They're lonely is all."

Sarah Jane, with her haunted eyes and reserved nature, portrayed a woman who knew something about loneliness. The conversations Mary had attempted with her seldom moved beyond what time Mary would come and how much she'd be paid.

"See you next week." The proprietress wiped a spill from the counter.

"Actually." Mary lowered her voice, aware that despite the rowdy talk and clanging of glasses, those near had their gazes and ears tuned to her. "I'm going to take a month off." She'd meant to say a week, but a month . . . the conviction solidified.

Sarah Jane frowned. "The men want you to come. It's all they talk about during the week." She handed Mary a glass of water. "Don't be upset about tonight. There's been one skirmish over a girl since I been here. That's a year past now. After the lawman came and asked questions, things settled."

Comforting that it had taken official action.

Matthew appeared beside her. With a hand to her back, he sidled unusually close.

"You all right?" he asked.

She didn't like the way his whisper tingled in her ear. "Of course." She finished the water and set the glass down. "I'll be back in a month," she told Sarah Jane. Maybe with some time away, the men would develop greater gratitude for music.

Matthew took her arm and wove her through the crowd to the door. Outside, the night air, free of body odor and alcohol, smelled gloriously fresh.

He turned her to face him. "You didn't deliver the milk to Shanty last week."

The reproof in his tone took her aback. "I sent Luke."

"I know."

According to their last conversation, Matthew was leading the squad at the south camp, nowhere near the main camp and Shanty's cabin. That he'd noticed she hadn't delivered the milk — even that he cared — seemed out of place.

"He came over asking if we needed anything done," Mary said. "I think he was hiding from Paul."

Matthew's eyes narrowed. "I doubt that was the reason."

"Then again, he might have been hiding from Johnston. This sheriff business has him burrowing like a badger. It's as if he doesn't realize the honor of being sought out and is shoving the nomination back at Pine Creek." Luke as sheriff of Pine Creek was an image that shone like a masterpiece painting in her mind. "This could be the answer his family has wanted for keeping him home. Papa was the first mayor of Pine Creek, and if Luke would take advantage of this opportunity and be the first sheriff, then . . ."

"Then, what?"

She struggled to find a conclusion to the thought. "I don't know. Then that would be special."

Why that would be special wasn't necessary to analyze.

"I was hoping to see you when you delivered the milk." His chastising tone had returned.

This wasn't a side of Matthew she'd been acquainted with. "I can't do everything on my own." She couldn't be expected, while running the dairy without dependable help from Papa, to complete all her usual tasks in her usual ways. She'd employed the help of neighbors and friends.

"And you shouldn't have to." Matthew's voice relaxed. "You need to talk with your father about selling to us. It's the only way."

"The timing hasn't been right."

"The timing is now." His touch to her elbow softened the retort. "Tomorrow. My father wants to build an extension of the camp closer to Pine Creek. We're increasing our output to meet building demands in Wenatchee, and if you're not willing to sell, he's going to seek another option."

Raindrops splattered the edge of the boardwalk. Mary tucked her lightweight cloak around her and pulled the hood over her hair. From the hitching post, Holly blew out a breath and tossed her head.

"We'll let you rent the house and barn for a fraction of your current mortgage and make sure you have the pasture you need."

Matthew's insistence stirred possibility in her. Papa wouldn't resist an opportunity like this. He couldn't.

In the distance, thunder turned over the sky, low and long.

"I need to go." Mary rushed down the stairs to Holly.

"Let me escort you."

Her throat expanded, and she concentrated on breathing. That thunder had been miles and miles away.

"That's not necessary." She'd be driving Holly hard, hunched over and focused on the path ahead. Matthew's trailing wouldn't keep the thunder from rolling.

"Too bad. I'm going to."

She pushed out a shaky smile as she mounted and gripped the reins. "Thanks, Matthew. You're a true friend."

Luke swigged another cup of water. The aroma in the kitchen tantalized his appetite. After the work he'd done that day, any aroma would provoke a growl from his stomach. They'd spent the height of the afternoon branding spring calves. The ranch was turning into the worst place he could have come to let his shoulder heal.

Paul expected him to put in a good day's work, and Luke wasn't going to turn yellow and cry about the dull, continuous ache. Paul wanted him more involved on the ranch, and Luke would sweat blood in order to show he loved this place. A person could love a stretch of land without feeling called to spend his years on it.

He walked to the stove and poured a cup of tepid coffee. Leaning against the pie safe, he reached into his pocket for the letter Grace had brought back from her trip to town. His captain's scrawl stretched across the front. Luke read the single page document for the fifth time, the coffee rolling bitter in his stomach. The Rangers had collected depositions, including one from a member of McNelly's crew who'd mentioned seeing Luke traveling with the Fowler Trio. *With* the trio, as in, part of them.

The coffee felt sour in his stomach.

Captain Finch, ever the calm and understated leader, appeared confident Luke would be acquitted if he waited and let the investigative committee do their work. In other words, Luke was supposed to do nothing, which seemed like a small man's move. He'd rather defend himself. Head south and show what loyalty looked like. But now wasn't the time to question orders. Maybe later, if things took too long.

"Uncle Luke?" Helen skipped into the kitchen. Paul trailed behind her.

Luke folded the letter and tucked it into his shirt pocket next to Father's book of Psalms.

"Greetings from Texas already?" Paul's question hinted

at more than curiosity. "Could it be that my brother's found a woman to put up with his wandering?" He stopped at the basin and splashed water over his hands.

Paul seemed intent on Luke finding a woman, probably because he thought it'd force Luke to put down roots. Paul had plans to hire a new crew in the fall when he purchased another hundred head of cattle, and though he'd not asked, he'd hinted at Luke managing the workers. Him, a manager? He didn't supervise people. He hunted them down and arrested them.

Luke set his mug down on the table. "What good is a woman going to do me?" A woman needed things he didn't have to give. Stability. And other things. Things he couldn't name but felt pulling inside him. Marriage came with demands.

"Most men find marriage and fatherhood an attractive venture."

"I'd rather have *adventure*."

"Let me say it another way." Paul offered a rare, unrestricted smile and swung Helen into his arms. "Most men find marriage and fatherhood the grandest adventure."

Helen squealed as Paul nuzzled her cheek with his and set her down again.

"You wouldn't know adventure if it nipped you in the—"

"Uncle Luke."

Helen tucked her small hand into his. Her almond-shaped brown eyes brought to mind another pair of eyes whose owner was the embodiment of adventure.

"What's up, little one?" He pulled his hand from hers, shoved it in his pocket, and leaned against the pie safe.

"I want to have a party for Grace's birthday and invite all her friends to celebrate."

"Sounds fun."

Abigail walked in to the kitchen and opened the oven, releasing a heavenly gravy smell.

Helen pulled his hand out of his pocket and swung it back and forth. "You're going to put on a show."

"Is that so?" He freed his hand and lifted her into his arms, setting her on his hip. "Do I have to sing and dance?"

Paul snorted.

Helen cupped his cheeks with her hands. "You're going to shoot."

"Now this sounds like a good show."

Paul wrapped his arms around Abigail. She settled against him with a sigh, and for one second — no more than that — Luke's heart veered a dangerous direction. One that involved his arms around someone.

Resting his hands on Abigail's rounding belly, Paul looked at Helen. "I don't think we'll have a shooting show at Grace's birthday."

Helen scrambled from Luke's arms. "Then Uncle Luke can teach me to shoot."

"Sorry, but you're not old enough." Paul moved Abigail from his embrace and rested his hand on Helen's head. "Clean up your blocks before supper."

The four-year-old stalked toward the door.

Abigail followed, glancing over her shoulder. "We're eating early tonight because Grace is helping Mary with milking."

The Smiths needed to unload that dairy, and Randall teetered on the verge of that decision. As long as Mary didn't persuade him otherwise. That girl needed a lesson in letting go.

"Besides." Abigail leaned against the doorjamb. "You two could use baths. The odor in the kitchen is far from appealing."

Luke sniffed. "All I smell is sweet cinnamon and savory meat."

Abigail shook her head and disappeared.

Paul studied him, a muscle in his temple throbbing. "Why do you do that?"

Luke frowned. "I don't have a clue what you're talking about since you can't mean complimenting your wife on her cooking."

Paul held up his hand and shook it. "Helen. She likes to hold hands, and you're always pulling yours away."

"I don't hold hands." Luke made a fist in his pocket. "It's awkward."

"If you think holding hands is awkward, you're not ready for the grand adventure of marriage. You'll have to do a lot more than hold hands."

"What's this about holding hands?" Their mother entered, a load of linens in her arms. "Your father and I used to hold hands all the time."

Exactly. Summer evening walks had been about family, handholding, and stargazing. Father and Mother led the way, Grace skipped with her basket, convinced she might catch a falling star. He and Paul trailed last, throwing pebbles at each other. But always, always, Father and Mother had held hands.

Mother put the linens in a basket. "Set the table, would you?"

Luke raised his brows and stared at Paul, who shook his head and pointed at Luke.

Mother bent to retrieve the bread from the oven. "One of you. It doesn't matter who."

Paul smiled and grabbed a pile of dishes. "I'll set. Luke can go wash his hands. Or is that awkward, too?"

Luke glared. "I have no problem with cleanliness."

"We'll see about that." Mother brushed a strand of hair off his forehead. "You could use a haircut."

What he could use was a good resolution to this mix up with the Rangers and those bullet wounds in his shoulder to heal.

Luke tucked the parcel under his arm as he exited Rod's, feeling more like an errand boy than a son. Paul had been set to send him to hard labor, but his mother had intervened and asked him to pick up some items from the mercantile. His tired shoulder thanked her.

Brightly painted letters, *Bridges Lumber*, splashed across the side of the fancy wagon parked in front of Rod's.

"Look who it is!"

An arm dropped around Luke's shoulder, and he turned to greet Davis. "Davis. Mary said you were back. You staying out of mischief?"

"Come on, now." Davis hooked his thumbs into his belt loops. "Heard you got in a tussle." Davis bumped his fist against Luke's shoulder.

Luke swallowed the pain, not about to give Davis the satisfaction of a wince. "Things happen when you're a Ranger."

"What about when you're a sheriff?" Davis laughed and leaned against the side of the wagon. "Yep. Johnston's been talking about you."

Davis's shoulders had broadened, and the boyish features that dressed his face had been edged with toughness. He remained a good six inches shorter than Luke, but made up for it in swagger.

"If you're going to be like you were that time at the bonfire, tense and uppity, you're not getting my vote." Davis paced to the back of the wagon and scanned the contents.

"I'd be exactly like that, so don't vote for me."

"Relax." Davis circled the other side and back to Luke. "What happened to the boy that could joke with the best of us?"

He'd grown up, committed his life to working for peace.

"I'll see you around." Luke nodded his head. "'Till I head south again."

Leaning forward in the pew, Luke rested his forearms

on his legs. Reverend Newton pitched his voice high and low as he pontificated on the story of Joshua crossing the Jordan into the Promised Land. The aging circuit preacher only passed through once a month, and to make up for it, preached four sermons in one.

Beside Luke, Paul held Helen on his knee. She twined a thread around her fingers, pulled it straight, and repeated the action. Luke looked away, dizzy with the monotonous motion. Across the aisle, Matthew Bridges sat rigid, and Luke followed his gaze to Mary, three rows up. Frowning, Luke tried to focus on the message, but frustration was a skilled diverter.

Nothing he'd said to people had made a difference. Johnston pushed forward with his agenda, and Mary was no help, either, campaigning for Luke everywhere she went. He couldn't go to town without someone questioning him about the election or wishing him well, as had been proved by his run-in with Davis.

The talk suffocated him. They didn't know.

They could know. Today. Now.

The conviction stormed his conscience, rumbled through his body. He could choose to tell the truth and accomplish two things: throw off the burden of carrying such a secret, and silence the expectations. Truth set a person free, according to scripture. That's what he was counting on happening in Texas.

When the final hymn was announced, Luke stood with the others. His eyes strayed from the hymnbook to Mary. He'd return to Texas when his name was cleared, so if the town hated him after his confession, he'd deal with it.

But Mary. The idea of disappointing her nearly sunk his courage.

Reverend Newton offered the benediction, and Luke's hands clammed, the moment upon him.

Don't think about it. Just act.

"Attention please." He strode to the pulpit, pulse in his

throat. "I'd like to say something."

Conversations ceased. A few smiled—Johnston, Mary, and his mother—probably assuming he'd finally agreed to run for sheriff.

"When the church burned down eleven years ago, the town assumed lightning to be the cause. But it wasn't."

Mary's smile slipped from her face. He angled his body so she was out of his line of sight.

"I'd taken shelter in the church when the thunder started. There were some matches sitting on a table." He gripped his arm, feeling the burn all over again. "I lit a few to pass the time, and . . ." He shoved back the fear, the urge to run. He wasn't a hider. "Things happened . . . It was an accident."

His face flushed beneath the stares of the congregation. Over the silence in the room, he heard his heart trying to beat its way out of his chest. He gritted his teeth and resisted turning toward Mary or his family.

Any second, the protests would start; the disbelief would turn to glowers, and the questions would unravel his shame, seek to reveal more than he wanted.

"I was wrong to keep it a secret. It' just . . ." No excuses. No falling back on the fact he'd been a wounded boy. "I want you all to know how sorry I am."

And now it should be obvious why he wasn't running for sheriff.

"Well, that's a surprise." The elderly widow Mrs. Lunsford stepped from her pew near the front and made her way forward. "That was a hard summer for you, wasn't it? Oh, when my Charles died, I wanted to burn down the house we'd shared, so great was the grief in each room." She took his arm and faced the congregation. "A boy makes mistakes. But it takes a man to own up to them."

"Absolutely correct." Johnston squeezed past his son into the aisle and paced to the front. "This, Pine Creek, is a man who knows how to amend his ways." He reached the front and pivoted to face the congregation. "Who hasn't done something daft?"

Muttering accompanied the stares of the people, and then a few *amens* skipped through the room.

What was happening? They were supposed to condemn him, not excuse his behavior. He'd been wrong, and he'd hidden the truth.

Preacher Newton put his arm around Luke's shoulders. "Far be it from us, the congregation, to hold a grudge where the Lord does not. My son, your sin is forgiven."

A smattering of applause started in the back and rippled forward, growing in strength.

Luke nodded and met the gazes of those near the front, careful to keep his eyes from Mary.

"You'll make a fine sheriff, son," Reverend Newton said.

Luke shook his head. "I'm not running."

"Oh, come on," a gruff voice cried from the back of the room.

A chorus of agreements echoed.

Incredible. He'd meant to gain a fraction of peace and free himself of their attention, but he'd secured them in greater measure. The watching, judging eyes he'd expected hadn't manifested. Instead, forgiveness. Compassion. Acceptance like this should thrill him, shoot joy straight through his heart, not constrict like an invisible noose.

He pushed down the aisle and ducked out of the church.

"Luke."

It was Paul's voice that called after him, but Luke pressed into the woods, out of sight of the others exiting church.

"Luke, wait, please."

He slowed but didn't stop, allowing Paul to catch up. "I suppose you want to tell me how foolish I was."

"No. I never knew you carried a burden like that."

Paul wouldn't have known. He'd been too busy taking over Father's job.

"I'm sorry."

Luke didn't need pity, didn't want his brother feeling sorry for him. He stopped and faced Paul, but Paul's somber expression bore an openness, perhaps even a hint of respect, though how could that be?

"You did right, owning it."

Luke's heart swelled. He leaned back against the trunk of a maple and held Paul's gaze until Paul looked away.

His brother pawed the ground with his boot. "Maybe now that your secret's out, you might consider staying?"

Luke wasn't accustomed to hearing such hesitancy in Paul's voice. Paul was a man of statements, not questions. Unfortunately, too many secrets remained for Luke to stay. The false accusations. The burn marks on his arm, which he'd never showed anyone.

Besides, staying meant settling in with his family, and he didn't want to be with them. Not when it kindled that sense of vulnerability he hadn't been able to shake since Father's death. Family. Home. Those were temporary things that couldn't be trusted.

"I'm needed in Texas. It's a wild place where the work of justice wakes you each morning eager and puts you to bed each night exhausted."

Paul raised his gaze, brow furrowing. "How about being woken up by your daughter wedging between you and your wife? Or going to bed next to the woman who's carrying your child. That's a good way to live, too."

Luke shoved off from the tree. "I never said what you have isn't good. You've done great things with the ranch. Father would be proud. But your life isn't for everyone. I've found my place, and it's good."

The town had offered him an alternative place, and their request honored him, but he'd committed to Texas, and if the Rangers would have him, he'd go back where he belonged, where life had been safe, despite the whizzing bullets.

CHAPTER SIXTEEN

The sun glowed below the mountains as Mary set aside her shawl and set out the pails for the evening milking. Drops of water hissed on the stove's surface as it heated. The door to the house slammed, and she spun around and peered through the open barn doors. Papa held his shoulders back and walked across the yard. She waved him off, but he shook his head.

He put his hand on the door and took a deep breath. "Sometimes a man's got to push through the pain."

Refreshing words from the same person who'd said a strong man knew when to relinquish. The Crawleys had rescheduled their visit for next week, and Papa intended to go and see this Seth Millwood. The time to talk about Bridges's offer had come, and the best way to do it was straightforward . . . with a bit of pleading intermixed.

"I talked with Matthew," Mary said. "And he told me more about their desires to expand."

Papa was shaking his head before she'd finished her sentence. "We can't wait around to see if they're going to need more milk in a couple months. That's not the answer."

She moved the water to the back of the stove and ladled some into several pails.

Papa carted one of the pails to the nearest stall and began cleaning hooves. She took her pail to the second stall, dipped her rag, and washed Mud's udders.

"They want to buy our land."

"I know."

"You know?"

Papa looked up from his washing. "Emory came several weeks ago while you were doing deliveries. I turned him down."

Why hadn't Papa said anything? Or Matthew. Shouldn't he have known? Maybe he had known and wanted her to influence Papa, change his mind. "Why would you do that?"

Papa's lips parted, and his gaze wavered. "I want to sell to someone who will use this place like we have. Someone like this Seth Millwood."

"You don't even know him." She huffed and moved to the next stall. "If we sell to Bridges, we get to stay and rent for a reasonable rate. He doesn't need a house, barn, and pasture. He wants the trees."

"Emory never said we could stay."

"That's what Matthew said."

He shook his head. "Let's not argue."

He'd ended the conversation, and time to convince him was running out, but she'd try later, appeal to his love for this place, his sentiment toward Mama.

A bark sounded in the distance, and thirty seconds later, Gus ripped around the corner of the doors. Apparently, either Grace or Luke had come to help. Her heart turned over, and she wished for the latter. She'd not seen Luke since his Sunday confession. A confession that still shocked her, and which she planned to ask him about sometime.

Luke sauntered around the entrance. Mary feigned a yawn and turned her back on him, needing a moment to decide if she were grateful her heart had gotten its way.

"Is that a way to greet your help?"

Flipping a rag over her shoulder, she spun back to Luke. "I have ten-day old cookies with mold if you'd prefer."

"On second thought, a yawn's not bad. I've been greeted with worse." He tossed his hat toward a hook. It missed and fell to the floor.

"I see you aren't perfect." Mary tipped her head toward the first stall on the south side. "Start with her . . . And thank you for coming."

Luke slung his hat over a hook on the way past to her papa. "Randall. Fine evening for milking."

Papa chuckled.

"Almanac's saying June's going to be a dry month. Maybe you'll finally get your visit to Mr. Millwood."

Mary glared at Luke for bringing up the subject.

"I plan to go next week." Papa groaned as he lowered himself onto a milk stool. "We need an answer soon."

Bridges had given them the perfect answer and could likely pay more than a commoner with a vision for a farm.

"Received another letter from him," Papa said. "Says he'd travel as far as Clifton on a daily basis to deliver milk."

"Ambitious," Luke said. "He'll need a team of workers if he's going to deliver that far."

Mary bit her lip to keep from lashing out at Luke. This had been his idea. Find someone to carry on the dream, he'd told Papa. Hogwash. Luke knew too much about passing things on and not enough about hanging on to what mattered.

"Hey, Contrary, maybe you could work for Mr. Millwood. Then you wouldn't have to say goodbye to your true loves." He jutted his chin toward the cow.

If Papa weren't here she'd be tempted to throw something at Luke. A woman was never too old to put a loudmouth in his place. Maybe she should do it regardless of Papa's presence. After all, if Luke were comfortable enough around Papa to tease her, she should feel free to defend herself.

The evening serenade of birds broke through her fuming and attempted to mollify her. She hummed along with a chickadee until the tightness in her chest lessened.

Papa stood slowly. Pain carved the wrinkles on his face a little deeper, but he pursed his lips and emptied the milk into the large can.

Mary stared at her trained, swift-moving fingers. Papa's hands had been this quick once, and she imagined Mama's hands had been as well.

Papa eased back on his stool next to another cow. Resting his elbows on his knees, he took a moment to catch his breath.

An ache wormed through her heart. It wasn't fair to resist his desire to sell when his body needed the relief. But she wasn't resisting his need for relief. She was redirecting. Selling to Bridges was the better choice and would enable them to hire help, so Papa could enjoy the dairy without the pressure of the work.

"This here is the definition of beauty." Papa patted the velvety jersey on the side.

Mary smiled across the aisle, grateful that his voice sparked with life despite his struggles. "I know Luke has a problem with exaggeration, but I didn't think you did."

Luke grunted. "I never embellish."

Mary rolled her eyes. "Beauty is defined in a sunrise. Or by these mountains. Fresh snow. Or someone like Cecily, if we're going to talk about people."

A burst of laughter came from Luke. "You think Cecily's beautiful?"

Everyone knew Cecily was beautiful, as much as they knew Mary was audacious. It wasn't a disputed issue, like whether or not the Great Northern Railroad would make Pine Creek rich.

Luke chuckled, and his cow shifted. He steadied his bucket and pushed back until the cow settled.

Mary drained her pail and leaned against the post of Luke's stall. "You don't find her beautiful?"

"Beauty's a strange thing."

Not as strange as Luke and his issue with holding hands, something she'd picked up on through the years. Or not as strange as Luke holding on to a secret for eleven years and then deciding the time was right to confess.

Mary swung her pail by the handle and moved to the next stall.

"You know Cecily thinks you're beautiful?" Luke asked.

Mary snorted. Definitely not a beautiful sound. "Stop lying."

"I don't lie."

So he'd conversed with Cecily about her.

She settled on her stool and bent to look around the rear of the Jersey to Luke. He'd rolled his sleeves to his elbows, revealing toned forearms. With muscles like that, he should be milking quicker, but tonight he sat crooked and favored his right arm over his left.

Her hands took hold and began the rolling motion. "Let's be honest—"

"You're nothing if not honest," Luke said.

A shot of laughter from Papa reminded her of his presence.

"I'm not ugly," Mary said. "But the word *beautiful* should be reserved for sophistication and glamour, the likes of which I saw on the boardwalks of Portland daily. And I am neither."

Luke moved to another stall, dropped the stool, and toed it into place. He sank down and spun to face her.

She met his gaze, feeling the defiant sparkle liven up her eyes.

"You got one thing right, milkmaid. You're not sophisticated or glamorous. But your idea of beauty is warped. Physical beauty's a matter of opinion, but real beauty is an issue of worth and significance, and it originates from the goodness of God."

Whoa. The depth of that thought, coming from a man who kept his spiritual comments holstered with his six shooter, shocked her boots off. Almost as much as his confession Sunday had. Did she even know this man?

She cleared her throat. "I guess Cam will have

competition on Sunday."

"Don't change the subject."

"Fine. Beauty is about worth. I can accept that." She stopped milking and wiggled her tired fingers. "And Cecily is worth more looks than other girls."

Chuckling turned her attention across the aisle. Papa leaned on the post, and though his body looked like one more ache might topple him, amusement lightened his expression. His gaze settled on hers.

"Would you like to go inside?" she asked. "We're almost finished."

He frowned and pushed from the post. "I wouldn't *like* to, but I should. My hands feel like they're on fire."

Mary set her pail aside and walked the few steps to him. She took his hands and rubbed her thumbs in circles around his joints. The irregular milking schedule he'd kept the past months, along with the salve the doctor had given him, had lessened his calluses. Papa let her massage for a few moments and then pulled his hands away.

She hugged him. "I'll be in shortly."

Luke tugged the cart to the springhouse and ducked inside. Gus turned circles by the door before disappearing into the darkness. Hanging the lantern from the hook on the low ceiling, Luke observed the crocks of butter that lined the troughs. Mary must have churned three straight hours today. He transferred the cans of milk from the wagon to the troughs.

She'd not said anything about Sunday. He'd had eight visitors to his home, thanking him for his honesty. Not that what he'd said had been easy, but it'd been easier to admit than the rest of the story.

He reclaimed the lantern and left the springhouse, cart in tow. The light swung with his steps, casting out and drawing back. It danced across a honeysuckle clipping, and Luke stopped. The uncrushed blossom rested on the earth in front of the barn doors where, moments ago, he'd towed the cart out. He frowned.

Honeysuckle blossoms turned up every time he came to help the Smiths. And then there'd been that one next to Rod's when he'd been listening to Mary play, odd considering there wasn't a honeysuckle bush anywhere close.

He plucked up the blossom and shoved it in his pocket, ignoring the unease that attached to him. Perhaps Mary plucked them throughout the day whenever she passed a vine. She could easily have dropped one outside Rod's.

The wheels of the cart creaked as he pulled it into the barn. Stools hung on the outside of the stall posts, and pails were rinsed and on their hooks. But no Mary.

Movement sounded from the rear of the barn.

"You want me to grease these wheels for you?" he called out.

The back door squeaked, and a gust of wind slammed it against the wall. He wandered back and peeked over the closed stall that held the calf, expecting to see Mary admiring the new baby. It was unlikely she'd head inside without saying good night, but not impossible.

He turned at the end of the aisle and crossed to the door blowing in the wind. Breeze had picked up. Beyond the open door, moonlight bathed the field, and he caught the sway of the swing under the large maple tree.

Mary, swinging at night in that standing position she favored. She had to be different than the other girls who sat and pumped their legs. The long ropes and wide-planked seat cut a deep, slow path back and forth.

He shut the back door, returned to the main part of the barn, and doused the lantern. Stepping outside, he exchanged the darkness of the barn for the muted glow of stars. Wood smoke rode the breeze, tandem with a sense of change. Cool temperatures blowing in, probably another spring storm. He secured the front barn doors and whistled softly to Gus, who stood sentry in the shadows, alert and facing toward Mary.

161

Gus didn't move.

Luke slapped his thigh. Gus still didn't move. Deaf old dog. Luke stalked over and leaned against the side of the barn, confident that the shadow hid his presence from Mary. She stood on the flat wooden board, hands gripping the rope, swaying back and forth, gazing up at the starry sky. She'd unbraided her hair, and he knew why. She'd encouraged Grace to do the same while swinging.

What good is swinging if you can't feel the wind in your hair? she'd said.

He didn't get the whole wind-in-the-hair thing. The Texas wind had whipped the short ends of his hair against his face and shredded through his shirt plenty of times, and it made him feel like his head was about to be ripped off.

"Come on, boy." He'd not interrupt her sweet moment for a goodbye. He turned the corner of the barn, trusting Gus to follow. His steps moved past the paddock and down the path, but when he reached the road, he stopped. Gus caught up and ran on.

He couldn't leave. Not when he'd found another honeysuckle blossom. No matter that he'd tried to make light of it, push away the unease. Something seemed off, and Mary seemed unaware of it, or more likely, distracted by other struggles — the dairy, her Papa's health.

Luke turned around, marched back past the paddock and past the barn. He'd blend in with the shadows, let her swing in peace, and ensure things were quiet on the property. But despite his decision to stay out of sight, something compelled him to keep going. The energy in his step took him by surprise as he hurdled the horizontal shaft of the fence and chased the moonlit path across field toward Mary and the swing.

What are you doing?

His heart increased its assault against his chest, the urge to be with Mary like one of the bulls-eye impulses he'd been praised for as a Ranger. Later, he'd investigate this crazy whim, but for now, he let whatever was at work in him tow him forward.

No doubt she saw him now, the lone figure advancing. No doubt she figured he had a purpose to tell her off, set her straight, put her in her place.

No doubt he wanted to kiss her.

Texas, I miss you.

Where his thoughts knew their place and his body and mind worked together for a single purpose. Justice.

Not this. Whatever this was.

He was within the radius of the swing's arc now, and when it moved away, he chased it, let the momentum of his jump move with it. He grabbed the ropes, and settled his feet on the outside of hers. She gasped, the movement shaking her balance. With one hand to her back, he steadied her, ignoring the pain that ripped through his shoulder.

"Something you learned in Texas or with the circus?"

"Same thing, according to you."

The corner of her mouth turned up. "I'm glad it's clear where I stand on the issue of you in Texas."

She'd missed him.

"Away from your family, that is," she added.

Nice cover. Because admitting she'd missed him would kill her?

"I missed you, too." He'd meant the words to sound humorous, but the raspy thing his throat had done changed the delivery from lighthearted to intense. All right. So now she knew he'd sincerely missed her.

She straightened her arms and leaned her body away from his, head tipped back to look at the sky — or to put distance between them.

"You see more stars in Texas where mountains don't block the horizon," he said.

She pulled up in one quick jerk. Her eyes widened. "I'm dizzy."

Talk about feeling shaky, his heart wobbled on the edge

of insanity. He'd have to put a curfew on himself if he was going to act half-witted after sunset. Swinging double with Dairy Mary Quite Contrary made him forget the Fowler Trio. Almost made him not care if he were kicked out of the Rangers.

Definite madness.

They swung into the wind, and his hat blew off. Mary's hair fluttered across his face, and he sputtered. Rocking back and forth, he coaxed the swing higher. To forget the dull ache in his shoulder, Luke seized her attention and stared hard at her eyes. He liked the way they turned up at the corners, even when no smile painted her face. He'd never been close enough to notice. No, he'd been this close to her — right before her fist had pummeled him. But a thirteen-year-old boy isn't interested in the shape of a girl's eyes. Not in the way a twenty-four-year-old, controlled by some untamed and unseen impulse, seemed to be.

"You know what's truly beautiful?" she asked.

The sight of someone he'd once considered a nuisance swinging in the moonlight with her head back and hair blowing. It wasn't the circumstances themselves that flabbergasted his heart, but the way those circumstances revealed things. Her luster and spunk. His visceral response.

He scowled. *Settle.*

"Don't glare at me."

Not at her, but at a thought that would be as unwelcome to her as it was to him, if he'd the gumption to tell her. She'd push him off the swing as he'd pushed her off the fence several weeks ago.

He worked to relax his expression. "What's beautiful?"

She looked past him. "This place."

She didn't mean the beauty of the cottonwoods by the river and the layout of the house, barn, fences, and springhouse. She meant the intangibles of home and dreams.

The things muddling his life.

"More than that," she continued. "The thought that

Mama and Papa started with several small, old cows." She turned her eyes back to his. "Did you know Mama's family were dairy farmers?"

He nodded. "I heard the story the other night." When Mary had been off doing whatever mischief he hadn't figured out yet. Unquenched curiosity wasn't something he let go. "I hadn't realized your Mama had brought that heritage with her to this place."

"You wouldn't have known. She'd only been here two years before it happened."

It happened. "Your birthday?"

"The day I entered the world. The day she left."

The leaves rustled in the breeze above them, and her hair lashed his face again.

She shook her head, attempting to subdue the strands. "I've got to cut this mess."

"Don't."

She raised her gaze to his. Her lips were too close. He needed a distraction.

Thunder sounded faintly beyond the mountains, a perfect distraction. Mary sucked in a breath. He stopped pulling his arms back and forth, allowing the swing to slow. Instead of waiting for it to stop, she jumped backward and made for the house.

He chased her across the yard and snagged her sleeve. "It's not close. The sky above is still clear."

She looked up, and her hair blew across her face like a dark blanket.

He pulled strands from her mouth, his finger brushing her cheek, and smoothed them behind her ears. "Can you imagine sleeping under one of those mammoth summer storms?"

Her eyes slipped closed. "Thank you for planting such a wonderful thought in my mind. I'm sure that won't cause any issues tonight when I try to rest in peace."

She was beautiful even when fear striped her

expression.

"I've survived plenty. Here, you're inside, and the mountains offer protection."

"Luke." She opened her eyes. "I know it's irrational. You don't have to try to talk me out of the fear."

"Why?"

"It is what it is."

He shook his head. "I didn't mean that. Why is it a fear? Do you remember the first time you were scared during a storm?"

"Do you remember the first time you panicked when someone held your hand?"

Fear hadn't disrupted her wit. "That's not the same thing."

She laughed, a melody that would have been delightful if not for the anxiety tightening it.

Another growl of thunder. She spun and ran.

"Mary."

She didn't stop until she'd reached the door. Glancing over her shoulder, she clutched at her chest.

He approached and rested his weight on one leg. *Sleep well* didn't seem like a fitting goodbye, considering. He settled with holding her gaze, which had *wild* as its main ingredient. He shifted forward under the impulse to hold more than her gaze, but her right hand thrust to the side and fumbled for the doorknob. Licking her lips, she unlatched the door and slipped through.

He knew his place in Texas, atop his mount with a rifle swung across his lap, patrolling the frontier. No laws existed in this new game of figuring things out in Pine Creek. No theories explained why his hands were shaking, and he hadn't wanted to rip his gaze from hers.

The frontier of the heart didn't tame like Texas. Another reason he needed to get south again. He'd not wait for word from the marshal more than another month.

Mary closed the door and stared at the empty place against the wall where the piano had sat. Tears thickened her vision.

When Luke had started for that swing, aiming to jump, her stomach had bottomed out, and her knees had weakened.

As they'd swayed back and forth, she'd come close to apologizing for not speaking kinder to him, for letting loose her moodiness on him too many times. For calling him the last boy she'd ever marry. But she'd not been able to break through the spell he'd cast—his charge across the field, moonlight, the gentle rocking of the swing, being so close—which is probably also why she'd not brought up his words from Sunday.

Then again, maybe she'd been too proud to open her mouth and say *I'm sorry.*

"I'm so confused."

The silent house accepted her confession.

Conviction had pressed in, but she'd ignored it. He'd had the humility to come clean before Pine Creek, but she couldn't grasp the same courage. Her sins remained buried beneath years of relating to him through snide comments and wit.

"Lord, help."

Apologizing meant changing. Trying to subdue the cursory banter that jumped in on her interactions with Luke. But take away the banter, and what was left? Something scarier. Something deeper.

Attraction.

Like Claire had hinted at.

Thunder punctuated the realization, louder than when she'd been outside, but still a ways off. Her throat constricted, making it hard to swallow.

"Mary?" Papa's voice reached her from down the hall.

"I'm inside now."

167

Another growl from the impending storm.

Papa entered the front room and lit a lamp. They knew the routine. When storms came through at night, Papa met her in the front room, sat with her while they passed.

She settled into her usual chair. "Luke asked me if I remembered the first time I was scared during a storm." Mary tucked her legs under her. "I don't."

"It stormed the night you were born." Papa's hands gripped the sides of the chair. "We've never talked much about that night. Not in detail."

The labor had been long, Mary had come out breech, Mama had bled to death. That was the extent of what Mary had wanted to know.

"It thundered. Hailed. The wind was fierce and the lightning continued for hours."

Mary's hands grew sweaty. The talk of storms, of the night Mama had died, was as harsh as the actual rolls of thunder to the south.

"I sat with Emeline for six hours. Mrs. Woods, the midwife, held you."

"Did . . ." Mary's voice cracked, and she cleared her throat. "Did I cry?" A ridiculous question. Newborns cried.

"At first, but Mrs. Woods gave you sugar water and swaddled you. The next time it thundered, though . . ." Papa shook his head. "That wailing of yours made the cows bawl."

A tear slid down Papa's face.

"Please don't cry." Mary slid from her chair and knelt before him, brought to her knees by the rawness of Papa's sorrow.

"I've not taken seriously the connection between your fear of storms and the night you were born." Papa coughed. "I thought you'd grow out of it like children outgrow fears."

Yes, she should have outgrown it, but one didn't grow out of loss. One dealt with it, but it never went away.

Her lip trembled as she took Papa's hand in her own. His work-worn fingers wrapped around hers, and Mary studied the scars on them. This hand, once strong, had held Mama's, most likely even while Mama strained in childbirth. Mary's focus shifted to her own sturdy hand, and she thought of all the notes it had pressed on the piano, the daisies it had plucked, and the cows it had milked.

Had Mama, weak and near death, reached for Mary's tiny fingers, caressed them, squeezed them? It had. Mary felt it like a lightning strike to her soul.

She raised Papa's hands to her lips and kissed it. "Thank you for sharing."

"Knowing might help you to heal."

A flash of light preceded a short clap of thunder. Her body jolted.

"Then again, healing takes time," Papa's hushed voice was half-drowned beneath the rain pelting the roof. "And more important, it takes an act of grace."

CHAPTER SEVENTEEN

Mary beat the rug, sending a plume of dust skyward into the sunshine.

Papa rocked in the chair she'd lugged from the porch. His laughter, which at times seemed crippled with arthritis much the same as his fingers, sounded light as birdsong today. "With all the things needing to be done, beating the one rug we own doesn't seem like a priority."

She walloped the intricately woven carpet she'd draped over the clothesline. A few more whacks and she might manage to ease the tightness in her chest, though dwelling on the unending list of tasks would clamp it up again: stalls and a chicken coop to clean, cream to churn, a trough to fix in the springhouse, and a kettle of soup that had simmered too long on the stove. Neighbors helped when they could, and someone from the Thomas clan brought over a loaf of bread every day, but she risked wearing out their generosity.

Let him reconsider Bridges's offer. . .

Even as she prayed, the awareness of this place as home slipped like sand through the cracks of her heart. And what a fissured mess her heart had become. Broken with trying to understand why letting go of this place seemed worse than death. Splintered with thoughts of Luke that wouldn't cease.

Luke in the morning when first light broke over the barn. Luke at midday meal, dinner, and again after evening milking when she huddled at Rod's in the dark, playing melodies that seemed alive enough to be friends. And Luke when she stocked the wood stove and pondered his confession from Sunday.

When he'd faced the congregation, a mixture of humility and detachment in his stance, she'd suspected a simple playing-with-matches incident was not the entire story. The things a person held back were often more important than the things spoken.

"The Crawleys will be traveling to Peshastin on Monday." Papa leaned back in the rocking chair. "This isn't a decision I'm making without prayer."

Or without Luke's advice.

And there he was again, infringing upon her thoughts.

She pounded the rug, turning her head to the side when a pocket of dust clouded the air.

"It's later in the spring than I'd have liked," Papa said.

Summer was knocking on the door, and though the Lord had been gracious to send rain, delaying the trip so that Papa might reconsider, Papa hadn't shown signs of doing so. Pushing him further seemed disrespectful.

"Mary. Will you say something?"

"I wish Luke had never returned."

I wish Luke would get out of my head.

Papa stopped rocking and smiled. "You don't mean that."

She closed her eyes against the breeze and remembered Luke on the swing with her, the back and forth like the swaying of her heart. Luke's return had engulfed her with emotions, one of which was, undeniably, delight.

"Here comes Matthew Bridges."

"What?" Mary turned and peered beyond the house.

Matthew rode his horse across the field, coming from the direction of the Wenatchee. She watched until he pulled behind the rug and dismounted.

Ducking around the frayed edge, he tipped his head at Papa. "How are you feeling today, Mr. Smith?"

"The joy of the Lord is my strength."

171

"I admire your optimism."

"It's more than that. It's truth."

Papa's curt response turned Mary's attention from Matthew. With pursed lips, he lowered his gaze to his lap.

She set aside her beating stick and waved at Matthew. "Would you help me in the barn for a moment?" She strode across the yard, trusting him to follow.

Matthew fell in step beside her. "I didn't mean any offense."

"He's not offended. He's weary of people asking about his health, drawing attention to his weakness."

Something Luke never did. He assumed Papa could do something unless Papa asked for help, which she supposed was why Papa liked when Luke assisted with the milking. "He's learned to live and function with the arthritis."

"And the shortness of breath?"

"The doctor doesn't have an answer for that, other than to say he should only do as much work as he feels able to do."

Matthew led his mount into the paddock next to the barn. "Considering his struggles, surely you're ready to move forward with negotiations with my father."

"Papa isn't interested. Evidently, he's had a conversation with your father."

The coolness of the barn closed around them as they entered. Mary looked back to see Matthew's reaction, but his expression maintained the usual friendliness. Perhaps Matthew had been unaware that Papa had talked with his father.

Mary picked up the broken post from the first stall and dragged it toward the wall. Matthew took the beam from her and stood it in the corner. "Want this chopped into firewood?"

"You're kind, but not now. I could use your help in securing the new post." She moved the milk cart out of the way. "Unless I'm keeping you from your work."

"You aren't keeping me from anything."

She shifted her eyes. "What about your men?"

"They'll manage, as long as Davis behaves, which . . ." Matthew shook his head. "That boy's trouble."

She'd broach no argument.

Leaning against the wall, Mary watched Matthew adjust the post. "I'm hoping I might be able to convince Papa to think again about your family's offer."

A bead of sweat dripped from Matthew's curls as he strained to wedge the new post in place. He gave the post a final shove and lifted his gaze to hers, offering an expression more intense than she'd seen from him. "Find a way."

She withdrew at the edge in his voice. "I said I'd try."

Matthew blew out a breath and smiled. "I know." He wiped his sleeve across his forehead. "Your family and mine make a good match. We'd accomplish more together in this valley than we can apart."

"I agree." Given the circumstances of Papa's body breaking down and her own inability to keep up with the work.

"I'm glad." Matthew's gaze grew bolder, provoking her, and she felt as though he expected her to read his mind.

She turned and headed out the doors, crossing from shadow into sunshine. In the past, Matthew's gaze had brought nothing but assurance, but the eyes he'd turned on her a moment ago carried an unfamiliar message. She wasn't interested in more mystery.

"There's something else you should know," Matthew said behind her. "I put in my name for sheriff."

She whirled around, dress strangling her legs. "You?"

He scowled. "Don't you approve?"

"No. I mean, yes. It's . . ." Last week she'd touted Luke's abilities to Matthew, unaware of Matthew's decision. She didn't doubt his qualities, but Luke . . . The thought of Luke as sheriff satisfied her.

Matthew's frown deepened. He spun away and whistled for his mount. "Luke doesn't want to run for sheriff, let alone stay in Pine Creek."

The quiet words couldn't have been more forceful if they'd been yelled.

"We need a sheriff who understands this town," Matthew continued. "Who's grown up here and won't accommodate Johnston's every idea. That candidate from Wenatchee isn't fit. And neither is Luke. He's never laid claim to this town like I have."

Town's weren't claimed. They were inhabited and cared for, called home.

Mary stumbled out of Matthew's way as he swung into the saddle. Without a goodbye, he nudged his horse.

"Matthew."

He reined in, spinning back to face her. The sun washed out the pale blue of his eyes. The intensity of moments ago had faded into hollowness. She'd hurt him.

"If being sheriff is something you care about, I'm happy for you," she said. "I was just surprised."

A smile relaxed the sternness from his face. "The unexpected is a good thing. Trust me."

She'd trusted him since the day he'd pulled the splinter from her palm her first year of school. Nothing should change that now. So then why was there hesitation in her spirit?

* * *

Luke rolled his pants to his knees and waded into the shallow waters of the Wenatchee. Aside from the swimming hole around the bend, the waters west of town were wide and no deeper than five feet, perfect for cooling off and fishing. He baited his hook and cast his line into the current. Afternoon sunshine warmed his back as he waited.

Now days, his life centered on waiting. Waiting on word from Texas. Waiting for his mind to stop thinking about Mary. Waiting for his shoulder to return to normal.

His line tensed, and he finagled in the trout, a modest ten-incher. He'd fried up a fish many a night around a campfire, rock at his back, legs outstretched, insects humming in the bushes. The reminder of Texas would taste delicious tonight. He tossed his prize in the pail, rebaited, and waded farther from shore. Cold water rushed above his knees, soaking the ends of his pants. Leafy cottonwoods and tall, skinny pines lined the shore, offering scattered shade and the privacy he'd craved after working with Paul all morning. In a setting like this, he could imagine himself alone, miles from civilization.

"Luke the Duke!" Mary called from the woods behind him.

Not alone anymore.

And not sure what I think about that.

He waved a hand over his head, not turning to face her. So much for waiting for thoughts of Mary to flee. Had he had a chance, anyway? She'd set up camp in his mind the night of their reunion weeks ago.

"Grace said I'd find you here."

Evidently his sister hadn't taken seriously his parting comment, *I'm going fishing; I need to be alone.* A morning spent roofing the accommodations they were building for the new crew with Paul had necessitated an afternoon of seclusion.

Though this interruption might not be so bad.

"Are you going to say something?" she asked.

He grinned. "What do you want me to say?" He tried to picture what dress she wore. Probably her usual rose-colored work dress.

He spun around. Wrong, but fighting her hold on him would have been easier if he'd been right. The white ruffled blouse hugged her form, emphasizing her narrow waist where it tucked into a sage skirt.

"I like the new outfit." He quirked his mouth at the bold comment.

She beamed and smoothed her hands down the front. "Grace has been hard at work." Mary walked to the edge of the water, as if waiting for him to join her.

Too bad. He wasn't in the mood for company, even hers. He was on a mission to catch fish for dinner. He returned his attention to his line. The bait had disappeared, so he pulled the line in, reached in his pocket, and remedied the problem. Casting the line again, he wondered if she had a purpose for seeking him out or if she planned to watch him fish. In un-Mary-like manner, she'd not shared her opinion on his confession, and he'd wager she had plenty to say.

"Guess what?" she asked.

Ah, she had news. "What?"

"Matthew's running for sheriff."

Luke jerked his head around.

She propped her hands on her hips and smiled. "How's that for news?"

"Surprising." More than that. Alarming.

A badge implied obligation and demanded integrity and courage. Beneath a veneer of chivalry, Luke doubted Matthew's commitment to justice and his stamina to handle the pressure of the job.

He turned back to his line. "What do you think about it?"

"I was surprised as well."

That didn't tell him anything. "And?"

"You're still my choice."

The words wormed through his defenses and made him think about what being her choice could mean — if he twisted her meaning. He closed his eyes. The unmarryable one wasn't her choice. Which was fine, because he was going back to Texas.

Water splashed behind him, and he twisted around. Mary sloshed through the river with her skirts knotted to the side of her calves.

"Of all the . . ." he muttered and shifted his gaze heavenward. Her unconventionality had no end.

One hand clutching her skirt, the other held out for balance, she meandered over the stones, watching her steps.

She'd worked her way to within four feet when she tripped and lunged forward, arms outstretched. He reached with his free hand and caught her shoulder as her hands seized his belt. He slipped his arm around her waist and pulled her up.

She raised her gaze. Not even falling into him and nearly pulling his pants off had brought a blush to her face. A normal woman would have blushed.

Drops of water sparkled on her face as she smiled. "I don't like not being able to see your eyes when I talk with you."

His heart stuttered, and he released her and stepped back. She could see them now.

The bottom half of her skirts were soaked. She wiped the water from her cheeks and studied him evenly. "You were brave on Sunday."

His grip tightened on his rod.

"After all these years, why now?"

He stared at the opposite shore. "It was past time."

"And maybe you hoped to distance yourself from these people? Discourage them from voting for you?"

She'd read him with uncanny accuracy.

"But it didn't work. Pine Creek loves you."

"That's the irony, isn't it?" He met her satisfied smile with a wry one of his own. "They shouldn't be so quick to forgive."

"You were a child, and you'd lost your father."

"Those are excuses." From the moment a child toddles, he learns not to play with matches. But Luke hadn't been just playing with matches; he'd been numbing the loss of his father, and that's what people didn't know, *couldn't* know. What kind of person inflicted harm on himself?

Mary stepped in front of him and peered at his face. "What's the rest of the story?"

He shook his head. "That's not important."

"So there is more."

He looked down at the fishing pole handle, and his

eyes caught the tail of a scar jutting from beneath his rolled up sleeves. His breath hitched, and he reached over and smoothed his sleeve down. The underside of his left upper arm told the rest of the story.

Mary sighed, a contended sound. "How long has it been since I've waded?"

He had no idea.

She leaned forward and glided her hands across the surface of the water. "It's almost warm enough to swim."

"Not even close." He turned a stern eye toward her, discouraging whatever wild thoughts were brewing.

His line stiffened, and he pulled on it. Fish two, within his grasp.

A torrent of water splashed him from behind, soaking him from lower back to knees. Gasping, he dropped his rod.

Mary shrieked and pranced after it, stepping high to run through the water. He stomped past her, eye on the swiftly moving pole that rode the choppy rapids downstream. The current carried his rod into the bank, where it hooked on some protruding roots. He slowed, glancing over his shoulder. Mary had yielded the chase to him and stood gripping her skirts in the middle of the river. Ever playful, her smile provoked him. He snatched his pole, stepped onto land, and paced up the shore. At his pail, he dropped his rod and lunged into the water after her.

She shrieked again and took off upstream. She'd been the instigator from the day she'd stolen his cookie and blamed him for having stolen hers.

When he caught up to her, which took all of five seconds, he clasped her around the waist and hoisted her over his good shoulder. Her giggles sounding close to his ear, he marched to shore and headed downstream.

"No, Luke!"

"That's right. You know what's coming."

She might have gotten him first, but he'd get her best.

"No, no, no, no . . ."

She tried to kick at him, but he tightened his grasp on her legs. Veering from the water's edge, he rounded the boulder, and on the other side, met the river where it curved into the swimming hole.

"Almost warm enough for a swim?"

Her fists pounded his back. "Now's the time to call upon your hidden chivalrous qualities."

He halted so suddenly that she stilled her squirming, a mistake since the lack of movement only emphasized her curves against his back.

"Huh." He pretended to think. Shaking his head, he started off again. "Didn't find any."

A smooth, flat rock the size of a small cabin sloped into the water. He waded to his ankles, a foot from the drop off, and turned to offer her a view of the greenish pool soon to be her demise for splashing him.

"Luke!" She wriggled against him. "Don't."

Her lighthearted pleas wouldn't get anywhere with him. He lowered her and shifted his hold to her waist. She clamped her arms around his neck. Tugging on her vice-like grip with one hand, he kept his other arm anchored around her middle. Her elbow dug into his bad shoulder, and he cried out.

Her arms unlocked from his neck, and she drew back. "I'm sorry."

He was sorry, too, as he gazed at her in his arms, looking haphazardly beautiful with mussed hair and glints of mica on her cheek. Sorry he'd reacted to her teasing without thinking about what touching her would do to him.

He let her go, stepped back. Shaking out his arms, he glanced at the sky. "You should get home to chores."

That sounded as lame as an overworked mule.

She shook her skirts out. "Yes, well, duty doesn't wait."

He retraced his steps with long strides. Near his pail, Mary's stockings bunched next to her boots. He'd seen stockings hung on the line, and his eyes hadn't lingered, but now . . . they looked dainty and suggested a vulnerability he didn't often associate with Mary.

Thomas, you're thinking too much.

He'd gone from not thinking enough to over thinking. He snatched his rod, waded ten feet into the river, and made sure his back stayed toward Mary.

"I'll leave you in peace," she called. "You'll catch more fish without me stirring the waters."

Her stirring the waters wasn't the issue as much her stirring his heart and dimming his love for Texas.

"Bye, Dairy Mary."

He strained to hear her footsteps above the water's rush, and as he did, his mind turned to why she'd sought him in the first place.

Matthew for sheriff. Luke grunted and tossed his baited hook downstream. From the standpoint of a lawman and a citizen of Pine Creek—a former citizen—Matthew's passive, conflict-avoiding personality wasn't a fit for sheriff. The quiet ones were never quiet on the inside. They churned through thoughts and emotions while maintaining an external pretense of calm. They were unpredictable. Private. Unlike Mary, who vomited whatever thought came to mind, an image she'd not appreciate.

For the life of him, he couldn't fathom what Matthew stood to gain by putting in his name for sheriff. In a strange, underhanded way, Matthew joining the race curled Luke's insides, made him want to step up and fight for the position.

Stay the course. You don't want this.

He had Texas to think of, his reputation to clear, and an expanse of people awaiting his protection and service.

He couldn't explain it, and he shouldn't have to defend his emotions to himself, but being Pine Creek's sheriff just wouldn't work. And he had the scars to prove it.

CHAPTER EIGHTEEN

Luke flipped the post into the new hole and wiped his hands on his trousers. A morning of digging holes and hammering posts was enough for him to know he'd chosen the right profession. Give him a gun and a skirmish any day. Sweat and toil deserved a better reward than cash and fat cows, something like justice and peace.

His shoulder throbbed as Luke grabbed his shovel and filled dirt around the post. Another few whacks with the mallet, and he secured the last of the forty he'd replaced. Blowing out a breath, he cuffed the back of his neck where sweat trickled. Grace had cleaned up his mop yesterday, and he'd not grown used to the absence of hair on his neck.

He rolled his shoulders as he studied the puffy clouds floating beyond the ridgeline. A new lump had developed the past weeks beneath the scarred skin of his front two bullet wounds. The tissue damage caused by three bullets had been intense, but he hadn't imagined it'd take two months to heal, or that after feeling better, he'd relapse. He'd refrained from using his left arm, but a man needed to work. Sitting idle and mulling over how his case was going down in Texas wasn't an option. If not for those ridiculous accusations aligning him with the men who'd shot him, he'd be patrolling his territory.

He whispered a plea for God's intervention. Prayers for resolution came and went through him, cycling with his breath.

"Uncle Luke!" Helen skipped across the field, braids bouncing. "Uncle Luke! Mama says . . ." She slipped and sprawled face-first in the mud.

He jogged over and pulled her to her feet. Cow patty decorated the front of her blue calico. She looked down and sucked in a ragged breath. A trembling lower lip warned him seconds before the wailing started.

"Nothing your mama can't wash out." He patted her shoulder, not knowing how else to offer comfort.

She wiped her dirty hand across her face, leaving a trail of mud, and reached for his hand. He swept her into his arms instead. Cow excrement didn't intimidate as much as the thought of feeling that little hand in his.

"I'm going to mess you up." She sniffed tears and leaned back from him.

Nothing was more messed up than shying away from holding a four-year-old's hand. He pulled her closer. "Nothing my mama can't wash out."

Leaving his tools behind, he walked in from the field and rounded the house to a welcoming party on the front porch.

"The doctor's here." Helen gripped his neck with slimy fingers. "That's what I was supposed to tell you."

A man he didn't recognize stood with his arms crossed conversing with Abigail and his mother.

"It's getting close to time for your little brother or sister. Two more months."

"The doctor's not here to see Mama. He's here for you."

The doctor must have said something because his mother turned and waved him over. Luke took the steps and offered Helen to Abigail.

She drew back and frowned. "What is Uncle Luke teaching you?"

"How to slip and slide in the cow pasture after weeks of rain." Luke smiled and ruffled Helen's wavy hair.

Abigail gripped her daughter beneath the arms and set her on her feet. "Stay here. As soon as the others go inside, I'm stripping this grime off you and carrying you to the tub. Paul, will you ready the water?"

His brother nodded to the doctor. "Good to see you again." Descending the steps, Paul's gaze brushed off Luke's, veiled and narrow.

"Luke," his mother said. "This is Dr. James Fraser." She took Luke by the arm, pulling his thoughts from one problem to another.

The doctor looked no older than Luke, even with a trimmed beard and professional dress. Luke shook the man's hand, enjoying several inches advantage in height. "Welcome to Pine Creek."

"Dr. Fraser's starting an office in Clifton," his mother said. "He'll be traveling to Pine Creek once a week."

"I heard that a Thomas son was visiting from down south." Dr. Fraser's tenor voice was smooth and friendly. "Running for sheriff, correct?"

Running from. "Not exactly."

"Your mother mentioned you'd been wounded and were having some pain. I thought I could take a look."

Luke's gaze sought his mother's, but she studied her hands and picked at dirt beneath her fingernails. She meant well, and because he loved her, he didn't let out the grimace that threatened. "I'd appreciate that."

His mother's look of gratitude told him he'd made the right choice not to argue.

He led the doctor through the front room and into the kitchen, where he gladly stripped off his soiled shirt.

Dr. Fraser set down his bag and fumbled to open it with his slim fingers. "Your mother explained about your father."

"I have none of his symptoms."

Luke sat on the table.

Dr. Fraser poked around the three bullet wounds, two next to each other on the front of his shoulder, and a third several inches around the side on his upper arm.

"This hurt?" Dr. Fraser dug his thumb into the scarred

flesh.

"Doesn't feel great."

"But does it hurt?"

The aches had become customary. "It's not like the first week, but yeah, I've been more comfortable."

The stethoscope rested cold against his chest as Dr. Fraser listened to Luke's heart and lungs.

"Pain's not that bad," Luke said. "These things take time."

Dr. Fraser looked up. "You been shot before?"

"No." But time seemed to be the answer to anything. The summer Father had died, he'd been told to give the grief time. Grief didn't need time. It needed release.

The doctor straightened. "You sound good, and you're not running a fever, meaning infection hasn't set in, but—"

The back door opened and Mary swept in, whistling. She turned and shut the door. "I've been anticipating Grace's birthday for weeks. Do you know how long it's been since I've spent the night here?" She spun around. "I know you're—"

Her gaze riveted on his bare chest, crashed into his eyes a moment, then lowered to his chest again. She closed her gaping mouth, tipped her head and frowned.

"Excuse me, miss, but I'm in the middle of an examination." Dr. Fraser stepped toward Mary, arm out to usher her toward the door.

Mary's attention didn't alter from Luke as she pushed around Dr. Fraser and hurried to his side. He lunged for his shirt, not caring about the mess Helen had made it. Mary gasped, and her steps hesitated. He slipped his arms through the sleeves, praying she'd gasped at his shoulder, not his scars.

But when she reached and lifted back the left edge of his shirt, eyes widening, he knew she'd seen his marks of shame. He shrugged from her touch. Had she any couth?

She stepped back and met his eyes. For an instant, he expected her to ask about the scars, but then she licked her lips and swallowed.

"There's a bullet still in you." Her voice sounded harsher than normal.

"Three bullets entered, and three were taken out." The doctor in Texas had showed him the bullets.

She brushed her finger over the protrusion. He fought against a shiver. One touch on his bare shoulder shouldn't cause his muscles to weaken, and his body to shudder.

Mary turned Dr. Fraser. "That needs to come out."

Dr. Fraser cleared his throat. "I was about to discuss that with my patient when you —"

"Interrupted." Mary smiled.

Luke prodded the lump. "It's true?"

"I'm afraid so." Dr. Fraser glowered at Mary.

"I'll assist," Mary said. "I've sewn up many cows."

Luke rolled his eyes. "Dr. Fraser, meet Dr. Mary Smith, owner of Smith Dairy and fastest milker this side of . . . civility."

Mary blessed him with a mock sneer.

Dr. Fraser returned his stethoscope to his bag and raised his brow at Mary.

"I'm not a doctor. Luke exaggerates, among other things."

Dr. Fraser took Mary by the arm. "Would you mind waiting in the other room?" He ushered her toward the door. "I can handle the minor operation myself."

She yanked her arm away. "Absolutely, I mind. Give me one reason why I can't help."

"Experience with cows does not qualify you to assist in surgery."

"A life is a life." Mary turned her eyes to Luke. "Please, Luke. I won't say anything. You know how good I am with cows." Her voice adopted a frantic edge. "Your mama would want someone in with you, and it can't be her."

True. She'd faint. Now that Mary had seen the scars, he didn't have that as an excuse. And furthermore, she'd not relent until she got her way. "She can help."

Mary beamed. "So it's settled. When shall we slice him open?"

Dr. Fraser glared. "I will slice. You will watch and hand me instruments."

Mary slid next to Luke and laid her hand on his left arm. "I'm free for as long as I'm needed. I have the milking covered tonight."

Because obviously, she was an integral part of this operation.

Luke offered the doctor an apologetic smile before slipping off the table and heading for the stairs, his room, and an unexpected surgery.

* * *

Mary scooted her chair close to Luke's bed and refused to look him in the eye. She wanted to dig beneath that shirt and see those pocked burn marks, confirm her suspicions that he'd done it to himself. Anyone else might consider the scars the result of an accident, but she knew: this was the rest of the story from Sunday's confession.

"You don't need to be here," Dr. Fraser said. He'd tried three times to get her to leave.

She wasn't leaving.

Dr. Fraser's mouth tightened as he matched her fierce expression. He turned to Luke and eased Luke's clean shirt off. Mary avoided looking directly at Luke, trying to offer a bit of privacy.

"It's a simple procedure." Dr. Fraser lifted instruments from the pot of boiling water Mrs. Thomas had brought up.

"I'm not leaving." Mary stiffened her posture.

Dr. Fraser pulled out his scalpel, and Mrs. Thomas sucked in a breath. Mary rose and met her in the doorway. Taking Mrs. Thomas's hand, Mary ushered her back into the hall.

"Do you have any concerns?" Mrs. Thomas called to

Dr. Fraser.

"None whatsoever."

"If you're sure you don't need me . . ."

Mary nudged her toward the stairway. "I'll keep him distracted. He won't even know he's slit open."

The faintest twitch of a smile showed on Mrs. Thomas's pale face. "I'm sure you'll be a fine distraction, dear."

Mary returned to the room and settled in the chair beside the bed, forcing normal breaths. The stench from the bottle of antiseptic Dr. Fraser had uncapped choked her.

Luke's bare shoulder, shrouded in goose bumps, stuck out from the blanket.

She studied Luke briefly while his gaze was elsewhere. He wore his muscle well. Not at all in an unmarryable fashion. Which reminded her of the apology she'd been waiting to issue, the one she should have offered when they'd swung in the dark, and then failed to offer again yesterday when he'd been fishing. Splashing him had seemed easier. Nor was now the time, distraction as it might be. Not when she was attempting to see Luke as nothing more than a jersey in need of a few stitches.

Dr. Fraser held a syringe. "This is a minor dose of morphine that will numb your shoulder. Tell me if you start to feel pain."

Luke sat up, blanket falling to his waist. "I don't want morphine. You said the bullet's at the surface?"

Dr. Fraser nodded.

She peeked at his scars. Five, maybe six that she saw beneath his left arm. None on his right side—that she noticed.

"You need anesthesia." Mary averted her eyes.

"I'm not having morphine."

"It's safe for medicinal use and not addictive in this case," Dr. Fraser said.

"No morphine." Luke relaxed back in bed and pulled the covers up to his chest.

Mary's stomach flipped as Dr. Fraser bent over Luke

187

with his scalpel. Forget privacy; she couldn't look away, despite the dizziness that filled her senses.

Luke flinched.

"You have to stay still," Dr. Fraser said, scalpel hovering above Luke.

Nausea warmed its way from her stomach to her chest. She'd reached into cows and pulled out calves. A small slit on the shoulder had nothing on that bloodiness. But the issue wasn't blood or mess. It was the man beneath the scalpel.

Luke closed his eyes and sucked air through half parted lips. The one who apprehended criminals and faced guns shouldn't be nervous.

Dr. Fraser placed the tip of the scalpel into Luke's skin.

Luke's hand rested on the bed close to hers. She reached for it, but as soon as she touched it, he jerked it away.

Dr. Fraser drew back. "Keep still."

Luke opened his eyes, piercing her with a look. "No hands, Dairy Mary."

"Get over your fear."

He lifted his head off the pillow, a better position for glaring. She pushed his head down and kept her hand resting on his temple.

"A preference is not a fear," he said. "I prefer not to have my hand held." He closed his eyes again.

"I can't keep up with you two." For the first time since she walked into the kitchen, amusement lightened Dr. Fraser's expression. He leaned forward. "No more silliness. Here I go now."

The fine point of the scalpel moved snail-like across the inch-wide lump in Luke's shoulder, Dr. Fraser's hand a sure guide. Luke's chest rose and fell with deliberate breaths. Her gaze roamed his whisker-free face, his trimmed hairline. He'd cleaned up, but a few snips couldn't eradicate his ruggedness. The blanket over his trunk slipped to the side, revealing a toned and tight abdomen. She set her hand on his middle.

His eyes shot open.

"Tell me again what the Texas sky looks like, and I'll try better to imagine it."

"It's . . ." His husky voice faded.

She drummed her fingers on his stomach, and his muscles hardened.

"It can be a dozen colors at once." His eyes fastened on hers.

A ping sounded in the ceramic bowl beside the bed, and Mary looked. The bullet rolled on its side, trailing a red stream of blood across the bottom of the bowl.

"What type of colors?" she asked.

"At daybreak or dusk, it's got the entire rainbow. Reds, oranges, and yellows on the horizon. Pale blue above fading into a deep blue on the opposite horizon that almost looks purple." Luke's eyes rolled back as Dr. Fraser pulled the needle through his skin.

She drummed on his middle again, and those hazel eyes fought their way to hers.

Luke's lips twitched. "You can feel the sky's curve above you, bending over, sheltering you, blessing you."

"That's a much better image than eating you alive or smothering you in your sleep. You're surprisingly poetic."

"Maybe you don't know me as well as you think you do."

She wanted to tease that she knew him better than she knew herself, but he'd hidden scars, carried a secret about the church fire. "Maybe I don't."

Dr. Fraser pulled the stitching taut, and Luke groaned. Scrunching his eyes closed, his lips trembled as he blew out a breath.

"I'd like to see a Texas sky," Mary said.

A brief, strained grin tipped Luke's mouth. "Would you?"

All his stories and descriptions had stimulated her appetite, not that she'd let on. She'd built her reputation when they were schoolchildren on goading him for wanting to run off to Texas with his gun and good intentions.

"Mary?"

She brought her gaze back from where it'd wandered to the window. "I would."

The tension loosened from Luke's face, and something about the way his heart escaped through his eyes made her want to cry.

"And I'm done." Dr. Fraser put down his needle and thread.

Mary stood. "I'll let the others know everything went well."

"Thanks, Dairy Mary." Luke's voice stopped her in the threshold. "For making life more interesting."

Life was definitely more interesting. She let her gaze dip to where he clutched his arm tight to his side. She'd get that story from him before he took off for Texas again, even if she had to tie him up.

***

Despite the numerous reassurances to his mother that he felt fine, she'd asked him to stay in bed for Grace's birthday dinner. What could he do but honor the woman who'd fought to keep the peace between him and Paul since his return, and not only that, but who'd resisted prying when she must suspect things weren't right in Texas. Hence, he'd balanced his plate on his lap and ate along, listening to the loud shouts of laughter and noisy conversation from below.

Luke shoved another bite into his mouth, studying again the flowered wallpaper they'd put up for Helen when she'd taken over his room. The busy design made the small space more constricting, reminded him he didn't have a place here anymore.

Heavy footsteps and slamming doors announced the end of the meal downstairs. They'd be moving out to the campfire, a tradition on Grace's birthday. Grace and her love for flame and warmth. It ran in the family.

A creak sounded on the stairs, and a moment later, Mary swept around his door, carrying her plate. Without meeting his eyes, she propped herself in the same chair she'd sat in earlier and picked at the scraps of remaining food. Her attention wandered to the window as she chewed, evidently in no hurry to join the others.

He looked at her until she shifted her gaze to his.

"What?" she asked. "You shouldn't be alone on Grace's birthday."

So she'd left the celebration to be with him. And those sitting around the campfire would notice.

He set his plate aside, swung his feet over the edge, and peered out the window. Paul heaped wood on the fire as the dogs paced around him. The others had settled in chairs rimming the pit, their laughter riding the breeze through Luke's open window.

He stood and made his way toward the door, testing his shoulder with a stretch. Sore, but not bad.

Mary's cleared throat stopped him. She eyed the sling at the end of his bed.

"It'll be fine."

"Dr. Fraser said to wear it for a week."

"Surely Dr. Mary can give me a pardon."

"She could, but she won't."

Mary set her plate on his, stood, and picked up the sling. She slipped the strap over his head, and fidgeted with the band at the back of his neck. The sensation of her fingers at the top of his spine seeped down to his toes.

"Today, Contrary." What was so difficult about tightening a strap?

Her brow furrowed. He could lean forward and kiss it. That would hurry things along—among other things. He honed in on the dull ache of his incision, resisting the direction his thoughts wanted to take him. His favorite direction was south, toward the familiar. Not toward romance with a woman who . . .

He cut off the false thought before he could finish with *annoyed him.*

She didn't irritate him, never had, not in the way she claimed he irritated her. They'd developed an ease since his return, despite the wit that coursed between them.

"There." She stepped back and smiled.

Looking at her large brown eyes, he rebuked his thought about developing an ease with her. The awareness that flowed beneath the interactions of the past month demanded strength of heart he couldn't muster.

He walked out the door, shrugging away the imprint of her touch. On his neck. Against his middle during the procedure. The bonfire would reset his priorities and clear his head. Being under an evening sky would remind him of the life he'd left in Texas.

And what if you can't get it back?

He didn't have an answer. Then again, he didn't expect to be dismissed. Truth would surface.

Like it did with your scars?

He tried to suck in a deep breath but couldn't. Telling her about that summer was a journey he wasn't ready to make.

She led the way, and he followed down the stairs and out the front door. On the porch, he stepped into his boots but didn't lace them.

Mary set her hand against the small of his back. "You feel all right?"

He turned to face her. No. He didn't feel all right, but it had nothing to do with his stitches. "I'm fine."

She reached and unbuttoned his top button.

His heart galloped. "What—?"

"Someone needs to teach you how to button a shirt. It's crooked."

She fixed the buttons, swept past him, and made her way across the cobbled path to the glow of the fire. The wood popped and streamed sparks into the dusky sky. He settled on a stump across the way from the occupied chairs.

Claire laughed at something Barrett said and burrowed further beneath a blanket she shared with Grace. Helen climbed onto Mary's lap and set her head against Mary's chest. Cam and his mother talked about the railroad.

Luke took in Paul, who stood behind Abigail, hands shoved in his pockets, staring into the flames. The slump of his shoulders and his grimace articulated the burdens of being head of the household.

Maybe Luke had been too quick to anger over Paul's overbearing ways. They weren't that different, he and Paul. Boys broken by the loss of their father, determined to make good on the dreams God had given them.

Abigail reached back and drew Paul's arms around her, and the lines around his eyes softened. A good woman stretched a man beyond his potential, and Abigail had drawn out things in Paul no one else had seen.

Luke diverted his attention from the display of affection but didn't know where to rest his eyes. They wandered around the campfire, skipping over friends, family. Barrett had Claire. Paul had Abigail, Helen, and another child on the way, and his mother had a son running the ranch. Mary had Grace and Claire. And Cam, he bore the seasons of life like a boulder buffeted waves.

Luke didn't belong here. He'd staked his tent in Texas. Taken up residence in a career that suited his gifts, and the thought of being evicted from that home — terminated by the Rangers — turned his gut rancid.

His mother looked over, and he read the question in her eyes *are you all right?* All this care and concern, the questioning how he was, ate at him, made him realize he was far from all right. Hadn't been all right since shoveling dirt on Father's grave. While others had moved on, he'd moved his grief deeper. Burned himself.

"When does your father leave?" His mother asked Mary.

"Monday. It's going to be a long week." Sorrow tensed her voice.

Luke looked her direction. Her gaze caught his, and he held hers without restraint, with an intensity that hummed beyond the small talk and hiss of burning cottonwood. The holding back had worn him. His secrets, his issues with the Rangers, even his name from the ballot when he knew the town didn't have a good candidate. A man couldn't hold back without growing raw inside.

You'll feel the tug eventually, and it'll pull you under so fast you'll hardly have time to breathe. Mary's warning had been about home. Pine Creek. But she'd been the one to pull him under.

He didn't belong here . . . yet she'd acquired a grip on him from which he couldn't turn loose. The battle tugged from two directions, and he wasn't going to make it out in one piece.

CHAPTER NINETEEN

Mary rolled over in bed beside Grace and looked toward the window. Black. No matter how late the hour when she retired, habit woke her before the sun.

Grace had begged, in that subtle and gentle way of hers, to tell Luke about the honeysuckles and noises, but Mary had put her off again, promising to seek the marshal if necessary. That seemed like an overreaction.

A floorboard creaked outside the bedroom door. Curling her legs, Mary stared toward the window, waiting for a slip of light to tell her she could rise. When Grace stirred and turned on her back, Mary rolled toward the middle of the bowed mattress.

She didn't ask for the image, but it came like robins after rain: Luke's body next to hers instead of Grace's. How much more his body weight would pull hers to the middle.

She sat up. Dark or not, the time to rise had come, thanks to the obscene thoughts. She fumbled for the clothes she'd set on the chair after sitting by the fire so long she'd hardly been able to keep her eyes open, even with Luke's presence as incentive.

Her stocking feet absorbed the cold from the wood floor as she opened the door and peeked into the hallway. Luke's door stood ajar, a lantern casting a glow over his made bed. If she found him doing chores, she'd tattle so hard, he'd have to wear that sling a year.

A box poked from beneath his bed, and she recognized the worn picture on the cover, a horse and rider at full gallop.

Luke's Ranger articles. He'd treated those newspaper clippings like treasure maps.

After a glance down the hall, she slipped into his room and knelt by the box, pushed by her desire to peek at the stories which Luke had retold to her and Grace. The tattered lid lifted easily in her hands, and she peered inside. Old clippings piled three-quarters high. She smiled and picked up the top one. A severe, bearded face stared back at her. She scanned the article, set it aside, and chose another. Sentence after sentence peddled the accomplishments of Rangers and their regiments. The corner of one clipping was bent and worn, as if he'd fingered it again and again.

She gathered the clippings and moved to return them to the box. An envelope at the bottom, newer and less wrinkled, drew her attention. She reached for it, but hesitated. She'd moved beyond newspaper clippings into personal territory. Curiosity swatted away the counseling of her conscience, and she lifted it up and slipped the letter out.

Dear Luke,

As you know, on March the third, after the incident which caused your injury, the Texas Ranger Judicial Committee began an inquiry into your actions while on assignment trailing the Fowler Trio — namely, questioning whether you acted within your orders. I sent you back to Washington for recovery while I stood in your defense.

Unfortunately, a witness, which I will not name for reasons of confidentiality, has come forward and charged you with working alongside the Fowler Trio in several robberies, including the Fort Worth Bank robbery last October that led to the death of two Rangers. In regard to this new development, the committee has made your suspension official and requests that you remain where you are in Pine Creek while they investigate the role you played. You will be contacted shortly by a marshal in your area. I cannot emphasize enough the importance of staying put. This is not the time to be a hero.

I believe in your innocence and will continue to fight to prove it. Be patient with the system. A Ranger going rogue is cause for extensive investigation, even if the initial witness is questionable. I'll get you back here eventually. A man like you belongs in Texas.

Captain R. Finch

Luke, rogue? Preposterous.

She had a mind to whip out a piece of paper and set this Captain Finch straight. Luke had more character than anyone, wrapped up in unapologetic actions and a thirst for adventure. But for all the carelessness a lifestyle of adventure might portray, recklessness didn't motivate him. Passion did. And behind that passion, a sturdiness of character that denied self and pursued the good of others.

Even if she believed he'd run to Texas to avoid facing his father's death, she couldn't believe he'd chosen his destination randomly. Luke was more than an adventure-seeker, and nothing in his character, nor his actions, suggested he didn't take his responsibilities with the Rangers seriously.

"What do you think? Am I guilty?"

She gasped and twisted to face Luke. A smirk covered the remaining sleepiness etching his face. He reached for the letter, but she stood and held it away.

"Of course you're not guilty." She skimmed the convicting words again. "But it looks like you're wanted."

He managed to keep his expression calm, and she admired him for it.

"I'm not a criminal," he said.

"You are accused of robbing a bank."

"Of being an accomplice to a group that robs banks."

"Is that all?" She rolled her eyes.

His expression grew stormy, and he snatched the letter from her hands. "I know you're wild around the edges, but I thought going through a man's personal things beneath you."

She backed up a step and averted her eyes. "I'm sorry." The words sounded defensive. She tried again, reaching deeper. "I shouldn't have snooped. I was curious so I did it anyway."

Holding her breath, she kept her gaze down and waited to see if he'd offer absolution or push for a fight. A touch along her jaw lifted her attention. He offered something between a smile and smirk, his finger brushing beneath her chin. Shaking his head, he turned to his dresser, set down the letter, and reached for his gun belt.

She'd take that as absolution. "Has the marshal sought you out?"

He fastened on his colts with a few quick and practiced movements and grabbed the letter. "Yes. I've given a deposition." He sat on the edge of the bed, dropped the letter into the box, and kicked the box under with his heel. "The marshal said he'd be in touch."

Her heart settled back into a normal rhythm. "That's good news. If the Rangers had serious suspicions, you'd be taken into custody." This unnamed witness must be setting him up, and the Rangers weren't convinced the witness was reliable. It made sense to her. "Does your family know?"

"Why? So Paul can tell me that I got what I deserved for leaving?" His tone turned sour.

"What did you get, Luke?"

He rose from the bed and paced away. "I got all I wanted and more."

"Then you don't want much, do you?"

His chest shook with soft laughter. "Your goading has no end, but you're wrong. To stay here would have been to not want much. Going to Texas was wanting more than I had a right to want."

His short hair was mussed about his temple. She wanted to reach out and smooth it down. That would go over well.

"How does a person have a right, or not have a right, to want something?" She shrugged. "I wanted to study the piano, so I left. But I wanted to come back more than I wanted to study in Portland. So I did. Who grants me the right to want to keep Mama's dairy? I simply want it. Even if keeping the dairy turns out to be wrong, my desire to do so isn't."

He walked around her to the window. An eastern glow crept into the sky. "There's wanting, and then there's . . . *wanting*."

Much clearer. *Thank you, philosophical Luke.*

"If I'd stayed here and wanted something simple, like marriage and family and ranching, then I could have had those things and been satisfied. But I wasn't made to want the simple." He faced her. "I want integrity and truthfulness and righteousness. I went to Texas because I wanted the hard things."

She refused to be intimidated by the smoldering of his eyes. "You might love those things, but that's not why you went to Texas. After all, integrity and truthfulness and righteousness can be sought anywhere."

He advanced toward her, hands on his hips, and the nearer he got, the more his presence took over the room.

"Those scars on your arm tell me the truth." Scars she yearned to see again. "You ran away."

His jaw tightened, and she itched to flick it. Why not? He'd touched her chin. She tweaked his chin with her index finger.

He reached and snagged her wrist quick as he might draw his guns. "I don't run from things."

His eyes cuffed her with intensity even though his grasp around her wrist, held up between them, remained gentle. She had the urge to brush her lips on his knuckles. And why not?

Many reasons. This was Luke, who, regardless of motivation, had wanted Texas and had gone after it. Like she was doing with the dairy. One didn't flirt with someone who had no intention of staying. Her eyes fluttered closed, breaking from the image of his strong hand around her wrist. But she could still feel the gentle pressure. Feel his fingers faintly circling. Feel . . .

Warm breath fanned her wrist, a moment's warning,

before his lips moved across the tender flesh where her pulse betrayed her rising desire.

She forced her eyes open. He mumbled something intangible, and not letting go of her wrist, rotated his head and aimed his mouth toward hers. The touch of his lips to hers was so light she had a hard time imagining this was a man who harnessed criminals, roughed up resisters, defended the innocent. But then, he pressed his mouth to hers with more certainty, and she could suddenly imagine all sorts of things.

Dizziness made her balance unsteady as he trailed his lips up until they played along the ridge of her cheek bone. A rush of pleasure stole her breath. Stole her sanity.

"Luke," she whispered. "You can come home."

He jerked back, dropping her wrist. "My home is Texas."

Because Texas didn't require him to invest, put down roots. And Pine Creek did. Texas had people who needed Luke the hero. Luke the helper. Luke the justice-worker. Not plain, heart-on-his-sleeve Luke. That Luke had died with his father.

Luke snatched his coat from the spindle of the bed and vaulted past her and out the door.

Mary's breath returned, and with it, her wits. She grabbed the sling and set chase. At the back door, she caught him and seized his shirt. "You're not supposed to use this arm, silly."

Silly. It sounded like something Helen might say.

"You're being quite contrary, you know."

And like that he'd recovered from the kiss and returned them to the realm where banter kept a safe arms' length between them.

Refusing to meet his eyes, she adjusted the sling's strap around the back of his neck with more efficiency than she had last night. Her hands were inches from his face. With a little effort, she could reach out a finger and feel the smoothness of

200

his cheek.

That moment is past.

With a lot more effort, she could subdue that impulse along with the rest of these new urges that were surfacing in his presence.

"Now your coat." She took it from him, slipped it on his good arm, and tucked it around his sling.

He flung the door open, took a few steps, then glanced over his shoulder. "If you're coming with me, you need a coat."

She stared at him. She'd assumed he'd been going out to do chores. Or running from her. "Where are we going?"

"To visit our graves." His eyes crinkled at the corners, and his face hinted at a smile.

She answered his smile, knowing he meant his father's and her mother's. "I didn't bring a coat, but I'll be fine."

His eyes meandered over her thin sleeves and down to her toes. Shaking his head, he returned and snatched Abigail's coat from the hooks next to the door. "Here."

She pushed it away. "Not necessary."

"Not an option." His commanding tone arrested her full attention.

"Is that your Ranger voice?"

The dim light of dawn couldn't mask his full grin. "It's my Mary voice."

The smile stretched wider across her face, and she plucked the coat from his hand.

He set off across the yard at a rapid pace, and she shrugged into the coat while struggling to keep up.

Maybe he wanted to be alone but had felt compelled to invite her. "I don't have to come. I won't be offended if you want to be alone."

He spun around, his gaze tightening on hers. "I don't want to be alone."

She wouldn't read into those words. But they were said low and certain. While looking at her.

You're not reading into those words.

———————————— ✤ ————————————

Luke forced his stride to shorten and match hers.
I don't want to be alone.
How much more pathetic could he seem?
You kissed her and ran from the room.
That's how much more pathetic.
After an action like that, he couldn't have slipped off to the graveyard without her and let her believe she was right to accuse him of running—from Pine Creek or anything else. So he'd let her catch him at the door. Let her loop that sling around his neck like she were lassoing his heart. Lord, help him—he wanted to flee her desirability and the way she tied up his thoughts and cut off his intelligence.

Dawn spilled across the eastern horizon and shone through the wisps of fog as they walked in silence to the hillside cemetery. He prayed the silence meant she agreed that what had happened in that bedroom didn't need to be spoken of and should not be repeated.

Because what good was a moment of pleasure when commitment wasn't possible?

He opened the rusted gate and allowed her to enter. She wound around the stones and sank in front of her mama's, using it as a backrest.

"Wrapped by Mama."

He mouthed the words with her, unwittingly replacing 'Mama' with his own name.

"Are you going to tell me about your arm?"

He collapsed onto the grass across from her, bent his knees to his chest, and avoided her eyes. He'd hoped she'd settle into storytelling about her mama like she sometimes did, not open the full breadth of her curiosity on him. But talking about his arm was safer than reliving the feel of his lips on hers.

He gripped his knees tighter. "I burned it."

"Why?"

He smirked. "I thought you had me figured out."

"I thought I did, too, but you're going to have to help me with this one." She pulled on the end of her loose braid. "Please."

The soft appeal, a request to know him deeper, dismantled his resistance.

Luke folded his arms across his knees. "I know it sounds silly, but do you know how soothing it is to watch a match burn? At first, that's all it was. A distraction. I struck matches until my hands were raw, but then watching didn't ease the tension anymore, and neither did running my finger through the flame." Did she really want to hear this? What a mess he must seem. "When I held the match to my skin, I didn't feel the loss of my father. Only the burn."

Morning birds serenaded, a sweet juxtaposition to the sting of his confession.

"Do you still . . . ?" Her question lingered.

He swallowed and looked down. "I've lit some matches since coming home, but I haven't burned myself." Because after four, five, six scars, a boy buckled beneath the weight of shame, figured out that one pain didn't cancel another.

"Take off your shirt."

"What?" His gaze jerked to hers.

"I want to see your scars again."

"I don't think so."

"But—"

"It's not appropriate."

He stretched his legs out, and she leaned her elbow across the top of his boots.

"You're right," she said. "But I'm curious."

And honest. Eccentric. Beautiful. She made him laugh, wheedled him into talking about things he'd not talked about with anyone. And the absence of condemnation in her expression made him feel safe. Understood.

Dangerous thoughts, Thomas. Thoughts like that didn't

203

free a man to return to his job.

He arched his back against the cold gravestone. "How do you feel about being alone next week?"

A shadow flickered in her eyes. "You did me a disservice with your *pass the dream* spiel to Papa."

"Letting go is hard."

"Didn't seem so hard for you when you left."

He cocked his head. "Graveyard rules."

She managed to look half chagrinned. "Besides, you don't let go of roots. They're the ones either holding on or letting go of you."

Yeah. He knew. The dream of being a Ranger had wrapped its tendril around him and vined its way into his heart. "Have you considered that God might have something different for you, maybe something better than you expect? Something that requires you to let go of the old, requires you to trust?"

Clearing her throat, she produced that whimsical grin of hers that had the power to coax a dormant bush into bloom. "I could say the same to you, that God's waiting for you to let go of Texas."

She circled his words back on him without any effort. Relentless, she was.

"And you know this because you spend hours in prayer each day and the Lord tells you his plans for everyone?" he asked.

She huffed. "Hours, right." Her brows drew inward, and she blinked several times. "It's all I can do utter a cry for help."

His heart loosened a notch, letting in a breath of compassion. He imagined being forced to resign, never returning to Texas. She had dreams much the same as him. And dreams didn't detach from the heart without a fight.

"Would you like to pray?"

Mary's smiled slipped. "Now?"

"Sure." He mentally slapped himself for suggesting

such an intimate thing, as if he needed more proof that his judgment slipped in her presence.

She shrugged and sat up from her position leaning on his boots. "I suppose."

He bowed his head and listened to the rush of the Wenatchee beyond the hillside. His mind turned over, searching for a Scripture that might ease the awkwardness of praying aloud with Mary—or with anyone. Other than at mealtimes, he didn't pray with others.

The verses that pushed from his memory were those he'd read that morning by candlelight on the front porch, the tree by streams of water in Psalm one. The tree that flourishes, bears fruit, no matter the season. Ironic, since he wanted to pray for her to let go, not sink roots.

"Lord . . ." A simple start. He leaned his head against Father's stone, and loosened his hands in his lap. "We delight in your word and ask that you would make us fruit-bearers wherever you set us. For Mary . . ." And for him? He could admit it. ". . . that might not be the place she's known as home. Bring your peace into the situation, that she might know you as trustworthy and good, and that she might be assured of your purpose for her. Whether in desert times or fertile times, may she know your streams of grace are sufficient for all her needs." And then, because no other thoughts came except wordless emotions that needed no examination, he opened his eyes. "Amen."

She'd locked her jaw, presumably to hold back tears. "No one's prayed for me like that."

"I pray for you every day."

"You do?" Pink tinged her cheeks.

"Whenever I think of you, which . . ." was by the hour, by the minute. Was she ever out of his mind? "Which is every day." He'd pictured the day he'd bring a flush to her cheeks, and prayer hadn't been part of the equation.

"I don't know what to say."

"Please don't say anything."

She'd come up with something sassy. Or worse, profound. Something that might contribute to their mounting intimacy. Like he'd already done that day by drawing his lips across her face. Unwise.

Wonderful.

"I'm growing in the virtue of silence," she said.

He laughed, stood, and without much of a second thought, held out his hand.

Her gaze traveled from his hand to his eyes and back, questioning. He encouraged her with a nod, and she placed her hand in his. She tried to retrieve her hand after he'd pulled her up, but he kept it tucked in his as he led her toward the gate. He could make it to the gate. A hand was a hand. Five fingers. A palm.

Heat washed his face. A man wasn't supposed to have such a visceral response to something that was *nothing more* than five fingers and a palm.

But it was so much more. He held a part of Mary, and for whatever reason, the joining of their hands felt more intimate than placing his lips on hers. He'd kissed his mother on the cheek, Helen, too. But his hand he'd kept back from others.

He passed the gate and kept going down the sloping path with her five fingers wrapped in his five fingers, palm against palm. Something like this should shoot panic through him. It didn't.

She kept pace beside him, letting the distant chopping of wood, the birdsong, and a scampering squirrel provide the noise. When they reached the fork in the road that split to their homes, Luke stopped, stared at the hand in his, told himself the time had come to let go.

Mary pulled hers away. Round eyes on his, she stepped back one step, then two.

He nodded once, turned, and left, refusing to let his eyes linger on Mary. As for his heart . . . He'd given up telling it where it could or couldn't linger.

CHAPTER TWENTY

Six years earlier, 1886

Luke had barely pulled the new team into the barn before Mary jumped down and took off toward the Thomas house to avoid the impending storm. They'd been out testing the young horses when the clouds had slunk over the mountains and darkened the sky, along with Mary's mood. Not that it took much to darken her mood. He handed Grace down and began unhooking the team, pleased with his brother's purchase. The horses rode with enough energy to keep the driver occupied but remained disciplined.

When he became a Ranger, he'd need a horse with a calm disposition, yet one with enough intensity to get the job done. A black one. Or a gray. Something different than the common chestnut, but not white. Maybe it'd be a paint. Not too big as to be slow. Not to small as to be weak.

"You going to stand there and daydream?" Grace slipped around him.

She'd caught his mind roaming to Texas more than once.

"Half the time I think you can't wait to leave us," she said.

"It's not like that." Luke grabbed the brushes and tossed one to her. "You know I need a more active life than what Pine Creek and this ranch provide."

"I have no idea what you mean by that."

Of course she didn't. Contentment mantled Grace the same way adventure mantled him. No one understood his yearning. No one since Father.

He had gifts that needed to be used. A great shot. A fearless heart. He was tougher than the average man, and he was only sixteen. God hadn't made a man like him to sit around a ranch.

The rain started as he and Grace finished brushing the team, a minute of slow and quiet fall before the deluge. The pounding on the roof was deafening. Dimness filled the barn and made it seem like dusk, though the time was five hours shy of dusk.

He walked to the barn doors and stared at the sheets of water separating him from the house. "You coming?" he called to Grace.

"I don't want to go out in that."

Neither did he, but he wanted to read the new articles the Rangers had sent him. Since he'd written them when he'd been twelve, explaining his interest, they'd fed him articles in batches. The latest batch contained five newspaper clippings. He was midway through his fourth reading, scouring for anything he'd missed.

Grace scaled the ladder. "I'll wait in the loft with Stella."

"If you can find her." That cat was almost as scared of storms as Mary.

Luke sprinted through the yard and up the porch steps. Water dripped down his hairline, and he brushed it off.

Mother came out the door, a basket of corn on her hip. "Don't even think of coming in with those boots on."

"Hadn't crossed my mind." He sat down and pried the muddy boots off.

The house was dark and quiet when he entered. "Mary?" No answer.

He heard whimpering from Grace's room. Strange. When storms rolled through, the dogs cowered in the kitchen next to the stove. He strode across the room and poked his head in the door.

Maggie lay outside Grace's wardrobe, head on paws, crying.

"Come on, girl." He patted his leg and backed up.

Maggie lifted her head and sniffed at the wardrobe doors. That dog could sniff out a mouse in the barn from her corner of the upstairs bedroom. Grace would squeal if she knew a mouse had taken up residence in her wardrobe. Mary, on the other hand would catch it with her bare—

Mary.

He walked the seven steps to the wardrobe and flung the doors open. She sat on the floor, knees drawn to her chest, head down. The urge to tease swelled, but he managed to keep his mouth shut.

"Go away." The muffled words sounded stuttered, as if she'd been crying.

A rare moment of compassion hit him, the compassion he reserved for Grace . . . or his mother . . . or sometimes his horse. But he'd never had it directed at Mary, the girl who had to have the last word, who challenged his patience. Compassion wasn't close to what she pulled from him.

Lightning flashed, followed one second later by thunder that sounded like it crashed on the roof. Mary's arms squeezed her knees, and she twisted her body to the back of the wardrobe. Dirt stains dressed her back where she'd landed after falling from the wagon earlier in an attempt to ride standing on the edge.

He knelt beside her and put his hand on her shoulder.

She flinched. "Leave me alone."

"Stop pretending to be tough." He yanked her arms from their locked position around her knees and pulled her toward him.

He expected resistance and harsh words, but she flung her arms around his neck and buried her tear-stained cheeks into his chest. He fumbled for balance.

Dairy Mary in his arms and crying like a baby. Nothing could be more awkward. He forced his muscles not to stiffen.

God, let this storm pass quickly.

For all their sanity.

"Did I tell you about Major John B. Jones?"

Mary grunted.

"A man of impeccable character and discipline. Never touches tobacco or strong drink."

"Must be the only one in Texas."

Even in a storm, mind crazed with fear, she managed to insult his dream.

"Plenty of Rangers are model citizens."

"And plenty have only a smidgen more virtue than those they chase."

He ignored her invitation to argue and kept his voice calm. "Jones was put in charge of seventy men, called the Frontier Battalion, and sent into an area where at least one hundred settlers were killed each year."

Another clap of thunder rattled the windows. Mary's fingers dug into the back of his neck. He sucked in a breath; she had claws like a raccoon. He didn't want to offend her by moving her arms, so he shifted his weight in hopes that she'd also shift. It didn't work. Her dead weight moved with him, but her claws remained fastened into the flesh at his neck.

This was what it must feel like to be a Ranger. To offer help in the midst of someone's desperation.

You don't deserve to be her helper.

The barb struck from the back of his mind, bringing with it a memory that he'd locked away more times than he could count. But no matter how many times he locked it up, the flames found a way to escape, burn their way into the present.

He pushed aside the grinding accusation. He had every right and ability to offer help when it was needed. "When other law enforcement officers were afraid to arrest a federal judge for murder, Jones went in and made the arrest. That's what a Ranger does. The things nobody else likes to do."

Like comfort a girl with an irrational fear of

thunderstorms even if she usually tested his last shred of patience.

Even if a guilty conscience tried to tell him he wasn't worthy. He could be stronger than the past.

Luke settled off his haunches onto the floor and pulled Mary with him into his lap. He told the stories of the clippings with as much detail as he could remember. With each tale, she relaxed, and the storm grew more distant. Her hands slumped from behind his neck to the front of his shoulders. The rain on the window softened until he couldn't hear it anymore.

The front door slammed.

"Mary?" Grace's voice.

Mary jerked from his embrace and stood. He wiped a hand down the front of his tear-soaked shirt.

Without looking at him, she straightened her shoulders and marched out of the room. The tough girl had returned, and he knew they'd never talk about this moment. There was nothing to say. The circumstance had called for comfort, and he'd given it. Whether he should have or not.

CHAPTER TWENTY-ONE

Present day

Mary snagged a sheet off the clothesline and folded it against her chest.

Papa had left that morning with a spark in his step she'd not seen since she'd returned from Portland last August. Hope had lifted the weight of arthritis, albeit temporarily.

The scent of cow wafted from the field on the same breeze that fluttered the last two shirts on the line.

True to her word to Matthew, she'd mentioned Bridges's offer once more to Papa that morning.

His brows had turned in, shadowing his thin face.

"Please reconsider," she'd said. "You're not in shape to take a trip in the wagon. We can draw up papers and have the deal done by the end of the week."

Shaking his head, Papa had gestured for her to come close.

Kneeling on the wooden floor before the stove, she'd taken his hands in hers. "Please, don't do this, Papa."

"Do what, child? What I think is best for my family?"

"I can do more." The urge to confess about her playing in Clifton had surfaced. "I've been—"

Papa's hand covered her mouth. "You shouldn't have to do more."

"I don't want to lose our home."

"Home isn't something you lose. It goes with you, in here." He'd patted his chest. "It's in the abiding."

John chapter fifteen again.

He'd left with the Crawleys promptly at seven.

She'd made two trips to town in the past eight hours, and each time she'd returned, the heaviness of solitude had been her only greeting. With so many cows, a flock of chickens, horses, and several cats, the dairy shouldn't seem abandoned, but she'd never been here without Papa overnight.

Hoisting the full laundry basket on her hip, Mary set off toward the house. Would a third trip to Rod's be excessive? Yes. She couldn't justify a trip for social reasons when work remained undone at the dairy. She rounded the corner and took the porch steps, her eyes drawn to the piece of paper fluttering on the rocking chair. A fist sized rock pinned the note in place, and she freed the thin square and picked it up. A honeysuckle blossom fell from between the folds.

Her heart raced, and her attempt at a swallow failed. She opened the note and stared at the simple sentence: *Love is strong as death, its jealousy cruel as the grave.*

Mary dropped the page as if it had burned her and kicked the blossom over the edge to the ground. True admiration didn't hide behind the anonymity of a note that sounded as creepy as it did romantic. *Death* and *grave* weren't words she'd choose for a one-sentence love note.

She hauled the laundry into the house and locked the door. No more secrecy. When Papa returned, she'd tell him her suspicions, and the next time Marshal Swensson passed through town, she'd let him know what was happening.

You're overreacting.

So someone left honeysuckle blossoms, and she'd heard a noise one night outside her window. And now this note. She forced the anxiety from her mind.

She had an admirer. It was that simple. Better to deal with this privately than unnecessarily alarming Papa. Or Luke, as Grace would have her do.

Words from Luke's prayer reverberated in her mind, and she wished for another dose of it. But she didn't need another's prayers. She had access to the Lord as much as Luke.

Hitting her knees before Papa's chair, she poured it out. The oddity of the blossoms, and this note that sounded like something out of Song of Solomon; her yearning for God to provide a way for them to keep this beloved place of Mama's; and whatever was happening regarding Luke, his issue in Texas, and the grip he'd secured on her heart.

She rested her forehead on the soft padding of Papa's chair and listed all the concerns that flooded her conscience. Grace's apparently unrequited feelings for Cam. Johnston's bossy shenanigans. Claire's family way. The vain pursuits she witnessed in Clifton.

When concerns dwindled, praise began, escorting in a peace. Honeysuckle, notes, and all the rest—nothing severed the Lord's presence. She'd be fine without Papa for five days. And if he returned with news that he'd sold the dairy to Seth Millwood, well, she'd . . .

An ache fissured her heart, disabling her from confessing something that wasn't true. She wanted to be fine, but maybe she wouldn't be. She'd deal with it then. For now, fear wouldn't keep her from enjoying life.

She rose, enlivened in a way she hadn't felt in months, and opened the door to retrieve the note.

But it was gone.

* * *

Luke strode from the barn to the house, the sling strangling his neck. Cool night air accentuated the ache in his chest. Too many days had passed since he'd given his deposition. He'd give the Rangers another week or two to contact him, and then he was going after whomever had tarnished his name.

He shut the door and hung his coat. Grace sat at the kitchen table, her thin fingers wrapped around a cup of cider.

"Can't sleep?"

The clock ticked past ten, and the dim light of the single lamp magnified the lateness of the hour.

"Waiting for you."

He'd taken off for Barrett's after supper, convinced that sitting the evening with friends would be better than getting into an argument with Paul, but watching the affection between Barrett and Claire had triggered the same longing he'd experienced that one night he'd returned home and had overhead Paul and Abigail talking.

He took a seat next to Grace. "Are you all right?"

"You've been home weeks, and your shoulder is healing. You avoid us in the evenings and seem restless." She drummed her fingers on the table. "You're planning to leave, aren't you?"

He averted his eyes. "Truthfully? I'm in a bit of trouble."

He heard Grace's quiet gasp, felt her staring at him.

"My loyalty's being investigated, thanks to a piece of false testimony."

After a minute passed, and she hadn't said anything, he looked up. She wiped a tear from her eye.

"Aw, come on, Grace." He scooted his chair closer and arched his arm across the back of her shoulders. "There's no evidence, because it's not true. Things will get cleared."

"And if they don't?"

"Don't borrow trouble."

She offered her cider. The sip stung his throat, and he coughed. "And please don't tell anyone." Mother had worried enough about his shoulder, and Paul . . . Luke didn't want to think how Paul would twist this news to make Luke look guilty of something.

Grace slumped against the back of her chair. "First, Mary, and now you."

"What about Mary?"

She took back her cup and finished the cider. "Where did you go tonight?"

215

Avoiding the issue. "Is she hiding something?"

"Luke, please, don't push."

Maybe he'd not push Grace, but this was the second time Grace had implied Mary was holding something back from him, from others. "I went to Barrett's."

Grace ran her finger around the rim of the empty cup. "Was Cam there?" Pushing her cup away, she shook her head. "Never mind." She stood, her expression pinched. "He's not interested in me, and it's all right."

The uncharacteristic agitation he saw in Grace meant she was anything but all right. She'd mentioned Cam in her letters, and he'd read her heart behind the words, but these weeks at home had clarified what had been uncertain. Cam didn't return her feeling. Nothing had happened between them. Nothing would.

Luke rose and enveloped her in his arms. "Things will work out for our good." He kissed her forehead.

She clung to his waist and rested against him. He hadn't held Grace like this in years, and he knew Paul, who wasn't demonstrative like Grace or their mother, didn't embrace anyone but Abigail and Helen.

"You can be assured that whatever plans God has for you are good plans." Luke smoothed her hair back from her wet cheek. "Because he's good, and he can't act against his character."

She knocked against his chest. "You hide a lot of depth in here." Pulling back, she looked up at him. "But do you believe your own words?"

"Absolutely." He'd never had an issue with God's goodness, never doubted God's plans.

But that belief didn't keep him from wanting his name cleared. Or from feeling trapped in this place that roused the shame of years past and made him want Mary like she was a glass of cold water and he'd been lost in a desert.

"What if you lose your position?"

"I might go to jail." If they found him guilty of robbery,

but how could they? They might dismiss him based on his disobedience, even if they acquitted him of the false accusations. "But if I don't go to jail, then I guess we better build on to the house, make sure Helen and the new little one have a place to sleep."

"You'll stay?" Her eyes danced.

"I almost think you want me to be dismissed."

She chuckled, but her expression sobered. "I couldn't want that for you, same as I don't want Mary to lose her dairy."

He moved the cup to the wash basin. "Is that her secret?" Had Randall already signed a deal?

"No." Grace hugged herself, biting her lip.

"Tell me, if it's bothering you."

She waved him off and pushed in her chair. "If you stay, you could be sheriff."

Against his will, her words sewed a thread of excitement in his heart. "'Night, Grace."

He entered the darkness of the stairwell and made his way to his room, avoiding the creaky boards. Oppressive air greeted him when he opened his door, courtesy of the closed window that had trapped the heat of the day. He slid it up, letting in a rush of sticky wind.

He stripped off his shirt, sat on the edge of his bed, and stared out the dark window. Lightning blanketed the horizon, dull behind the band of clouds that had played on the mountains all evening, building, disbanding, building again. They'd continue to form until they broke open and splayed sheets of rain over the valley.

Mary.

He frowned and stretched out on his quilt, ankles crossed and hands propped behind his head. He loved a good storm, when a downpour cleansed the stale, dusty air. Maybe that was a metaphor for his current situation. Old things were being washed gone, making way for new things.

Instead of the defensive spirit he'd expect at thoughts

of change, hope breezed through his heart.

Lord, cleanse me.

Truth was supposed to set a person free, but despite knowing her fear of thunderstorms traced back to the night she was born, Mary couldn't help the instinctive responses.

Another roar echoed across the valley. She could hardly breathe, but that didn't stop her from burrowing deeper beneath the covers.

It's only a storm. Lightning, thunder, and rain. A bit of wind.

The roof groaned.

More than a bit of wind.

You're safe.

Her renewed prayer from the other day life was supposed to replace worry with praise.

More rattling of the eaves drowned her pitiful attempt at calming herself. A branch clamored against the window, scratching twiggy fingers on the glass, and causing her fingers to wrap tighter around the wad of sheet as sweat tickled her neck.

You're stronger than this.

Desperate to regain control of what had become a ridiculous and irrational fear, she threw back the covers and pushed herself out of bed. Her clammy feet stuck to the planked floor as she rushed from the room and down the hall. Another flash of lightning illuminated the living room, casting a bluish hue over Papa's chair. In the kitchen, she stoked the stove and moved the kettle to the center. Lighting a candle, she focused on relaxing her muscles. First her jaw, then her shoulders.

That's better. Excellent.

A pounding on the door returned her muscles to spasm. Nausea fisted her stomach. As if thunder weren't enough to stop her heart and put her in the grave, a visitor —

her admirer?—had to disrupt the wee hours of the morning.

She glanced around the kitchen for a weapon while the pounding continued. A fork? A crash of thunder rendered useless the modest mental ability fear afforded her. She snatched a rolling pin and rushed into the front room, eyeing the door as if someone might barrel through and kidnap her.

"Who's there?"

"Mary?"

She threw open the door. "Luke Thomas, you imbecile. It's storming." Rolling pin poised in one hand, she yanked him inside and slammed the door. Water dripped from his hat and off the shoulders of his duster and puddled on the floor. "Is Grace all right? Your mama?" She gasped. "Is the baby coming already?"

"Everyone's fine."

Lightning split the sky. She squeezed her eyes, cringing at the expected thunder.

"Except you."

She opened her eyes and forced her tightened muscles to form a smile. "I'm fine." The thunder shook the frame of the house, and with it, her insides. "Other than it being three in the morning and stormy." Did her voice shake? Stupid, stupid fear.

He shrugged from his wet coat and let it fall to the mat in front of the door. When he reached to take the rolling pin from her hand, she tried to let go, but the fingers she'd wrapped around the handle were locked in place. She lowered the makeshift weapon to her side.

"Let me help." His quiet words found a way beyond the thrum of rain. He captured her hand and lifted it, eyes not leaving hers. His wet fingers encircled hers, and he pried her fingers back until her muscles understood and relaxed. "Come on." Luke set the pin aside, grabbed her elbow, and settled her on the couch. He took a seat at the far end, but the distance still seemed too intimate.

She drew up her knees and hugged them to her chest,

her bare feet tucked beneath the hem of her nightgown. Between the howling of the wind and the constant rumbling of thunder, the storm was impossible to ignore—even with Luke, a formidable distraction. He'd ridden through this. For her. He shouldn't have. It wasn't proper. Why did he have to go and do something as foolish as being chivalrous at her expense?

She'd had several opportunities to speak the apology on her heart, yet she'd not been able to get it out. God had sent another opportunity, wrapped within a thunderstorm and the kindness of Luke.

He snatched the afghan at the end of the couch and draped it over her, probably thinking her trembling was a result of being cold.

"You didn't have to come," she said, putting off the apology. One didn't launch into a confession without small talk.

He leaned back, stretched his legs, and crossed his ankles. She wished he'd launch into a lecture, distract her, but instead he laid his head back and closed his eyes.

"Really, Luke. I'm a grown woman."

This time he laughed.

"I fail to see why that's amusing."

His eyes shot open, connected with hers. "It's not."

He stood and walked to the kitchen. The whoosh of air as he strode past the candle extinguished the flame. She ducked under the blanket and buried her head in her knees before the brilliance of lightning had opportunity to intrude upon the darkness. Her breaths came quick and steamed her face.

Between crashes of thunder, she heard the creak of the tea kettle and Luke's footsteps.

He tugged the blanket off her head, and peered into her face, his hazel eyes sparking with more energy than the storm. He'd relit the candle and set a cup of tea next to her. She swallowed and reached for it. One sip. Two. Words pulsed in

220

her heart, demanding to be spoken. "Luke."

His name came out raspy. She downed more tea, gulping the hot liquid until it burned a path to her stomach. He'd confessed to Pine Creek, discussed difficult things with her, and she couldn't get out a simple apology for some harsh words spoken years ago?

His steady eyes were unreadable. Or not.

She diverted her attention, afraid she'd seen disappointment of some sort. "I want to apologize." A terrible start. "Rather, I *am* apologizing." She'd welcome an interruption from him, even teasing about the unlikelihood of her apologizing. "I've sinned against you."

When he didn't respond, she looked up. His forehead creased, but the corners of his mouth hinted at a smile. Even in her most solemn moments, it seemed he couldn't take her seriously.

"Remember that day of the picnic, I was up in the tree . . ."

He nodded.

"I said some things I regret. I was wrong."

He raised his brows, which widened his eyes, eyes that had recently become fuller in their expression around her, and yet retained a hidden meaning she couldn't discern. Though heat rushed her face, she couldn't look away. "I said no sane woman would ever want to marry you."

"Cream that won't churn to butter?"

"Yeah, I said that."

"A seed that won't grow."

He remembered word for word. She cringed at the renewed shame and nodded.

"And you're sorry?"

So sorry she ached. "Grace told me you wrote to her about Rachel, but then you said Rachel turned you down." And why that should bring her fresh courage in the midst of her emotional storm, she couldn't figure. "I'm afraid I cursed you," she whispered.

"What?" He leaned his head back and laughed. With a quick movement, he reached out and tugged a strand of her hair. "You amaze me with the things you come up with."

Either he'd complimented her or she'd made a fool of herself. She pressed herself against the end of the couch and played with the frayed edges of the afghan, needing to reverse the curse with her next words. No, that was God's prerogative, but she could offer blessing. "You're . . . hard working, just, sacrificial . . ."

"Handsome."

Powerfully so. "Don't push it." She tossed the blanket off. The heat in the room stifled her senses.

"Why can't I push it? I'm going to enjoy this rare moment of humility."

Was she that proud? Evidently she'd crossed the fine line between confidence and pride. "I've felt guilty about that day for years."

He studied her for five seconds. Ten. She forced herself to maintain a normal expression and not shrink back. How long could a person stare at another person and not blink?

"You think you're the reason I'm not married."

She shrugged. Seemed obvious enough. Luke had never had issues with attracting female attention, and surely in his line of work he encountered an excess of available women in each town he and his brave steed swept through. Not that he ever stayed in one place for long.

He shook his head. "That's not . . ." Frowning, he stood. "Drink your tea." He stalked into the kitchen.

She set down her cup and followed. The apology had been spoken, but she wasn't finished speaking the words of blessing that sought release from her heart. One more comment.

The candle's glow from the front room trailed through the doorless entryway. Luke stood with his back to her, looking out the rain-splattered window and probably seeing nothing considering the darkness.

"You're not unmarryable." A start, but there was more that wouldn't be pushed down. "You're the most marryable man I know, and any sane woman can see that."

A soft chuckle stole its way into the silence, and he turned. "You volunteering?"

Her lips parted. Teasing, at a time like this. Another moment to add to the thousands of others.

But when he took a purposeful step forward, her breath hitched. Staring at his chest, unable to lift her eyes, she took in his woodsy scent, or rather, it overtook her with the same vengeance as the thunder. She searched her heart and found desire.

Not understanding how an apology led to the same cliff they'd teetered on the other day in his bedroom, she closed her eyes and waited. Hoped he'd kiss her again. Though she anticipated his touch, when his finger grazed her cheek, she gasped. The trail it blazed beneath her eye and over to her ear weakened her knees. She turned her face until his finger rested near her lips.

Her mouth formed the words, *Kiss me,* and with the way her pulse struck her throat, she wasn't sure if the words came out as a breath or with sound. Her eyes slid open, and her gaze focused on Luke, a portrait of stoicism.

He must regret kissing her the other day. Of course he would. He'd be back in Texas as soon as his name was cleared—and she had no doubt it would be cleared.

She jerked back and returned to the front room for her cup. When she'd returned, Luke had picked up the teakettle and was pouring himself a drink. He downed the liquid with one, long swig

The rain had slowed, but her heart still raced.

He set his cup down and crossed his arms. "Things been all right around here?"

Had Grace mentioned anything? Luke looked as if he knew something.

She nodded. "I suppose."

223

Hands on his hips, he entered into one of his interrogating gazes.

The honeysuckles and note. The noises.

What if it's him?

The thought caused the walls to close around her. No. Luke wasn't secretive or deceptive. Except for the church fire. But he'd not lied about that; he'd held back a story because it bore witness to his wounds and shame.

His mouth twitched, and he strode past her into the front room. "Storm's mostly passed." He pulled on his wet duster, stepped into his boots, and laced them. "It all right if I leave?"

His leaving had never been all right with her. She'd used a flood of anger to hide the way his leaving for Texas had upset her, made each dawning of sunlight a little dimmer. "Yes. Thank you. It wasn't —"

"It was absolutely necessary." He shoved on his hat and flung open the door. "And I don't regret a moment."

He stepped into the rain, and in moments, the night swallowed him.

The sun that greeted the morning left no tale of the nightmare of last night's storms, although if Mary considered the lightning and thunder a nightmare, she had to be fair and consider Luke's presence — and whatever else had happened — akin to a dream. Something from a fairytale where the prince shows up when all is lost.

All would still be lost if Papa came home and said he'd shaken on the deal with Mr. Millwood.

She had six more nights to wonder, and she prayed those six nights were not stormy, or they'd be sleepless as well, and not merely because of fear. She'd never experience a thunderstorm again without reliving that scene in the kitchen with Luke.

The facts were plain as the black coffee she sipped from

the teacup Claire had given her: things happened when Luke was around. Magnetic things that altered her sense of reality.

Mary gulped the last of her coffee and tied her boots. Her morning's help would arrive in the next thirty minutes. Work waited to be done, and dwelling on each breath and glance of the previous evening accomplished nothing—for the dairy. Her heart, on the other hand . . .

She shut the door behind her and padded down the steps. The wind had downed branches from the trees near the house. She gathered the sticks that had blown against the porch, and then made her way around to the back, clearing debris as she went. A limb leaned against the house next to her bedroom window. She reached for it, but stopped short, breath hitching. Clear footprints pressed into the soft ground. Man-sized and unfamiliar. She knew Papa's boots. Without making a conscious effort, her eyes scanned for honeysuckle. She found none.

Luke had been here last night, concerned for her. No doubt he'd walked around the house, making sure the storm hadn't caused damage. She wasn't willing to entertain another explanation.

Chapter Twenty-Two

Luke pushed through the mercantile doors on Thursday afternoon. A painted sign hung above the counter: Luke Thomas for sheriff. His jaw clenched, and he turned to the man walking out the door, a stranger with thinning silver hair and a round face. "I'm not running for sheriff. Don't believe what you hear."

The man raised an eyebrow and shuffled around him.

Luke beat his hat against his thigh, shaking the dust off. Didn't think the sign had angered him that much, but five whacks of his hat later, dust plumed the air.

"Do you mind?" Cecily grinned, put down her cloth, and reached for the broom.

"Sorry. Didn't think it had that much dirt on it."

Her clear blue eyes sought to engage him. "You live on a ranch. What did you expect?"

Not to be worried about getting elected sheriff, considering his confession in church the week before. The townsfolk had been gracious with forgiveness, but their continual push for him as sheriff was about more than he could take. A couple more knowing smiles or good luck wishes, and he'd pack Gabriel and make for Texas. Forget staying put.

Mary's laughter sounded from the front walk, and a moment later, she pushed through the door, bumping into him.

"Do you mind?" He asked Mary the same question Cecily had asked him, smiling at Cecily.

"It's your choice," Mary said. "But it doesn't seem smart to me."

"What are you talking about?"

She looked too pleased with herself. "I thought you asked if I minded that you were standing in front of the door."

She twisted words with the skill of a conman. She was certainly making off with his heart as easily.

"Maybe you should check with Cecily. She probably doesn't appreciate you blocking the entrance." Mary swept past him and headed for the piano. "Although, you might be good for business. Aren't the most attractive items supposed to be in the window? And I think I remember you calling yourself handsome recently."

"I think I remember you agreeing."

She looked back and stumbled over a rake handle that had fallen into the aisle. She righted herself but not before pulling out a smirk that drew his attention to her lips. Lips he'd almost kissed the other night, until he'd pictured the hills of Texas, imagined himself in the saddle, on assignment.

He followed her to the piano and leaned against it as she settled into some finger-zipping piece. When she finished, she hopped from the stool and bowed to him, thrusting her arms to the side and brushing her fingers against his forearm.

"I'll assume you're applauding in your heart," she said.

His heart was doing something. Leaving Mary was going to be hard. He wasn't ashamed to admit it.

He dug into his pocket and pulled out the vine of honeysuckle he'd plucked on the way into town. The more he mulled over the blossoms he'd found at the dairy, and even in town, the odder it seemed. Her reaction would be telling.

He held out the blossom. "For you."

"Where'd you get that?" Her accusation was quick as his draw.

"I picked it south of town."

Each furrow on her brow confirmed what he feared: like him, she considered the honeysuckle appearances strange.

227

Her color paled as she stared at the blossom, and he wasn't sure she'd accept, but she reached with her thumb and index finger and pinched it from his hand. "Thank you."

He thought she shuddered, though it was slight, and he might have imagined it. He'd taken to imagining things around Mary, playing a what-if game he never won.

"Have you been leaving me honeysuckles?" She deposited the blossom on the piano and raised one brow at him.

"No." But someone else had. "Are things all right?"

She circled him and headed for the door, calling over her shoulder, "Positively wonderful."

The too-cheery voice didn't sit with him. He started after her.

Rod appeared in the doorway, blocking Mary's departure. "Did I miss the concert?" He shifted the crate in his arms. "I heard someone over at Clifton plays the piano at the Gold Mine sometimes. Classical, and such. I'm sure not as well as you play."

Mary pasted on a smile that would have had her kicked out of any theater troupe. She didn't do fake well. She did honest, in-your-face, unpretentious.

"I'll have to check it out." She rushed around Rod and through the door.

"Not on your own." Rod called after her.

Luke tried to slip by Rod, but the proprietor turned, blocking Luke's way.

"Clifton's had problems," Rod said. "A new batch of loggers from down south. Oh, did you see the sign? Johnston brought it by."

"I'm not running."

"You'll change your mind when you get elected." Rod thumped him on the back.

"Take it down, please." Luke nudged Rod aside, exited the store, and looked both directions. Mary was whisking her way up the street like bandits tailed her.

"Contrary."

She spun, and her skirts fanned and caught Mrs. Randolph walking the other way. "Make it quick. I've got a list that'd make your workday look like a lazy afternoon by the creek."

Which was why she'd stopped in at Rod's for a song or two.

He planted his hands on his hips and took his time surveying her hairline down the side of her face, past an ear with a pinprick mole on its lobe. How had he not noticed that before? Because before the past two months, he'd not made a habit of studying the out-of-the-way places on her skin.

"Do you mind?" Her sing-song voice played at impatience.

"The question of the day. And no, I don't mind taking time to look at you."

Her full lips arced up, and she turned those kiss-me brown eyes on his. They'd undone ninety-nine percent of his self-control the night of the storm. That one percent had earned him a medal for holding firm.

"If you want to go to Clifton and hear that piano player, I'll take you."

Her cheek twitched. "That's sweet, Luke. Thank you."

He'd anticipated her to argue that she'd go when and how she wanted, but she'd called him sweet, a far cry from the usual descriptions she used with him. *Sweet* made his chest expand. He'd become soft since returning to Pine Creek.

Mr. Winston stepped from the livery and looked at Luke. "I'd vote for you if you'd only agree to run. I'm afraid I'll have to cast my lot for our other local boy, Matthew, even though Mary came by yesterday, soliciting your vote."

Luke's gaze swiveled to Mary.

She shrugged. "Soliciting is a generous word. I've answered questions about your abilities honestly."

Mr. Winston laughed. "She said you'd make the best sheriff a small town could hope for, and I believe her. But I won't vote for someone so adamantly opposed to running. Doesn't seem right."

Luke nodded. "Thanks."

When Mr. Winston disappeared back into the livery, Luke fastened his hands on his hips and tipped his head, raising a brow at Mary. He couldn't pursue being sheriff, not with everything in Texas unresolved. "You know I don't want the position."

"You don't think you do."

Luke swung his gaze from Mary's, but his eyes circled back as if she pulled them on a string. He smiled and shook his head. Her words pinpointed the frustration he tried to ignore: Matthew running for sheriff. And the talk of the town was starting to shift toward the lumberman's son. Luke should be relieved.

"Fine," he said. "Part of me is intrigued by the position."

Her sharp intake of breath caused his chest to constrict. First, *sweet*, and now a breath that sounded both delighted and hopeful. Something was happening beneath his ribs for which Mary was directly responsible.

He put a finger underneath her chin and closed her gaping mouth. He didn't need her campaigning for him. "I might admit to being intrigued, but keep your mouth closed. It's driving me crazy." *That came out wrong, dunce.* "Your chattering about me, that is." Heat splayed his face. "Any word from your father?"

"No." Her curt answer slammed the door on further inquiry.

No problem; he didn't mind opening doors. "And if he comes back having sold your home?"

Mary offered her profile to Luke and stared at the street. "I don't understand why he won't consider Matthew's offer."

"Matthew made an offer?"

The heir of the local lumber baron wanted to be sheriff

and run a dairy. That didn't make sense.

"Bridges wants to buy the land and will allow us to stay and rent at an affordable rate."

"Emory said this?"

Mary's mouth tightened as she shook her head.

"That doesn't sound like Emory," he said.

Emory Bridges, though not cruel, ran his business with profit and advancement in mind. Neighborly benevolence didn't fit that model.

"Papa has turned him down, but Matthew wants me to talk to him again."

Just how much had Matthew been talking to Mary? Feeding her information that may or may not be correct? She wasn't gullible, except her anguish over losing the dairy seemed to have blinded her.

"This doesn't sound right," he said.

Mary huffed. "You've known about my desire to sell to Bridges. Why get upset now?"

"I'd assumed Emory made the offer, not his son."

"The son can speak for his father."

"Can he?" Luke stepped in front of Mary, but she spun sideways. Avoiding him. "I'd check your facts."

Mary shrugged. "Doesn't matter anyway. Papa's not interested."

Smart man.

Her hand hung by her side, inviting, prodding him to remember the day he'd held it. He grasped it and ran his finger over the back of it.

"I need to go." She backed away, eyeing him.

He stepped after her. "How many honeysuckles have you found?"

A fragment of surprise slipped through her gaze before she schooled her expression. "A few."

He wasn't falling for such vagueness. He firmed his mouth. "How many."

"Seven." Her voice cracked. "It's nothing. An admirer

231

who's too shy to come forward."

He kept the sick feeling in his gut from traveling up and blanketing his expression. Leaving flowers once or twice might be innocent, but leaving them repeatedly, in odd places . . . for heaven's sake, he'd found one outside Rod's when she'd been practicing, as if someone else had been listening. Jealousy joined the uneasiness carving out his heart.

He opened his mouth to question, but she waved him off.

"Too much to do." She turned and charged down the street.

She might not want to talk about the honeysuckles, but that wouldn't prevent him from keeping an eye on things. Starting tonight, he'd be patrolling the Smith property before settling into bed each night and again each morning before the sun rose.

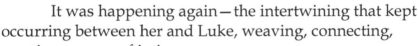

It was happening again — the intertwining that kept occurring between her and Luke, weaving, connecting, creating a sense of intimacy.

But for what reason? For him to thrust off the town's forgiveness and return to Texas? Plain and simple: Luke had never reconciled with his father's loss. The man who'd let go of Pine Creek had never let go of his father.

Mary maneuvered Holly around the sharp rock outcropping and down the winding path. Reining in, she opened her hand and rested it palm up on her lap. Sun filtered through trees and shone on the crisscrossed lines of her palm.

There was letting go. And then there was having something ripped from you. Both were loss. Both, an invitation to something greater.

Seizing the reins again, she urged Holly onward. Pontificating over Luke, loss, and letting go wasn't solving her present issue, that of seeking the truth from Emory Bridges. Luke's words had planted doubt in her that demanded an answer.

Why had she not looked into this deal?

Because Matthew had been the knight in residence at the schoolhouse. She'd considered him trustworthy. And she'd been desperate for a solution that would allow her to keep the dairy.

Mary dismounted and tied Holly in front of the Bridgeses' spacious, two-story home. Before she could knock, a housekeeper dressed in black and white opened the door.

"Good day, miss."

"I'm Mary Smith from Smith Dairy. I'd like to speak with Emory Bridges."

The middle-aged woman admitted her and led her down a hallway that boasted pictures of George Washington, Napoleon, King Henry VIII, and what looked like a dynasty of former family members. No other home had this affluence, excepting Johnston Brown.

"Wait here, please." The housekeeper gestured to a sitting room with tall windows that faced a mountainside half-cleared of trees.

Mary sat on the edge of a wingback chair, aware of the sweat and dirt on her work dress. Crossing her ankles, she perused the shelves of books. A large globe sat on a stand, hinting of adventure.

A door closed somewhere down the hall, likely Mr. Bridges exiting his office, and footsteps approached.

"Mary Smith, I declare. Do you bring me good tidings?" Emory Bridges, stout and tall with a moustache more tangled than a morning glory vine, swept into the room and dropped into the deep-backed couch.

"I'm afraid not. Papa is visiting the family that hopes to buy from us."

"A shame. I'd have loved to gotten my hands on your cedar forests. What a waste." He wiped a hand over his face. "How can I help you?"

No use delaying. "Matthew has spoken to me about

your generous offer."

Mr. Bridges scowled.

Not a good sign.

"What's he said?" Mr. Bridges asked.

"That if we sell to you, we could remain in the house and operate the dairy for a minimal rental fee."

Mr. Bridges murmured beneath his breath, words she didn't think she wanted to understand.

"We'd discussed the possibility, but I hadn't committed, nor did I feel Matthew's idea was sound business—nothing against you and your father, of course."

Mary stood. "I understand."

Matthew had lied to her.

But as surely as the thought came, defense for her friend argued back. He'd discussed it with his father and perhaps had felt permission to speak to her. It'd been a misunderstanding, not a lie.

He lied to you.

Not Matthew.

Mr. Bridges walked her to the door. "I know you would have preferred to remain, but it isn't practical. If I acquire your land, I'd build housing for workers in your pasture." He stopped, leaning one hand on the open door. "We're still your best option for profit."

Mary nodded. "Papa is set on someone taking over the dairy who would love it and use it like we did."

"We all have our preferences. Can't blame him for that. Just wish I could change his mind."

Mary said goodbye and descended the wide porch steps. The heavy door clicked behind her, a closing statement on Mama's dream. The finality overwhelmed her. There would be no selling to the Bridges.

This isn't defeat. It's surrender.

The hushed thought summoned her prayers as if God had netted her heart and whispered her to come, to let go. Relaxing her shoulders, she eased into the invitation, praying for strength to find home wherever God led her instead of in a dream of the past.

CHAPTER TWENTY-THREE

Seated in front of her mirror, Mary twisted her long dark hair at the back of her neck and secured it with a pin. She'd not looked this fancy in years. Too bad she couldn't take Luke up on his offer to escort her to Clifton. Little did he know she *was* the piano player.

After her month-long break, she'd sent word to Sarah Jane that she'd come for one more performance, and then no more. Considering yesterday's discovery about Bridges, and her subsequent surrender, she saw no need to continue. Unless she counted her desire for an audience and love of music, but that had been more of an excuse than a valid reason to play at a saloon for a group of men who probably had more on their minds than good music.

The knock sounded on the front door as the clock finished its five chimes. Mary quieted the rush of her heart as she strode to the door. Likely, Jake and his brother had arrived for the evening milking.

Mary opened the door, and Grace burst in, followed by Claire. "You're wearing my dress!" Grace set her sewing basket on the floor and turned a circle around Mary. "It's beautiful."

"Like it was three days ago when I tried it on at your house."

Grace had turned the putrid material into a beautiful, ornate outfit that came off more sage green than rotten apple.

"To what do I owe the pleasure of you two showing up on my doorstep?" Mary led the way to her room.

"We're going with you," Claire said.

"What? Truly?" Mary spun around. She'd made a casual remark to Claire last week about wearing her new dress to Clifton for a final performance. "That's wonderful! It'll be an adventure." She swept into her room and settled before her mirror to finish pinning her hair.

"I don't do adventure well." Grace sat on the edge of Mary's bed.

"Nor do I," Claire said. "But with the three of us together, I assume things will be fine. I've held my own with thirty-four children. How different can it be?"

Grace's face paled, and she sent Claire a look that argued.

"Both of you have a superb capacity for adventure," Mary said.

Grace crinkled her nose. "What an honor to hear the queen of mayhem say such a thing."

Mary checked her finished image. Good enough. She rarely looked half this put together. "One of you moved a thousand miles from the city to a small town, and the other has lived her entire life rubbing shoulders with hardworking men of the rougher class. Just because a man is unkempt and likes a shot of whiskey doesn't necessarily mean he's a menace."

Grace folded her hands in her lap. "I've never been close enough to rub shoulders with a rough man."

Mary laughed. "You live with one."

"I'd ask which one of my brothers you mean, but that's not necessary. And he's nothing like the men of Clifton. He has ounces more integrity. If he knew you were comparing him—"

"But he doesn't, and he won't." Mary winked at Grace and reached for the vial of perfume she'd brought back from Portland, a gift she not yet used. The flowery fragrance was strong enough to confuse bees.

"What are you doing?" Claire took the bottle from her

and set it aside. "Are you going to play the piano, or do you have something else planned?"

"I need to look professional. Refined. Not like a barn girl who spends more time with cows than people." To borrow a childhood accusation of Luke's.

"A professional what?" Claire asked.

"I need to look like you with your fancy dresses and perfectly pinned hair."

"Mary, don't take this the wrong way." Grace fixed the cuffs on Mary's sleeves.

"Yes?"

"You look . . ." She stepped back and inspected Mary.

"Is there a stain on my new dress?" Mary glanced at the flounces of green material that made up the skirt.

"No, no. It's not that." Grace's voice wavered.

"Are you disappointed in your work?"

Claire cleared her throat. "You have more curves than Grace and I put together. That's what she's trying to say."

Mary turned sideways and looked at her figure in the mirror. "Are you calling me rotund?"

"Not even close," Grace said. "Look at this waist." She grasped Mary around the middle. "Wonderfully accented with your stays."

"These stays are stealing my breath."

Grace smirked. "I made the dress loose enough so that you wouldn't have to tie them too tightly."

Mary shoved Grace's hands away from her waist and grabbed her reticule. They'd caught her trying to look beautiful. "I simply want to look nice."

Claire snagged her attention in the mirror. "Luke thinks you're beautiful."

Mary took her time folding her handkerchief and wedging it in her reticule as if her hands weren't shaking and her heart wasn't about to race out of her chest. "Oh, really?"

Mary sensed Grace's stare but didn't yield her attention. She had nothing to confess to Grace.

"I overheard him talking with Barrett and Cam," Claire said.

Mary's heart stuttered on the edge of crazy, but she maintained a casual persona. "What did they say?"

"I heard one comment in passing." Claire leaned toward the mirror and smoothed her red curls. "You weren't the main subject of conversation, if that's what you want to know."

Mary shrugged, despite the plummeting of her emotions.

Grace rounded Mary and peered into her face. "Are you keeping something from me?"

"No." A rare rush of heat flooded her face, and she spun away.

She had no secrets about Luke. Correction. She had one small secret, the kiss they'd shared in his bedroom. But that wasn't a gossip-worthy secret. These feelings of infatuation were no more valid than the schoolgirl crush she'd had when she'd sat up in the cherry tree and tossed down daisies. *He loves me. He loves me not.*

Nor she, him.

He'd leave, and Mary would add the memory of swinging with him and her near *kiss me* utterance, to the memory of him locking her in the Thomas's attic and hiding her mother's ribbons.

"I'm ready." Mary gestured to the door.

Grace walked out and down the hall, but Claire lingered, a simple arch of her dainty brow all the question necessary.

Mary rolled her eyes. "I might love him."

Claire smiled. "You might."

Luke sat across from Barrett in the smithy and stifled another yawn. He'd walked the perimeter of Mary's house and barn twice a day the past two days, before the sun rose and after the sun set. Nothing had seemed out of place, but his suspicions wouldn't rest.

Cam pumped the double bellows and the fire flared. He shoved an axe head into the forge, hung his tongs, and picked up his mallet. The broad man expended more energy than a team of oxen and had the muscles to prove it.

Luke popped another of Grace's cookies in his mouth. "Don't you ever get hungry?"

"He's too busy for the distractions that usually plague men. Food. Women." Barrett leaned on the back legs of his chair.

Cam pulled a sandwich down from a shelf, raised it toward the boys, and took a bite.

"You got a woman hiding somewhere, too?" Luke asked.

Barrett laughed. "I can't wait for the day Cam lets a woman hide in his smithy."

Cam grunted and yanked a strip of metal from the end of a plow. Sweat stained his shirt down the middle. "You hiding yours in Texas, Luke?"

"Don't tease him when he's grumpy," Barrett said.

Luke tipped his head toward his immobilized shoulder. The doctor had been by to check on his progress. Not satisfied with the healing of Luke's stitches, he'd splinted and wrapped Luke's left arm to his body. "I should be doing more than eating cookies and watching you work."

"All this sweat making you jealous?" Cam wiped his brow with a gloved hand.

Luke stood and paced to the open doors. This prescription to refrain from work had made him antsier than Mary in a thunderstorm. He pictured her the other night, hiding under her blanket. The stripping away of her usual self-assuredness had humbled him. That he'd been allowed to see her at her weakest, and that she had seen him—his scars— created a false sense of intimacy. False because it couldn't last. He needed to get back to Texas, clear his name.

"There is something you can do," Cam said.

"No." The election was Monday, and he wasn't changing his mind.

"You'd rather Matthew or that other guy?" Barrett asked.

Luke kicked the doorframe.

Barrett shrugged. "At least Matthew's not as crabby as his father."

Luke relaxed in the chair again and tipped back on its hind legs, matching Barrett's position. "He's too quiet. Too polite. Doesn't seem real to me."

Barrett laughed. "You sure that's not the Ranger in you seeing things?"

"I agree with Luke." Cam stoked his fire. "You seen the way he looks at Mary?"

Luke slammed the chair legs to the floor. "What do you mean?"

"I mean that it's distracting when I'm preaching to look up and see a man ogling a woman. He's burning through her skull with those eyes."

Luke had seen Matthew looking at Mary once, the Sunday he'd confessed about the fire, but usually he'd been stuck in the second pew with his family. No more. He'd be in the back of the church, ready for action—for the last Sunday or two he'd be around.

Cam hung his mallet. "Luke, you got any time to fish tomorrow?"

"What about me?" Barrett asked.

"You have a ranch and a woman," Cam said.

"I like the sound of that, but what does that have to do with fishing?"

"You gave up your free time."

"What do you call this?"

"Sulking." Cam tossed the hot metal into water. Hissing tore through the air. "Poor boy doesn't have anything to do when his wife goes socializing."

"Where's Claire?" Luke asked.

"With Grace and Mary at your house."

Luke leaned against the doorjamb and stared at the evening sky. "Not at our house. Grace took off right after supper with her sewing basket."

Barrett groaned. "Claire will be out half the night if Grace gets her distracted with fashion."

Cam grinned. "This is what marriage does to a man. Makes him cry when his woman's not around."

The Pearson brothers ran past the smithy.

"Hey," Luke called.

The boys stopped.

"You been out helping Mary?"

Jake shoved his hands in his pockets. "She's not there tonight. Took off on her horse with Miss Grace and Mrs. Clarke."

"Took off where?"

Jake shrugged. "Toward the lumber camp. She was fixed up and all. Looked really pretty."

Fixed up? Since when did Mary get fixed up? "Thanks." He waved as Jake stalked off. This sounded like a Mary scheme.

Scowl lines crossed Barrett's forehead.

Luke held his hand up. "Don't look at me. I don't have any control over Grace."

"I wasn't thinking of Grace." Barrett snatched his hat.

"Both of you relax," Cam said. "Claire and Grace have enough sense to counter whatever Mary might come up with."

Luke stormed from the smithy, Barrett by his side. He turned back to Cam. "You coming on the search?"

"The search for what?" Cam picked up his mallet. "You're overreacting."

Luke shook his head and walked away. He didn't ignore his instincts, and instinct said Mary was up to something.

"Bear. Luke," Cam called.

Luke turned.

"Let me know if you need anything." Cam nodded and returned to work.

The hammering chased Luke as he walked south, hand reaching habitually to check his gun. His *gun*. He hated that this bum shoulder took away one of his shooters. The pain was all but gone, despite the slow healing of his stitches.

"Think we need a horse?" Barrett asked as they approached the Y in the road.

Luke paused, looked in the direction of the Smith's, then grunted and turned toward home. "We'll take a couple of ours."

They marched in silence, and his mind took him a thousand directions, none of which made sense. Jake could have misinterpreted which way the women had headed. Maybe they were at Claire's, and Barrett didn't know it. Maybe they'd simply gone for a ride around Smith property.

All fixed-up with evening soon passing to night? That's what bothered him most.

If they were headed toward Bridges, she might be visiting Matthew, but with Claire and Grace along? The only thing past the camp was Clifton, and what would—

The pianist who'd dazzled the miners and lumberjacks.

Luke took off at a sprint, his bound arm hindering, elbow digging into his side.

"What?" Panic shot from Barrett's voice.

Luke rounded the bend and pushed up the grade to the barn. He tore through the doors, out of breath and with shaky legs, praying Paul wouldn't be there to question him.

He spun toward Barrett. "Unbind me."

Barrett worked at the fastening around Luke's arm, shoulder, and side. "What are you thinking?"

"Clifton. The Gold Mine."

"Claire's smarter than that."

"Mary's not. And Claire's ignorant enough about

243

mining and lumber towns."

Luke fiddled with the last of the bindings and threw them on the floor. Good riddance to things that held him back. "Start saddling."

Only minutes passed until they exited the barn on horseback and cut through Thomas pasture to get to the road to Clifton, but Luke's mind had managed to run a dozen scenarios. The pale blue sky arched over them, and a trail of light filtered through the trees to the west. The rhythm of Gabriel's hooves stirred his imagination, threatening to send his thoughts out of control. He'd been in too many saloons, arrested too many drunk men, to not worry what situation Mary might be creating for herself by showing up in fancy clothes and playing the piano.

Luke narrowed his focus on the path ahead, nudging Gabriel faster. He hadn't succeeded as a Ranger by melting under adversity, and he couldn't lose it now.

Possibility didn't mean probability. Just because Mary was entertaining — a terrible word choice — men, didn't mean they were mistreating her. She had grit. No one crossed her without a fight.

Outside of Clifton, they descended into a gorge. The river swept through with a roar exaggerated by the narrowness of the canyon. Clifton was tucked against the bottom wall of the basin, a town that offered a bar, a store, and rows of houses for miners.

Luke reined in Gabriel and coerced his heart to settle. Cam had been right. "I'm overreacting."

"Are you?" Barrett's two words belayed more tension than his silence.

They looked over the few buildings lit by lanterns. If not for the river's sound, he'd be able to hear Mary rapping out Beethoven across the way. Luke nudged Gabriel onward and fought a moment of panic that they wouldn't find the girls here.

But when they descended the last twenty feet and

crossed to the bar, he saw Holly and Buttercup tied out front, meaning two of the girls had ridden together.

Luke left Gabriel at the crowded railing, trusting Barrett to follow. He couldn't reach the doors fast enough. Laughter and conversation pulled him in, but not the sound of a piano. He needed to hear the piano.

The blessed sound came as he pushed through the doors. His gaze honed in on Mary at the center of the room. Men circled the piano, packed elbow-to-elbow. She'd fixed herself up in a new green dress, courtesy of Grace. His sister stood to the side of Mary looking more serious than a displaced Puritan, and when the man seated behind Mary reached to touch a strand of her hair, Grace glared. Bless her.

"A drink, sir?" A middle-aged woman in a plain dress offered a glass to him.

He shook his head and marched around the outside of the room until he could see Mary's face. Between lopsided hats and tangled mops of hair, he took in the enjoyment that dressed her features. Her sense of pleasure stirred his ire. Sure, it was enjoyable now, but what about in an hour when the alcohol began to work on these men?

"Where's Claire?" Barrett spoke by his ear.

Luke scanned the room. His hand went to his gun as he measured entrances and exits. Stairs scaled the side of the back wall. Instinct drove him toward them.

Halfway up, he heard the sounds of struggle. Grunting. Shuffling. He reached the top, gun pulled. Ahead in the dim light, a man with a protruding belly and suspenders pressed Claire against the wall. Using her stern teaching voice, she was trying to talk her way out of his advances while her hands clawed at his.

Luke lunged forward. "Hands off. Now."

The man stepped back and swayed. Glossy-eyes turned on Luke. "What's going on?"

"Nothing anymore."

Barrett pushed around Luke and inserted himself

between Claire and the stranger. He spun on the man and shoved him into the opposite wall.

"Not worth it." Luke held Barrett back. "Focus on Claire."

He elbowed Barrett toward Claire. Her dress wasn't rumpled, nor was her hair, hopefully implying things hadn't gotten far.

Luke snagged the drunken man by the collar and rushed him toward the stairs. He knew the type. A passive opportunity-seeker without much backbone for a challenge. Barrett might feel like pummeling him, but violence spurred by emotion forged a dangerous path. Restraint was as important as speed and accuracy. And knowing when to do what was the height of wisdom.

I could use some wisdom, Lord.

Shoving his gun to the man's back, Luke escorted him downstairs and into the main room where, Mary's lightning fingers were spreading melody over cheers and laughter.

A sense of the surreal closed around him. How many times had he apprehended men who'd overstepped bounds with women? Or broke up gambling in a bar, or settled arguments among drunken men? He'd trained for this, practiced his shot for hours.

And he'd never been as on edge as now. Not because imminent danger lurked, but because the what-ifs wouldn't let loose of his mind. What if they'd not chased the hunch and left Cam's? What if they'd not found Claire in time? What if Mary'd been . . .

Barrett ushered Claire around him and toward the door. One glimpse of her tear-stained face sucked any remaining *nice* from him. Mary had hauled two friends into this environment without thought for her safety or theirs.

"Everyone freeze!" Luke's voice thundered over the room, bringing instant silence.

Mary leapt from the stool and spun. Her eyes widened, and her mouth gaped enough to let in a parade of flies. Better the shock of seeing him here than the surprise of being absconded when she stepped outside to leave.

Luke narrowed his eyes at her before scanning the room. "Who's in charge?"

The woman in the simple dress, now standing behind the bar, raised her hand.

Great. A fifty-year-old woman who looked meeker than a saint was in charge of keeping a houseful of rowdies under control.

"I'm Texas Ranger Luke Thomas and —"

"We ain't done nothing wrong." The grumbled words came from an elder man smoking his pipe in the corner.

"Since when is it all right for a man to do anything he wants to a woman?"

Luke shoved the man who'd accosted Claire into a seat and walked toward the woman at the bar. "Is this what goes on here?"

She shrank back.

"What's his name?" Luke nodded at the perpetrator.

"Scotty Green."

"Is the marshal in town?"

The woman shook her head.

"I'm reporting him to Swensson, and you can all wager this man will be questioned and watched."

"You can't come in and stir things up just 'cause you're a lawman." A youth with a gap between his front teeth crossed his arms and rested his weight on one leg. "Maybe you ain't. I don't see a badge."

Steadying his grip on his gun, Luke stared at the mouthy youth. "Tonight's concert is over." Luke let his eyes linger until he was satisfied the youth was more talk than threat.

Mary gasped, and Luke's attention shot her direction. Several men close enough to breathe on her neck laughed. Luke had missed something, and with the way Mary smoothed her skirts and jutted her chin out, he feared it had been a swat to her rump or the like.

Luke moved as close to the piano as he could get, but twelve feet, and a lot of men, stood between him and Mary. The expression in Grace's eyes begged him to make things right.

"Let's go," he said. "Move." The command was as much for the men as for the girls to make an effort to part the sea of them.

The man who'd been sitting directly behind the piano stool stood. "Rhett here has a point. How do we know you are who you say you are? Maybe you're trying to take this woman for yourself." His gaze washed over Mary. "And who'd blame you?"

Mary glared at the offender. Luke expected her to speak on his defense, to say she knew him. Instead, she snatched Grace's hands and forced their way through the tables that sat closest to the piano. The men didn't so much as lean back and offer more room for the girls to pass, but neither did they grab them.

Mary reached him first, tripping over an outstretched boot. She grasped Luke's bum shoulder, and he bit back a grunt and cupped her waist. Once he'd steadied her, he pushed her past without meeting her eyes. She got the point and kept walking toward the door, shoulders rigid and mouth taut. When Grace stepped around the last of the men, Luke snagged her hand and looked around.

Amusement lingered in some expressions, confusion in others, and a few stared at him like he'd lost his mind. Had he? Other than words, they hadn't thrown anything at him. They hadn't gotten physical. The women were unharmed, and the men had even shown a certain protectiveness of Mary by questioning Luke's intentions.

Luke backed up, Grace's hand in his, until he reached the door. Satisfied the men wouldn't cause him any trouble, he spun around, pulled Grace with him into the night, and plowed into Mary. Stumbling, he released Grace's hand and snagged Mary's elbow.

She tried to push past him. "I need my money."

"Forget the money."

"She hasn't paid me for the last three times I've been here."

Incredible. He nudged Grace toward where Barrett had gathered their horses across the way.

"What does she owe you? I'll pay it." Luke moved his grip to Mary's upper arm and tried to guide her away, but she hesitated.

"There's no need for you to pay. Just let me—"

"No." He slung her over his good shoulder and stalked toward the others. Unlike several days ago in the river, Mary offered no resistance.

Grace had climbed on Buttercup, and Claire was settled on Barrett's horse. Luke set Mary down hard in front of Holly. "Mount up. Now."

She lifted her chin, matching his anger with a glare.

"You're welcome," he said.

"I didn't say thank you."

"If I waited for appropriate gratitude, we'd be here all night. So you're welcome. Now get on your horse before I throw you on."

With a huff that could have blown dandelion fluff across a pasture, Mary swung into the saddle.

He walked around to Gabriel and reached for the reins, but Barrett held them back.

"Your woman almost got my woman killed," Barrett whispered.

"Mary's not my woman."

It took more than a brush of the lips and an embrace in a thunderstorm to make her his woman, no matter how his heart argued against the words he'd shoved back at Barrett.

Luke caught the reins Barrett shoved at him and mounted. Once Barrett swung up behind Claire, Luke nodded for him to head out. Grace followed, leaving him to stare down Mary and make sure she didn't make a last attempt for her money.

"No way am I letting you ride last," he said.

"Your sense of trust honors me."

She'd drawn out the livid from him; an emotion he hadn't known himself capable of.

At the Smith's, Barrett and Claire kept on toward town and Luke sent Grace ahead. He had unfinished business with Mary. She crawled off her horse and didn't argue when he took the reins and led Holly into the barn.

"Go inside," he called over his shoulder.

Again, she offered no resistance. Not like her.

Luke settled Holly, fed her, and closed the doors on the barn. Now he had to close the doors on this evening. Not as easy.

Halfway across the yard, he paused, looked up at the stars and tried to pray, but every few words his mind strung together, his heart dismantled. His prayers stemmed from a mountain of yearning that had no words attached.

He walked to the open door and stopped at the threshold, not willing to enter and return to the night of the thunderstorm when heartstrings had tangled. That night was gone. She'd been vulnerable, and he'd been the hero.

Tonight was all about irritation and stupidity.

She stood several feet from him and hugged herself, her face pale in the moon-shadowed interior.

"I don't want to ask what you were thinking," he said.

She rolled her eyes. "So you'll comment on it instead. Is that how you get your criminals to talk?"

He took her bite as evidence she was under conviction. "Fine. What were you thinking?"

Her lips drew tight before she opened her mouth. "I needed the money. Don't berate me for using my talent to get it. If it helps, this was my last night."

"Out of how many?"

"Eight."

He groaned. She left him in the doorway and paced from the moonlight into the dark room.

Barrett's haunted eyes imprinted his memory.

"You endangered your friends. Let them down."

"Ha! You're one to talk about letting others down, you who left your family behind."

The accusation stabbed at him. They were talking about her choices, not his. Her stupidity. Once again, she diverted the attention to him.

"You took your friends into a place where they'd be vulnerable."

Movement sounded in the shadows in front of him, and a moment later, a match hissed. Mary lit a lamp and raised the wick, a soft glow filling the front room.

"Everyone is overreacting," she said.

"Do you realize what could have happened?"

"I *work* in a barn. I wasn't born in one. Of course I realize what *could* have happened. Could implies the entire realm of possibility, and letting possibility rule your life leads to a boring, locked up existence."

He shoved off the doorjamb, wise or not, and advanced into the room. Mary leaned against the wall, propped up like her legs had rebelled.

"We found Claire upstairs in the hallway in the arms of a less-than-honorable admirer." To put it softly, but by the drop of her jaw, Luke knew she understood. He rested his hands on the outside of her shoulders. "You're trembling."

"I didn't know . . ." she locked her jaw.

"Please acknowledge this wasn't smart."

Her gaze flitted to the side.

"Mary . . ."

"I admit, I shouldn't have taken others with me. But . . ." She shoved his hands aside and stormed to the center of the room. "Half the time I have grass in my hair or mud on my skirt. I smell like cows, I even look like cows—"

"That's an exaggeration."

She pointed at her eyes. "Did you or did you not say these were the same color as Gretto's?"

"I meant it as a compliment." They were beautiful brown eyes, expressive, deep as the swimming hole.

"I performed music, and they listened. Nothing untoward happened until tonight with Claire, who is beautiful and sophisticated." She smoothed a strand of hair away from her face. "I'm just an average pretty."

This woman was more messed up than he'd thought. He snatched the lamp from the table, wrapped his hand around Mary's arm, and escorted her down the hallway and into her room. Forget propriety.

Placing her on the chair in front of her mirror, he shoved the lamp close to her head. "There. You see that? Not average."

Her head dipped, and she stared toward her feet. He set the lamp on the table and gripped both sides of her head, brought it up until she raised her eyes to the mirror again. Beneath his fingers, her pulse strummed warm.

"I've been in and out of saloons—"

"The Gold Mine is an inn."

"I've dragged outlaws out of bed and away from their women, and I'm telling you . . ." His words veered in a direction that seemed irreversible, but with the way her eyes riveted on his in the mirror, he couldn't stop himself. The heart had taken aim and fired. And he never missed.

"I've never seen beauty like yours," he whispered.

She closed her eyes.

That was it? No tears of appreciation? No swooning look? Weren't those the words every woman wanted to hear?

"No one's going to bother me when I sit and play the piano. They'd rather listen to my music than . . ." her tone weakened.

"Touch your body? Wrong."

She grimaced, and he regretted his words. No, he regretted the need to say them. He'd never frowned upon bluntness. Truth was meant to be heard.

Mary pulled her head forward, out of his hands, and stood. He curled his hands into fists, resisting the urge to reach for her and pull her back. Here was proof—she was touchable.

"I push around one thousand pound cows." Resilience returned to her voice. "I think I can defend myself."

He must have dozed off and landed in a fantasy world. She couldn't be thinking she could boss around a potential abuser like she did a cow.

He gripped her upper arms, tightening his fingers enough to put pressure, but not enough to bruise. Backing her up against her bedpost, he invaded her space. Leaned into her. His every nerve screamed her nearness, reminded him of their kiss. But he'd not be distracted from the lesson.

"I could do anything I wanted to you, and you couldn't stop me."

He lowered his mouth a breath from hers, and she didn't blink. The stubborn woman didn't bat an eye. He released one of her arms, and fingered the top button of her dress.

Lesson gone too far, Luke.

She didn't flinch. Her steadiness portrayed trust in his character, but also challenged him to see what it would take to get his point across. He unbuttoned her top button, and her mouth twitched. Point considered. Shutting out the objections of his conscience, he reached for the next button and slipped it loose. Her hand slapped at his. Point received. To make sure she understood, he went for her third button. She swung into motion, tugging on his wrist, twisting her hips trying to get away.

He pressed closer, stilling her frantic movements. "Anything."

"Are you through? Because you're hurting me."

He released her arm and eased back. She must think him a monster.

Not taking his eyes from hers, he reached for her buttons again, slowly. She suppressed a flinch, but not before he caught it. He buttoned the second button, and then fumbled with the first. Her pulse hammered in the hollow of her neck, drawing his finger. He brushed the warm skin, wishing it were his lips and not his finger.

He lurched back, but no amount of distance could undo that image. Here he was chastising her stupidity when his thoughts surpassed all foolishness.

He stalked from the room, away from the fizzle of the lamp, the flowery scent that smothered the air with femininity. His long legs made short work of the hallway and front room and delivered him into the night. The cool air coated his dry throat.

"Luke."

The desperation in Mary's voice turned him. She stood in the doorway, her figure backlit by the glow of a lamp. He looked away and rubbed his fingers through his short hair. It wasn't her fault she looked like she'd walked straight from the Garden of Eden and the hand of God.

"Thank you."

He took the ten steps back to her and pulled her into his arms, crushed her against him. The way she burrowed into his hold fished more desire from him than he'd realized he possessed.

"I'm sorry." He whispered the words into her hair, his mouth brushing against the wavy strand at her temple. The fresh air had cleared his head. He'd had no right to handle her as he had, no matter that desperation to protect her had motivated him to scare her. "I was wrong."

He cradled the back of her head against his shoulder as if he could hide her from her own spirited decisions. But wasn't that what he loved about her?

The word 'loved' burned him, and he pushed her

away.

Her eyes latched onto his, and he couldn't look away even when it felt like she drew secrets from him that he had yet to understand. Texas had never demanded this much from him. After what seemed like twice the length of a Sunday sermon, she offered a half-mouthed smile, tentative.

Lord have mercy, he wanted to tuck tail and run from the revelation that jerked his heart from its rhythm. She spun away first and marched back to the house. His feet bolstered to the ground, and not until he heard the door shut, was he able to pry them loose.

You love Texas. Your independence. Your role as a peacemaker.

And he loved his family, on the fringe of which Mary had lingered all his life. Yet no matter how much he rationalized these surges in his chest, he knew the truth. Mary had dethroned Texas.

CHAPTER TWENTY-FOUR

Around three on Monday afternoon, the Crawley wagon rolled around the bend in the road. Mary stopped churning the cream and stood, waiting on the porch despite the urge to run and pry the information from Papa.

This must be what it felt like to stand before a judge, knowing his decision would determine your future.

Lord, be gracious.

Since the afternoon over a week ago when she'd hit her knees after finding that mysterious note, she'd made a habit of getting those knees to the floor several times a day. The more confusion plagued her regarding her attraction to Luke, the harder she prayed, as if releasing those emotions to the Lord might lessen them.

The opposite had happened.

She loved him more now than she had before he'd hauled her from the Gold Mine.

Mr. Crawley parked the wagon and helped Papa down while Mrs. Crawley waved. Mr. Crawley hiked Papa's travel bag up to the porch and let it drop with a thud. He offered Mary a nod and a smile before ambling back to the wagon and climbing up beside his wife.

"Thank you." Papa leaned on the back of the rocking chair as he waved.

"I'm glad the trip was worth it." Mr. Crawley turned and spoke to the horses, and they started forward.

Worth it. Meaning Papa felt good about what had happened with Mr. Millwood.

Mary turned, laying a hand on his arm, ready to get answers, but at the sight of Papa's pale face, she quelled the questions. The long ride had not treated him well.

"Come inside." She helped him turn and opened the door. "I'll make you some tea."

He waved off her help, turned inside, and settled himself in his chair.

When she brought him a cup of steeped nettles, perspiration beaded along his hairline. "Should I have someone ride for Dr. Fraser?"

Papa shook his head and took a sip. "The pain will lessen tomorrow."

She sat on the footstool before him, allowing him to drink in peace before her questions refused to wait longer.

"Did Luke visit?" he asked.

Her gaze skirted the room, looking for anything Luke might have left that had prompted Papa's question. "He was by several times. Along with Grace, Claire, and those you asked to help milk and do deliveries."

"Things went smoothly?"

"Fine."

Papa meant the dairy, but Saturday's images flickered in her mind, had never left her thoughts through yesterday or this morning. Luke taking charge in the Gold Mine. Luke pushing her against the bed. Luke unbuttoning her shirt. He'd made his point, and she'd spent Sunday afternoon making amends to Barrett, Claire, and Grace for her foolish decision.

Papa's gaze met hers above the cup. "I've agreed to sell to Mr. Millwood."

She squeezed her eyes shut, but her muscles were no match for the emotion that bottomed out her heart and dripped from her eyes. Snuffling, she buried her head in Papa's lap.

Hand resting on her hair, his thumb drew circles on the crown of her head. Amid ragged breaths and sobs, she inhaled the barn smell entrenched in Papa's pants.

It should have been Mama's head resting on Papa's lap, not Mary's. Things would be different if Mama were here. Better for Papa.

"I should have died." Mary's words came out choked, disjointed.

"What is this?" Papa lifted her head and cupped her face with his hands.

"Mama's loss cost you more. I was just a baby. You lost a helpmeet and gained an infant who had nothing to offer and everything to demand."

"Child." Papa shook his head and ran a gnarled finger across the wetness beneath her eyes.

"I tried to make it worth it, that I'd lived and she hadn't." Mary worked to speak despite the uneven breaths stitching her side. "I tried to keep this place that you and she loved. I wanted to make you happy."

Papa removed his hanky from his pocket and wiped her face. "I never once wished that Emeline had lived and you had died. It was never an either-or. Nor was it up to you to make me happy. No person can bear that burden."

She sucked in a deep breath.

"Neither can a place."

An earthly home didn't have the power to bring contentment, and the realization hollowed her.

"I've loved every day of our struggle on this land." Papa quieted his voice. "But God brings about new things and remains constant through the changes around us."

"I don't want to leave." Her voice cracked.

"I know. We'll miss this place." His gaze traveled the room and found hers again. "But we'll go knowing that another family will have the blessing of this home."

Mary frowned. "I thought Seth Millwood wasn't married."

"He's not, not yet. But he hopes to be someday. Are you volunteering?"

Luke had asked her the same question in regards to

himself when she'd declared him marryable.

"No. Definitely not." Not to Seth Millwood, and to Luke . . . if he'd not been teasing, she'd have said yes.

Papa eased from the chair and stretched the muscles in his back. He held out his hand to her. She gripped it, and he helped her up.

Cupping her face with his knobby fingers, Papa looked through the surface of her eyes and into her heart. "Home isn't simply the place you lay your head, but the people with whom you make a life." His smile deepened. "That's what Jesus does. He makes his home in our hearts and allows us to be heart companions with others. As long as you and I are on this earth, we won't understand why home hasn't included your mama, but I never want you to doubt that I love you."

Fresh tears pooled in Mary's eyes. "I know."

He turned to go, but she reached for his hand.

"Papa, there's one other thing." She tightened her grasp and watched for his reaction as she revealed her secret. "I've been using my Saturday evenings to play the piano at the Gold Mine."

"You played for a roomful of drinking, gambling men?"

"It wasn't wise, I admit. But I was intent on earning money for the dairy."

Papa's eyes closed, and he rubbed his furrowed brow.

"I should have told you," Mary said. "But I didn't want you to worry. I'm sorry."

The lines around his eyes softened as he opened them. He took hold of the back of the chair and looked heavenward. "Well, I'll be. Nothing should surprise me about you, and yet . . ." He shook his head, a smile brushing the corner of his mouth. "This wasn't your smartest moment."

"Luke seems to think no one has ever made a more irresponsible decision."

Papa laughed and swiped at the moisture that lingered in his eyes. "Luke doesn't know how to think anymore around

259

you. He only feels."

She bit her lip, but the grin pushed out anyway. "He's not far from the truth. I took Claire and Grace with me last time and things got" — awful, like a nightmare — "challenging. Luke and Barrett fetched us."

Papa's thin brows slanted. "I suppose I'll have to offer my gratitude next time I see them."

He held out his arms, and she walked into them. Strength reverberated in his embrace despite how his body had weakened. She laid her head on his shoulder and let him smooth her hair like he used to do when she was younger.

"It's going to be all right." His steady tone asked for her trust.

"What will we do?" The question begged to be asked, whether she was ready to hear the answer or not.

"I'll be heading back to Peshastin and going on to Wenatchee with Mr. Millwood to take care of the sale."

That didn't answer her question. "Where will we live?"

"Rod's allowing us to lease the apartment above his store."

Which meant Papa had talked with him before going to Peshastin, anticipating the need. She'd been too preoccupied with losing the dairy to have offered support when Papa had needed it.

"We can take a month or two while we stay above Rod's to decide our next steps," Papa said. "Mr. Millwood will need our help to get acquainted with the routine of the dairy."

Exhaustion mantled her spirit. Though midday, her body longed to stretch out and rest, digest the news of saying goodbye. Then again, too many last times waited. A last hike through the cedar grove. A last swing in the dark.

"I leave on Wednesday. Depending on how things go, I should be arriving with Mr. Millwood in a week."

A week. She had only seven days to say goodbye to Mama all over again.

Luke squirmed beside Mary on the narrow seat of the milk cart. He'd been a fountain of restlessness since she'd found him hiking down the mountain behind Barrett's and invited him to join her. Given the choice to wander into town and watch people vote or ride along with Mary on one of her last deliveries, he'd chosen Mary.

On second thought, the town would have been a safer choice than being hip-to-hip with Mary. Or was it heart-to-heart? He pushed his feet against the rim, wishing for more space to stretch his legs.

Mary guided Holly up the long, slow rise toward Mrs. Lunsford's. "You're more restless than Mud when she's calving."

Luke tried to shove his hands into his pockets, but his elbow jabbed her in the ribs. "Sorry."

What if he were elected sheriff? He'd tell them no, that he had to return to unfinished business in Texas. They'd move on, offer the position to the runner up, likely Matthew. And that was the rub.

Something was off about Matthew.

"Worrying won't change the voting," Mary said.

"I'm not worried."

"I see. This squirming is normal Texas Ranger behavior."

Mary had redefined his normal. She'd composed a song in him he couldn't quiet, which was why he needed to return to Texas and clear his name. He couldn't make decisions about his future until he'd resolved issues with the Rangers. With potential jail time hanging over his head, he didn't have a chance with Mary. And as certain as her hip rubbed his, he wanted a chance.

Meaning he needed to head south and work things out, no matter that they told him to remain in Pine Creek. He needed to leave . . . in order to stay.

He leaned forward and rested his arms on his knees to keep from going crazy with her nearness. "How are you doing?"

She let out a long breath. "The sorting and packing has been the hardest, knowing the place I've considered home won't be home next week."

He glanced over his shoulder at her.

Unshed tears glistened in her eyes. "Papa left this morning. Seeing his joy and relief has done more for my heart than I knew I needed." Her smile stretched. "I'm ready to let go, if you can believe it."

He almost couldn't, except for the genuine peace in her smile.

"You, on the other hand . . ." She stopped Holly past the creek that separated Clarke and Lunsford land and turned toward him as much as the shrunken space allowed.

Her knees rubbed his. He could do with several more feet as a bulwark from the softness of her . . . knees.

You're not thinking about knees.

"You could use a lesson in holding on. Maybe it'd help you stop running." Her smile gave off mischief like the sun gave off heat.

"I told you. I don't run." No matter that his better sense advised jumping from the cart and making for the woods. Confronting his feelings for Mary now meant jeopardizing his conviction to leave. "And I know how to hold on."

"I don't think you do." She raised her hands and showed him the reins. "See? I close my fingers like this." She made a show of squeezing them.

The sparkle in her eye tangled his thinking, provoked him to prove her wrong. Quick as he might draw weapons, he reached for her face and slid his fingers into her loose hair. Her soft intake of breath urged him on, and he drew his face within inches of hers until her breath warmed his lips. "This" — he clasped her face as if letting go meant falling from a cliff — "is holding on."

The depth of desire in her eyes reached like fingers around his heart, offered him an opportunity to cling. And then she was kissing him as if he were plummeting from that cliff, out of her life, and she had one chance to save him.

God help him, he wanted to be saved.

He savored her taste, sweet and smooth like cream. Holding her hand had felt right, but kissing her moved into the realm of perfection. His thumbs circled the softness of her neck behind her ears. She made a sound and pushed her body into his, but when he slipped his arms around her waist and demolished any last space between them, conviction seared him.

He couldn't guarantee his charges would be dismissed, had no idea if he'd be able to return, to own up to his love for her, and to defeat the vulnerability of this place with all its memories of Father.

Her breath spiraled across his face as she kissed his forehead, meandered a trail back to his lips. He'd allow himself a few more seconds . . . maybe a minute.

A dog barked in the distance.

"Mary." He pushed her face away with trembling hands. "I have to leave next week."

Mary shoved him back, picked up the reins from her lap, and pulled Holly from her snack of roadside grass. Focused on the bumpy road, she clicked her tongue and urged Holly forward.

His kiss burned her heart like the first swig of hot coffee in the morning, the heat that motivated her to get out the door and to the barn. But Luke's kiss didn't motivate. It broke. It shattered her belief that she didn't love him, her will not to love him.

Loving him is futile. You knew that. You knew he'd leave.

He might acknowledge the ways he was broken, the fears that kept him from sinking roots, but she'd no more get him to dig in and make home with her than she'd be able to reverse Papa's decision.

He'd determined to return to Texas.

"You read the letter about the accusations." Luke's gravelly voice sounded more intimate now that she'd kissed him. "You know I have to go back."

She'd rather know why he wanted to stay, if he loved her or had merely given in to some flimsy form of emotionalism these past weeks. "The letter said you're not supposed to leave Pine Creek."

He whipped his hat from his head and spun it in his hands. "I can't wait longer."

Meaning he'd had enough of Pine Creek, and though he'd been told to stay, he couldn't stand to spend another month here.

A warm breeze stirred the trees, and Luke hung his hat from his knee, bouncing it in a steady allegretto.

"I suppose that kiss is your way of saying, 'nice to see you again'?"

"*I* was practicing holding on." His words held a smile, and she turned to see the slightest raise of his cheeks. "*You* kissed me."

Her mouth gaped as she relived the sequence. He'd taken her face in his hands and drawn it close, an irresistible invitation. She *had* kissed him first. What did he expect with the way he'd breathed on her? Ezekiel's dry bones hadn't felt that much life.

His hat slipped off his knee, falling to the ground. He jumped off before she'd fully stopped the cart.

"What if you win the election?" she asked.

"I'm under investigation. How can I accept?"

"Those accusations are hogwash. You know the town loves you."

He smirked and reached beneath the cart for his hat. How could he not see that he was wanted here? How could he not care? She kicked the footboard, and Holly jerked forward.

Luke cried out, sitting back on the ground and holding his right hand.

She yanked the reins and jumped down. "What happened?"

"Cart rolled over my hand." He stood and shook out his hand.

Her heart pounded as she reached for his fingers, but he winced when her fingers grazed his and pulled his hand away.

"It's nothing."

The lines on his forehead and his quick breaths didn't look and sound like nothing.

"I'm sorry, Luke, really."

What if she'd broken the fingers of his strong hand? What if they healed wrong, and he never shot with the same accuracy again? He'd hate her. She'd hate herself.

"Hey." His non-injured hand cupped her shoulder. "It's going to be fine. I've had bruised fingers before." He climbed back on the seat and shoved his hat on his head.

"Are you sure?"

He shrugged. "Don't need this hand right now anyway. I'll be on a train for a week, then pleading my case to my captain."

She joined him in the cart and flicked the reins.

"Doesn't hurt nearly as bad as being shot."

She tried to smile, but her muscles wouldn't obey.

Keeping his right hand next to him on the outside of the seat, he reached with his left hand and cupped her chin. His finger stroked the soft flesh beneath her chin, luring her gaze to his. Good thing Holly didn't need direction because Mary couldn't concentrate on the road before them.

"I don't want these accusations hanging over me. If I want a chance here—and I do—"

"You do?"

"Then I have to go back."

He wanted a chance in Pine Creek? Mary stared ahead

and bit her lip to keep the grin from saturating her face.

"I'm coming back." His words were half-breath, half-sound.

She turned to him again. Her gaze wavered between his eyes and his lips. *Don't think about it. He said he was coming back, not that he loved you.*

Holly rounded the bend into Mrs. Lunsford's drive, and Luke blinked, sat back, and pulled his hand from her chin.

The elderly woman exited the whitewashed farmhouse, her bright red skirt catching the breeze. "You're just in time. Been wanting to bake some muffins for the election celebration, but I'm out of milk."

Mary hopped from the cart and grabbed a jug of milk from over the side of the back.

Mrs. Lunsford waited on the porch and waved at Luke. "You've arrived with my hero."

Mary's eyes sought Luke's.

He shrugged one shoulder. "I taught her how to shoot."

The grin that plumed across Mary's face was effortless. He'd once called himself *a real helper of the people*, and he was. Luke loved these people the same as they loved him.

He climbed across the seat and stepped down by her.

She flicked her gaze across the yard toward Mrs. Lunsford, then turned and spoke softly for Luke alone to hear. "You'd make a great sheriff, which is why I voted for you."

"Thank you."

His brows slanted in, the concentration of his expression heightening his ruggedness. Without warning, his finger trailed along the back of her hand. Breathing became difficult.

Looking at Mrs. Lunsford, he tipped his hat. "I'm going to cut over to Barrett's. Have a nice day."

Mrs. Lunsford waved again, pride in her smile.

With one last cast of his gaze at Mary, he turned and

left.

Mary strode around the front planter to the porch.

"There goes a good man." Mrs. Lunsford chuckled. "But I don't need to say that to you, do I? Because if I do, we're going to have a sit-down right now."

Unexpected tears rushed Mary's eyes. "That's not necessary."

"I didn't think it was." Mrs. Lunsford grinned.

After several minutes of chatting, which included Mrs. Lunsford complimenting Luke twice more, Mary returned to her cart and meandered the lane back to the road. Opening her hands, she stared at the reins. Lessons in holding on . . . turned lessons in kissing . . . turned injuring the man she loved.

The day could not get more emotionally exhausting.

* * *

Luke loosened his collar while he stared at passersby. Behind him, Cam pounded iron as if today was just another day. And for Cam, it was. He'd not been kissed into a stupor nor had his hand run over by several hundred pounds of cart. The smallest flex of Luke's fingers sent a stab of pain up his arm. Broken, not merely bruised.

Barrett exited the mercantile and raised a hand at Luke, escorting Claire around the throng of gathering citizens. Luke had tried to escape to Barrett's only to discover both him and Claire had migrated to town along with everyone else.

Horses crowded the railing up and down the townsite, and wagons littered the outskirts of town. No other day, except maybe the fall festival, drew as much attention as election day. Rod had set up a table with a sign that read *Vote Here*, and the community had filtered in from a ten-mile radius to scribble their preferences and stuff them inside a box. Johnston and Cam took turns guarding the table, as if a ruffian might try to take off with the ballots or vote multiple times.

Cam held up a hinge and inspected it. "Sure you don't want to eat?"

Luke shook his head. He'd suffered through midday meal at home, each bite that touched his lips reminding him of another sensation. That something so basic as eating used the same part of the body as something so divine as kissing had flustered his composure. Sure that his family could read his thoughts, he'd excused himself. He'd been hiding in the smithy ever since.

Cam washed his hands. "Voting's about to close."

A crowd was gathering outside the mercantile. Matthew had worn a suit, as had the candidate from Wenatchee. Luke crossed his arms, taking in the worn pair of trousers and cream-colored button-down that needed a good scrub. The fanciest thing he wore was the residue of Mary's kisses.

"They already took the first batch of votes to Johnston's office," Cam said.

Luke paced to the water bucket and gulped down two glasses. He tugged the Psalms book from his shirt pocket and opened to the middle, reading wherever his eyes darted, first to the upper left, then to somewhere in the middle. Words of peace interspersed with words of affliction, a suitable blend for his inner turmoil.

Sinking to his chair, he closed his eyes and leaned his head against the wall. Cam shuffled about, and Luke's ears traced Cam's movements to his desk. Voices of townsfolk drifted through the open doors, occasionally disrupted by a child's squeal.

Lord, I don't know if I can leave.

He'd been sure leaving was the right choice. Then Mary had kissed him and reordered each desire in his heart.

Chair legs screeched on the floor. Cam nudged Luke. "Looks like it's about time."

Luke ruffled through his hair, shaking out the dust of the smithy, and donned his hat. Stepping behind Cam into the sunshine, Luke shoved his hands in his pockets. At least a hundred and fifty people lined the street. Cam wove through the crowd toward Barrett and Claire who were resting beneath the shade of a tree, and Luke followed, but seeing Mary approach and hug Claire, he reversed directions and returned to the front of the smithy. He'd not recovered from his last encounter with her.

Johnston exited his office to a smattering of applause. Luke's jaw clamped, and he worked to relax the tension. From his place across the street, and with a sea of townsfolk in the way, he couldn't tell if Johnston was frowning or squinting into the sun.

Stepping behind the podium, Johnston held up his hands until the crowd quieted. "The results of the first sheriff election are in. Runner up, Luke Thomas."

Luke ducked his head, feeling like he'd been punched in the gut with one of Cam's hot irons. After all the begging for him to run, he'd lost? But he hadn't ran. He'd adamantly stood against running.

"And your new sheriff, citizens of Pine Creek, is Matthew Bridges."

Applause coursed through the crowd as Matthew took his place next to Johnston and shook the mayor's hand. Luke dragged his attention to Mary. She stood with her arms crossed, mouth drawn into a line. Her head turned his direction, and he whipped his back around, strode through the crowd, and approached Matthew.

"Congratulations," he said.

"Thank you." Matthew's pointed look tarnished Luke's manners.

He refused to let go of Matthew's gaze, meeting the pale blue of Matthew's eyes with the fire of his own. "A badge is a big responsibility."

Matthew edged back. "You must be relieved not to have it pinned on you."

As if he couldn't handle the responsibility? He could

handle it. And he wasn't relieved like he'd expected to be.

"I guess you can leave town now without a worry since you've no good reason to stay."

"On the contrary. I have every reason to stay." Luke held out his uninjured hand.

Matthew's eyes narrowed as he shook it.

"My best to you," Luke said.

"Thank you."

"Boss!" Davis squeezed his way from the crowd and slapped Matthew on the shoulder. "Who would have thought?" He shot a grin at Luke then returned his attention to Matthew. "Might need to do a little celebrating tonight. Take a trip to the old fire pit?"

Luke slipped down the alley between the mayor's office and what would soon be Matthew's office.

This is for the best. If you'd won, what then? You're not free to take the position.

Yet his heart bottomed out, betraying him. Mary's words from earlier in the week, *You don't think you do*, exposed him. He'd wanted to be sheriff. Against his will, he'd wanted it.

Chapter Twenty-Five

Luke leaned back in his chair and watched his mother dry the last dish and put it in the cupboard. If the Rangers wanted him, they'd have to come haul him away from Mary and Pine Creek. It had been three hours since the election results were announced, and every minute added strength to his conviction.

He couldn't leave her. He couldn't leave this town with a sheriff like Matthew Bridges, someone whose reasons for wanting to be sheriff seemed wrong. Not for the love of justice, love of people.

The more Luke considered how Matthew had pressured Mary to sell his family the dairy, how he'd stared at her in church, the more he believed Matthew to be her admirer. The one leaving the honeysuckles. Which meant, Matthew had run for sheriff either out of jealousy or because he believed it would impress Mary.

First thing in the morning, Luke would be getting some answers from Mary about the honeysuckles. She'd not brush him off again.

"Feeling better?" His mother set her hand on his shoulder.

Luke stuck his elbow out and rotated his arm. "Shoulder's great. The fingers, not so much." He tried to flex them, but the splint he'd rigged up earlier immobilized them.

He stood and reached to retrieve the broom from her, but she pulled it back. "You don't have to do this," she said. "It's been a long day."

She meant the fingers, the election. She had no idea about the kiss that had both invigorated him and depleted him more than if the cart had run over his entire body.

"I'm not an invalid." He took the broom. "Please let me do this for you."

She hung up her apron. "Thank you." She patted his cheek, hands still damp from dishes, and slipped out the door to join Abigail and Helen in the yard.

Through the back window, Luke watched them gather wildflowers. Helen's hair glowed like honey in the evening light.

Paul bounded down the stairs. "Guess you got what you wanted with the election. You don't have to worry about being trapped with your family in Pine Creek."

His brother's words rankled him.

Luke glared, set the broom aside, and walked out through the front room. He pushed open the door, sending it clashing against the house, and took the steps two at a time. Heavy footsteps rushed after him. After all the day had held— good, bad, and painful—he didn't want to add a confrontation with his brother. Luke circled the house and took the path into the woods. In three easy strides, he hopped the rocks and crossed the creek.

"Luke. Wait."

Paul's rare tone of regret jerked Luke to a stop. He spun, anchoring his hands on his hips, his stance coincidentally mirroring his brother's stance. Water rushed between them on its course over stones and sticks.

The lines around Paul's eyes deepened. "I don't mean to sound like I'm attacking. It's just . . ." Paul's husky voice rumbled across the sound of the creek. "It's hurt us, you being gone. It's felt like you abandoned us. Me. And since you've been home, you've only talked about going back."

"I never meant to hurt anyone." He'd not understood the way his leaving had affected his family, or maybe he'd been too hurt to put forth the effort to understand it. But regardless that he'd been drawn to the Rangers, that he'd had the skills, he'd left with the wrong attitude. "I'm sorry for the pain I caused, for the workload I left you with."

Paul ducked his head and wiped at his eyes.

Luke's chest cramped, making it hard to breathe. "You've been right about some of the things you've said since my return. I would not have come home if my captain hadn't sent me."

Paul looked up.

"Not because I don't love my family. I'd die for you, but being here reminds me of all we had before Father died. Being here reminds me of the stupid things I did. Being here is hard." Luke shifted his weight, staring past Paul to where Helen held Abigail's hand, swinging a bouquet of wildflowers in her other hand. He returned his gaze to his brother. "That said, being here is right."

Taking care of those he loved was right, even if it wasn't easy.

Luke crossed the creek and stood beside Paul. "I've decided to stay."

Without warning, Paul pulled him into an embrace. Unlike the one on the porch the night Luke had come home, this embrace wasn't offered from a brother's obligation. It carried a sense of forgiveness that shrunk the years of divide.

"Welcome home," Paul said.

"There's one issue." Luke stepped back and issued a wry smile. "I might be arrested."

Dusk hovered over the valley as Mary made her way from the barn to the house. She'd spent longer than usual with the cows, stroking velvet ears, peering into large, brown eyes, each milking like its own goodbye now that her days here were numbered.

Oh, stop. They're cows.

She'd promised herself not to let sentiment pilfer her

joy. Letting go of the dairy gave her an opportunity to hold on to something else, namely Luke—pending he loved her; she'd argued both possibilities since their kiss, a moment that hadn't left her thoughts, even after the disappointment of the election.

Mary entered the house and secured the door. The heat of the day nestled into the emptiness, and she cracked the windows of the front room and kitchen to admit a cross breeze. Three large trunks lined the wall, half filled with linens, dishes, and keepsakes.

Books were piled in the corner. Mary dropped into a chair and sorted through a stack of titles, placing special ones in a trunk, returning others to a shelf. After ten minutes, when she could no longer see through the dimming light, she lit a lamp and stretched.

The lush scent of honeysuckle drifted through the crack of the kitchen window, and her nerves tensed. What used to smell like heaven now clogged her thoughts with questions. She shut all the windows and latched them, checking twice to make sure they'd been secured properly.

Snatching the lamp, she moved toward the hallway, but the honeysuckle aroma intensified, stalling her steps. She scanned the room. There. On the table. A note wrapped with a honeysuckle vine had slipped between knickknacks waiting to be packed.

Someone had been in her house while she'd been in the barn.

She'd debated telling someone other than Grace about what had been happening, but she'd made too many excuses, pushed it off, not taken her questions seriously.

Stupid.

Her legs shook as she retrieved the note and slipped off the honeysuckle. The tackiness of the nectar stuck to the paper as she unrolled it.

I've won once today, and I must win again. My love burns like a fire, like a mighty flame. Many waters cannot quench it.

Matthew.

She threw the paper on the ground, heat expanding in her chest. She rehearsed his behavior, how he'd showed up at The Goldmine every time she'd played, the intensity that had taken her by surprise that day in her barn, and his insistence she sell to his family. The signs had been subtle but present.

Her deeply inhaled breath incited a spasm of nausea.

She couldn't stay here. While she'd half a mind to confront him, reason told her to go to Luke's and seek out the marshal. Matthew's secrecy felt like deception. He might be quiet and withdrawn, but why hadn't he tried to court her the normal way? She'd trusted him, touted his gallantry throughout the years. And he'd repaid her by creeping about and spying on her, too afraid to admit that he cared for her.

Anger thickened her throat. Carrying the lamp, she traversed the hallway. Papa's door stood ajar, but instead of the customary peaceful snores, silence emanated from his darkened bedroom.

You should have told him.

But Papa had been home only two days, and with the pending sale and move, it hadn't seemed pertinent. Until tonight.

Regrets wouldn't get her to Luke's faster. She strode through her door, but jerked to a stop upon seeing the window wide open. Her nightgown lay folded on her pillow.

He'd been in her room. He'd touched her things. Of all the eerie, sinister things . . . Her heart pounded so hard it ached.

The stench of alcohol wafted from behind, rousing a moment's premonition.

"What took you so long?"

Mary spun. "Matthew!"

Shirt untucked and hair on end, he looked about as civil as a coyote. His unfocused gaze coursed over her, and he pushed off from his position against the wall.

She backed up and tripped, then sat down hard on her

bed.

He advanced until his legs pressed against hers, pinning her in place. She looked into glossy, stormy eyes. The childhood friend that had solicited her trust seemed far removed. As far removed as the help she needed right now.

"You didn't answer my note." Matthew's voice slurred.

"That's hard to do when the sender doesn't leave his name." She worked for a steady voice while she considered her options. Scream and let loose some anger, though no one would hear. Or try to run, which wasn't feasible considering the way he was pressing against her legs.

He reached down and pulled on her arm, raising her up. The smell of alcohol might have knocked her down again if his hand hadn't been digging into her upper arm. She'd never known Matthew to drink.

"I want to celebrate with you."

"The election." Her voice scratched against a dry throat. She should try to pacify him with a congratulations and buy herself an opportunity to run, but she couldn't force out any well wishes.

"Do you know why I accepted the nomination? I did it for you. I knew you would like that." He spoke too loudly, the words rushing and tripping over each other, mixing syllables and sounds. "Did you vote for me? Please tell me you voted for me. I did it for you."

He'd lost more than his sobriety. He'd lost his mind. The panic-stricken way he spoke and the way he looked at her set her insides quaking.

He scowled. "Why aren't you grateful? Say something."

The alcohol had changed him into someone she didn't know, though maybe she'd fooled herself all along.

She pushed against his chest, vying for space he wasn't willing to give. "You're acting strange, and its scaring me. This isn't the Matthew I know."

His expression fell. "Don't say that. Please, don't say

that." He put his arms around her and cradled her head by his shoulder. "It's me."

She stiffened. "Let go of me. Now."

He grunted and pushed her away so suddenly her feet tangled and she fell back on the bed. His eyebrows stood on end, and his nostrils flared. She'd seen bulls look friendlier.

She scrambled to her feet and sidestepped him, heading toward the hallway. When his gaze slipped toward the nightgown, she bolted and raced down the hallway and out the front door.

"Mary!" His mournful cry chased her, along with loud, gaining footsteps.

He caught her in the yard between the house and barn, barreling against her and tackling her into the cool grass. Her shoulder jammed into a rock, and she kicked at him, but he pulled her to her feet as if she weighed nothing. She tried to pray, but panic fringed each thought. The most she could mutter was a simple, "Jesus, help!"

"Don't fight this, Mary." His voice rasped in her ears, void of the tenderness she'd expect from a man who'd left her honeysuckles and love notes. "I won an election today, and it's time to celebrate."

He gripped her upper arm and led her through the pasture.

"You won a position which requires you to protect people, not kidnap them." She dragged her feet. "This is wrong."

"This is right." He spun on her. "It's not kidnapping. It's putting together two things that are supposed to be together. You and me. He was always in our way. He picked on you, distracted you from me, but I always stood up for you."

Luke. *Oh, God, send Luke.*

Matthew wormed his finger along her forehead and brushed hair from her face.

When he bent forward as if he might kiss her, she

277

jerked back. "Let's go, then." She'd have to keep his attention diverted from her, and right now that meant following his plan to go wherever he had planned.

He slid his hand down her arm and gripped hers. She craved the touch of another hand in hers, and tears threatened.

With his other hand, Matthew brushed dirt from her shoulder and fingered a tear on her blouse. "Are you all right? I can carry you."

His mood changes had her head spinning.

"I'm fine." *Other than being kidnapped.*

She'd play along until a moment for escape presented itself.

He continued across the field, taking long steps that required her to rush to keep up. They passed the swing, illuminated by moonlight, and it invited memories of Luke.

"Yes, I saw the two of you swinging."

Nausea curled her stomach.

On the far side, Matthew angled into the woods and took the path toward the ravine where he and the boys used to have their fires.

"Watch out for the limb." He ducked beneath the protruding arm of a felled poplar. "There's a rock outcropping right around the corner." He walked with confidence, more evidence that he'd been striding around her woods in the dark for months.

"You left me honeysuckles."

"Yes."

"Why didn't you ask to court me?" Like a normal man.

Matthew grunted. "Everyone knew Luke was smitten for you."

She'd not known. "So you spied on me."

"No. I watched you to keep you safe."

Matthew's obsession had grown into such that he'd thought he was doing right by secretly observing her. He'd thought an anonymous approach would win her heart more

278

than an open confession. With skewed thinking like that, she had no idea what he might do.

Pulling out a flask, he grinned down at her. "This stuff will make you think you can run the world."

Evidently.

He held it to her lips.

"That's disgusting." She pushed it away, tripping over a root.

His grip on her arm strengthened. "Almost there."

A subtle orange glow showed in the distance.

"This isn't going to work, Matthew. You and me."

He growled and half dragged her the remaining hundred yards to the tucked-away cove where a bonfire greeted them. He'd set this up. Probably left the note, come down here and piled the wood high, then come back for her.

"Where are the others?" Not that she'd expected them, but he'd shared this place with friends.

"It's just you and me tonight."

"Why don't we invite them and make it a real celebration? I could go get Davis." Luke. She'd get Luke.

"It's you and me." Matthew yelled the words like a four-year-old whose will had been challenged.

Her arm throbbed beneath his tight grip.

"Will you run if I let go of your arm?"

"Yes." The truth slipped out before she thought to disguise her intentions.

The corner of his eyes turned down. In the firelight, his countenance appeared more sorrowful than angry. His unpredictability made him too hard to read.

He lowered himself to a log, pulling her onto his lap. Bile stung her throat. He wouldn't hurt her if he loved her, would he?

"I've waited years for you," he whispered into her hair. "I waited for Luke to leave, and then I waited for you to come back from those silly music lessons. I don't plan to lose you again."

He'd painted himself an imaginary world.

"You never had me." Her teeth chattered and beads of sweat formed on the back of her neck.

"I have you now."

Chapter Twenty-Six

From his bedroom window seat, Luke watched the final strip of light fade from above the western mountains. Disappointment about the election fused with the unknown of the situation in Texas. He'd hunt down Marshal Swensson tomorrow, send off an inquiry about where they were in the process of the investigation. Mary'd said they couldn't possibly find him a threat if they let him remain outside custody. She was right, which strengthened his conviction that he'd get out of this in a matter of time.

A soft knock on the door announced either Grace or his mother.

"Come in."

Grace shoved the door open, letting in the fragrance of fried apples and fresh sweet cream, a dessert his mother had whipped up as soon as she'd heard the news of his staying.

Grinning and tearful, his sister crossed the room and threw herself into his arms. "I heard you're staying. Tell me this isn't a joke."

"It's no joke."

She released him and did a little jump. "I think I could scream."

"You'll wake Helen."

"Fine. I'll refrain. What's this?" She lifted the vase of wildflowers from his dresser.

"A gift from Helen. As is this." Luke stood and plucked the honeysuckle necklace from where he'd tossed it on his bed and hung it around his neck. "My room's going to smell like a garden."

Grace leaned toward him and whiffed. "Or like Mary. Remember how she made yards of these when she was younger?"

He remembered more about Mary than he'd confess to Grace. Remembered things Grace didn't even know about.

Grace frowned and returned the flowers to his dresser. Her mouth opened as if to speak, but she shook her head and closed it again.

She took his hand in hers and made a face. "How do your fingers feel?"

Pain radiated up his arm whenever he moved them. "Not too great."

"Good thing you don't need your strongest trigger finger right now, or really, any trigger finger."

She flopped on the bed, and though fatigue weighted him, he didn't have the heart to tell her he'd rather sleep than talk about his future, which he suspected was on her mind.

"Where did you disappear to after supper?" he asked.

"Claire's clothes are getting tight, and I was helping her modify them. I didn't know I'd miss the announcement of the decade." Tucking her feet beneath her legs, she leaned forward. "Why stay? You love being a Ranger."

"Is this a test?" He turned a chair around and straddled it. "I love my family."

"And who else?"

He grinned. "I can hardly tell you before her, can I?"

"What are you waiting for?" Grace played with her braid hanging over her shoulder.

He had time now that he wasn't leaving. He'd plan it right, let her settle in her new place before telling her she'd ushered him straight to the heart of home, and he never wanted to leave again.

Then again, maybe he'd tell her tomorrow, after a good night's sleep.

Drumming the fingers of his left hand on the back of

the chair, he shrugged, playing down the urgency that screamed at him to rush over and tell her now, tired or not. "She's got some big things going on in her life." That was the reason he'd been telling himself since supper.

"You know? Thank God." Grace crossed her hands over her heart, and her eyes fluttered closed. "I thought she'd never tell anyone, stubborn as she is. Things are getting bizarre. He left a note, and then it disappeared."

His chest burned.

A note. This was what Mary had held back the other day in front of Rod's when he'd asked how many honeysuckles and she'd avoided the topic.

He locked his jaw, pushing down the questions and alarm and allowing his sister the space to reveal all she knew.

"The honeysuckles he left weren't a big deal, but one time he moved the shawl she'd left in the barn and she couldn't find it, and then another time there was the noise outside her window . . ." Grace shuddered, then whispered, "He watched her while she bathed!"

"What?" Luke sprang from his chair, and it crashed to the floor.

"Maybe not watched. All I know is that she heard a noise when she was bathing. She excused it as an animal even though I begged her to tell someone."

"How long have you known about these things?" he asked.

"Since the week after you came home." Grace frowned, studying his expression. "You already knew about them, right?"

He scrambled for his dresser and pulled open the drawer where he kept his guns. "Not everything."

"Oh, no. Oh, no. Oh, no." Grace jumped from the bed and hung on his arm. "What are you doing?"

"I'm going to get her and bring her back here. Her father left this morning, and she's alone."

Stubborn woman.

283

"You can't do that. I wasn't supposed to say anything. Wait until the morning, and I'll convince her to tell you. We can invite her to stay with us."

Ignoring Grace's protest, he strapped on only one of his Colts since his right hand was worthless. Just when his shoulder had healed enough to allow him to wear two guns again, Mary had to run over his hand with the cart. He fastened his ammunition belt across his chest, though he wondered how easily he'd be able to reload with a splinted hand.

"How could you keep this from me?"

Grace's lower lip trembled. "Mary didn't want me to say anything."

He scowled. His sister was faithful to a fault. "Something like this goes beyond the loyalty of friendship."

At the door, he turned to Grace. "Anything else you've forgotten to mention that I should know?" He regretted the sharp tone of his voice.

"The note was something from Song of Solomon." Tension had deepened the lines across her forehead. "Something about jealousy and love as strong as death."

His legs quivered with the familiar energy he'd thought he'd left in Texas. He rushed down the stairs and stepped into his boots.

"Luke." Grace called after him. "Any ideas?"

He finished lacing his boots. "Yes." One idea. One certain, beyond-a-doubt conviction that he should have realized earlier.

The shadows he'd seen the first night he'd returned, the stranger he'd chased through town after listening to Mary play. A good lawman would have paid more attention, not ignored his suspicion, but he'd been a distracted lawman, begrudging the trip home, anxious to get his name cleared.

He threw the door open and jogged across the yard to the barn. Forgoing a saddle, he slipped headgear and reins on Gabriel, mounted, and rode from the barn. The wind whipped his cheeks as he galloped down the drive and along the road. He took the shortcut through the creek, Gabriel's splash wetting his legs, and angled through a copse of aspens. The friction in his chest could start the forest on fire.

He pushed through the woods into the Smith's field. From a distance, the house appeared dark, as it should, seeing that Mary would be in bed by now. As he rode past the barn, the shadow of the front door came into focus — rather, where the front door should be. But it stood open, leaving a gaping, dark space.

Pulling on the reins, he dismounted before Gabriel had fully stopped, and ran up the steps and through the door.

"Mary!"

The glow of a lamp beckoned from down the hall, and he followed it to her room. An open window and mussed bedcovers bore witness to what he'd feared upon seeing that open door.

Matthew had taken her.

"Mary!"

His call went unanswered. Luke marched the lamp through the house, looking for anything unusual. Everything seemed out of place amidst the mess of the move, yet the crumpled piece of paper lying at the opening of the hallway stood out. Luke swiped it up.

I've won once today, and I must win again. My love burns like a fire, like a mighty flame. Many waters cannot quench it.

The fire pit. Davis had mentioned it earlier to Matthew. It'd been their place of celebration over the years.

Shoving the note in his pocket, Luke blew out the lamp and left the house. He checked the barn, though he didn't expect to find anything, before mounting Gabriel and galloping across the field.

Many waters might not be able to quench love, but Luke could do it with a pair of guns. *One* gun. A love that stalked and obsessed deserved more than a good dousing of water.

A faint glow appeared and Luke slowed Gabriel before the bend, keeping out of sight. Faint harmonica sounds and the crackling of a fire confirmed he'd guessed right. He strained to hear Mary's voice as he dismounted and sought his gun. Maybe he should take his splint off and transfer his gun to his right side.

Nope. He'd trained both hands, and a weak hand was a surer bet than a broken trigger finger.

He crept closer, and the aroma of campfire, usually a comfort, nauseated him. Rounding the trail, he remained outside the circle of light, which thanks to the pile of wood on the fire, was large. Matthew had Mary on his lap, one arm snaked around her middle, the other holding his harmonica. Other than a dirtied dress, she appeared unharmed. Thank God.

His heart rate settled a bit as he prayed for a peaceful resolution. As angry as he was with Matthew, he didn't want to have to shoot him. They'd grown up together. Learned geography and math together. It seemed surreal that Luke now had a gun pointed at him.

He snuck closer, light on his feet, attempting to be as quiet as possible on the dry vegetation. The sparse undergrowth beneath the tall pines meant he'd be exposed as soon as he ventured near enough to the light. From his perspective, he didn't know when that would be.

Matthew loosened his hold on Mary, using both hands on his harmonica, and she pushed him back and tried to run.

Matthew sprung from the log and snagged a handful of her skirt. "Don't do this."

"Let me go." She turned on him and slapped at his hands.

"Stop fighting me." He gripped her by the shoulders and yelled into her face. "Tell me that you love me."

Luke's hopes for a peaceful surrender faded. Matthew was drunk and out of control. Luke advanced another ten feet, now thirty feet from his target.

"I've never loved you, and I never will." Mary tipped her chin and spoke inches from Matthew's face. "I love Luke."

Of course she did, but as much as he wanted to hear the words, she shouldn't have spoken them to a man consumed with securing a confession of his own.

Releasing a mammoth growl, Matthew pushed her to the ground and reached inside his coat.

Instinct urged Luke forward. "Let me see your hands."

"Luke!" Mary clamored to her feet.

Matthew whipped out a revolver and jerked it in a wild path, searching the trees. "Where are you?"

"Doesn't matter. Drop your gun." Luke stepped close to a trunk on the edge of the circle of light. He could see Matthew, but Matthew was probably too drunk to pick out his shadow.

Mary pulled on Matthew's non-shooting hand. "Put the gun down."

He shook her off, waving the gun at her, and staggered a step toward Luke.

Mary must have sensed Matthew's mounting foolishness, for she backed away, stepping over the fallen log. Luke steadied his grip and kept his aim on Matthew, willing Mary to run, but her retreat remained slow, as if she didn't want to give Matthew a chance to panic and shoot her. No way would Luke let that happen.

I don't miss.

He'd said the words many times, but tonight they carried more weight.

Matthew raised his gun and shot into the darkness. Mary screamed. Glaring her direction, Matthew waved the gun wildly, finger resting on the trigger. His aim passed over Mary.

Luke's heart stumbled. "Over here!"

Matthew squinted into the shadows and lowered his gun to his side. "Show yourself like a man."

Said the one who'd hidden behind a note and some

flowers.

Luke hurled a rock as far as he could into the woods. Matthew's attention jerked toward the sound, and Luke stepped into the light, gun raised at Matthew. "Drop the gun. Now. You're drunk, and you're not thinking straight."

Matthew's hand twitched at his side, eyes wild and unintelligible. "I know exactly what I'm doing."

"You're getting yourself into a heap of trouble, that's what." Luke forced himself to speak calmly. "Put the gun down and make it easy on yourself."

Matthew stood motionless, and Luke thought he'd give in, but the fire popped behind him, and Matthew jerked his weapon up toward Luke. Without hesitation, Luke pulled the trigger.

Mary screamed as Matthew slumped to the ground. Luke rushed forward, took the gun from Matthew's loosened grasp, and rolled him over. A clean hit in the chest. Luke holstered his weapon and tore his shirt off. Pushing the material against Matthew's wound, he tried to slow the flow of blood. Matthew's chest heaved once, his breath rattling, and Luke's lifted wordless pleas to the Lord.

Mary approached him from behind and gripped his shoulder with a fierceness that caused him to suck in air. He glanced back. Her wide, unblinking eyes were fixated on Matthew. Her mouth gaped.

"Get back." He'd not meant the order to sound harsh, but — *Lord, please* — she didn't need to experience more trauma than she already had. "Please, stay back, Mary."

She covered her mouth, muffling a sob, and fled to the far side of the fire, where she dropped onto the log. Satisfied she was far enough removed, Luke returned his attention to Matthew.

The rasping breath had stopped, and the light from the fire reflected in empty, lifeless eyes. Blood had seeped through the shirt Luke had pressed against the chest wound. He felt for a pulse. None.

He'd not only shot a childhood friend. He'd killed him.

The situation shouldn't have ended like this. If he'd not been consumed with his own issues, would he have realized Matthew's obsession? If he'd pressed Mary with his questions . . . If he'd confronted Matthew's drinking years ago . . .

"Luke?"

She'd poured every bit of her anguish into the speaking of his name.

He tore his gaze from Matthew and strode toward her. "He's gone."

She lunged from the log and burrowed into his embrace with an intensity that undid his defenses. He rested his cheek against her hair, and a faint trace of alcohol assailed him, sending his heart beat into a frantic rhythm. He fought for breath that fear wanted to steal. Matthew could have shot her, brandishing that gun like he had. Or he could have ridden off with Mary, taken advantage of her . . .

Weakness stole over his limbs, but he labored to keep them from shaking—for Mary's sake. He was the lawman, the one who was supposed to stay calm. Nothing inside him felt calm. "Did he harm you in any way? Physically, I mean?"

"No." She trembled.

He tightened his arms around her. "It's going to be all right."

Sobs shook her body, and her warm, heavy breath seeped through his undershirt. He fisted her hair and held on until his heart rate settled and his mind let loose of its frenzied thoughts.

Mary wiped her face on his shirt and turned her head sideways, resting it against him. "I'm sorry—"

"No." Luke palmed her head against his chest. "You don't need to apologize."

"I should have told someone, but I didn't know what to say. I didn't want to be a burden. I didn't . . ."

He pushed her back and kissed the tear that streaked her cheek. "It's over. Don't trouble your conscience."

She'd done nothing wrong, and he'd not let her take a burden that wasn't hers. He was the one that had to reconcile that he'd been forced to kill his friend.

She wiped her nose with her sleeve like a child would do. "If only I'd—"

"Don't think about what can't be changed." Consternation played across her expression, and Luke bowed his head, closed his eyes. "Lord, we thank you for your protection and for your presence that never fails. We commit to you what has happened and release ourselves into your care. You've promised to lift up those who are weighed down, and I ask that now for Mary, that your Spirit witness the love of the Father to her heart. Amen."

Mary swayed forward and sank against him, her trembles stilled, and her breathing evened out. "How did you know?"

"Grace told me about the note and the bathing incident. I was already concerned about the honeysuckles, so I went to fetch you from your house and bring you to mine. When I found the door open and the note about the fire, I knew Matthew had you. I should have made sense of it all sooner."

She shook her head. "This is so humiliating."

Eyes watering again, she fiddled with the collar of his shirt. The feathery movement of her finger sent tremors down his chest and into his legs. Her bottom lip shuddered, and he set his mouth on hers, a gentle, undemanding kiss meant to comfort—that is, until she roped her arms around his neck and pressed into him. Thoughts of comfort faded, and he tasted the salt of her tears like they had the power to nourish his soul. The way her lips moved against his made him wish he had more to give than a devoted heart and an uncertain future.

He did have more to give. A promise.

He pulled back and gulped air. "I can't leave you." More tears fell, and he swiped his thumb across her cheek. "I love you, and I can't leave you. Not for the sake of my name.

Not for anything."

Mary leaned into Luke as they rode through the woods toward the Thomases' house. The fortress of Luke's arms around her reinforced the sense of peace which had begun to fill her as he'd prayed. Still, her body couldn't seem to stop shaking.

She'd been around death before. She'd watched the passing of a cow while delivering a calf, but she'd not witnessed a man die. It had left a barrenness within her which she imagined would take months to be healed.

And this was the life Luke had committed to — the likelihood of situations in which he'd be required to step into the fray of hostility, to pull the trigger.

"You don't miss." She traced the knuckles on his left hand. "I've never been so grateful for that truth, though for years, whenever you said that, I secretly hoped you'd miss."

The soft release of a breath, almost like a voiceless laugh, sounded by her ear, and she could sense his smile.

"It wasn't a difficult shot," he said. "Even you could hit the center mass of a person from twenty-five feet."

"With my weak hand? I think not. I was shaking uncontrollably."

"When pressure comes, instinct takes over. That's all."

He might dismiss his abilities, but his dedication to hone his skills had saved his life and maybe hers.

"I need to ride to Clifton tonight for the marshal."

"Please don't leave." Tightness gripped her chest. "Or at least take me with you."

"You'll be safe with my family."

"But the marshal will need my testimony." The night's trauma screamed in her mind, and the thought of being separated from Luke coursed panic through her.

"He'll want to talk with you, but he can wait out the night."

She wanted to climb into bed next to Luke, curl up with his arms around her, and not move until morning. Of course, that wasn't possible — or proper to think — but proper yielded to the extenuating circumstances of being kidnapped and having a gun waved at her.

"I'll be back by sunrise."

He pressed a kiss to her ear, and she turned so his lips met hers.

When they rounded the drive before the house, spots of light flickered in the darkness, evidence that someone had waited up. Luke pulled up to the steps, dismounted, and reached up for her. She slipped into his arms and tilted her head to meet his eyes, trying to garner one more moment of connection before losing him to the task she knew he had to do. His hands tightened on her waist, and the unguarded nature of his gaze reached around her heart and strengthened it.

The door crashed open against the house. "Mary?"

Luke released her, and she rushed to meet Grace on the porch.

"Don't be mad at me." Grace threw her arms around Mary. "I didn't mean to tell Luke. He was talking like he knew, and I was so relieved, I started babbling."

"What you said might have saved my life."

Grace thrust her away and searched up and down Mary. "Are you all right? You're dirty."

She couldn't answer. *All right* seemed too trivializing of what had happened.

Luke strode to the porch and took the arm of his mother, who'd silently come out and leaned against the doorjamb. He glanced at Mary and Grace and nodded toward the door. "Let's talk inside."

Mary followed the others into the dimly lit front room and sat on the couch next to Mrs. Thomas while Luke disappeared upstairs, and though only out of the room, angst replaced her fragile sense of peace. Her eyes glossed over as she stared toward the stairs, waiting. She'd rather ride all night on that horse, propped between Luke's arms, than be tucked in bed without him.

A hand grasped hers, and she looked at Mrs. Thomas. The woman's fingers settled around Mary's and squeezed.

Footsteps pounded down the stairs, and Paul appeared behind Luke, buttoning his shirt. "I'll ride with you."

Luke turned, and Mary expected him to argue, but he nodded at his brother. "Thank you."

Paul pushed through the door, but Luke joined them in the front room and settled on the edge of a chair. Leaning forward, elbows anchored on his knees, he directed his attention to his mother and Grace. "This is the short of it. Matthew came after Mary. He was drunk and armed, and he wouldn't give up his weapon. When he raised his gun to shoot me, I had no choice but to return fire. He's dead."

The pronouncement added weight to a reality that still seemed surreal. Grace covered her face in her hands, and Mrs. Thomas reached her arm around Mary and drew her close. The hand she rested on Mary's shoulder shook.

"Paul and I are going for the marshal." Luke rose and kissed his mother on the cheek. Kneeling before Mary, he cradled her face in his hands. "Even in the things that don't make sense, God is sovereign."

She nodded.

"Get some rest." He leaned forward and brushed his lips on hers.

She couldn't move, not even swallow, until the slamming of the door announced he'd left. And then she collapsed into Mrs. Thomas's lap and wept again.

CHAPTER TWENTY-SEVEN

Mary stirred, a cramp in her neck, and became aware of someone watching her.

"Good morning," said a small voice.

Mary's eyes darted open. A smiling Helen rocked back and forth on her heels.

"Did you sleep on the couch all night?" Helen laughed and held out her hands.

"I did." What was left of the night after she'd emptied more tears on Mrs. Thomas while Grace had stroked her back. "Is that funny?"

"Yes." The girl laughed. "But not as funny as Luke. He slept in the chair without even a pillow." Helen pointed to the chair that had been scooted flush against the foot of the couch.

Mary sat up, swung her stocking feet to the floor, and strained to hear sounds of Luke's voice, but all she heard was sizzling from a frying pan and mellow conversation beyond the kitchen door.

"Are you hungry?" Mary asked Helen, eager to find Luke.

"I already ate." She held her arms out, eyes wide. "It's almost nine o'clock."

Mary gasped and jolted to her feet. Her poor cows. She padded into the kitchen, her stomach's growls drawn out by the mix of salty and sweet aromas. Mrs. Thomas, clad in the same clothes as the night before, flipped griddle cakes while Grace poured coffee.

"Here. Sit." Grace shoved a mug into Mary's hands.

"There are cakes and bacon, and you're going to eat even if you don't feel like it. You've taught me to be bossy, and I'm going to put those lessons into practice."

Mary smiled, the strain of not enough sleep pinching her eyes. "I've got cows to milk, for a few more days, but thank you."

"You can't escape so easily." Grace steered her to a chair and pushed on her shoulders. "Luke left two hours ago to milk the cows, and that was after having slept not more than thirty minutes. Evidently, he loves you."

Mrs. Thomas chuckled as she turned with a plate of food. "Not much could be clearer." She set the food before Mary and kissed her on the forehead. "Now eat, and then we might let you go after him."

Nothing would stop her.

Luke washed out the milk pail and hung it by the others. Milking one-handed had taken longer than anticipated. He'd expected Mary to join him partway through, but after last night, she deserved every moment of sleep she could wrangle.

He rinsed and dried his hands, then rotated his shoulders. Stiff and a hint sore, but he attributed that to the strain of last night and the activity that had kept him out until dawn's first whisper. He'd collapsed in the chair next to Mary to doze until Helen had woken him with her warning not to sleep past chores.

Luke led the cows to pasture and rested his elbows on the fence railing. The early heat promised a scorching afternoon, not surprising since the Fourth of July celebration was a mere five days out, signaling the start of the hottest month.

"Can you think of any reason you need to leave my sight again?"

His heart jumped, and he spun to face Mary.

Hair mussed and hanging in a loose braid over her shoulder, she strode across the yard and up to the fence. Looping an arm around his neck, she drew his head down and kissed him. "I can't think of one."

When she acted like that, neither could he.

He leaned against the fence, and she wrapped her arms about his waist and looked up at him.

"Did you get things taken care of? Is everything going to be fine?" Her brows drew together.

"We fetched Marshal Swensson, returned for . . ." he cleared his throat, hating to draw her attention to all that had happened, though she'd likely be consumed by it for some days anyway like he would. " . . . the body, and went to the Bridgeses'."

Beneath her shadowed eyes, he sensed her reliving the trauma of last night.

"It's going to be all right."

"I know," she whispered. "But you're going to have say that at least a few more times before those images disappear. If they ever do."

They wouldn't this side of glory. "Stay by my side, and I'll love you so hard you won't have a chance to be anything other than all right."

Her gaze warmed, softening her expression and lighting it with tenderness. "By your side doesn't have to mean Pine Creek."

Birdsong underscored her soft, convicted words.

"I'll go with you to Texas," she said. "I'm letting go of the dairy, how much harder can it be to let go of Pine Creek? Not as hard as it would be to let go of you."

He loved how her heart had no hesitations about what it wanted, and wonder of wonders, it wanted him more than it wanted the home she loved.

He poked a strand of hair into her braid. "You honor me, but I belong here, and so do you." His throat thickened at the trust she demonstrated in her offer to go with him. "Show

296

me how to do this thing called home that you do so well."

She hung her head, and the sun glinted off her dark hair, giving it a glossy look. Taking his hands in hers, she opened them.

His splinted fingers ached.

"It starts with this." She kissed the palm of his uninjured hand and set it flat against her heart, covering it with her own.

His hand burned at her vulnerability. In Texas, vulnerability got a person killed, or close to it, and he had the wounds to prove it. But with Mary, openness beget intimacy.

"It doesn't matter where we lay our heads at night or wash our clothes or cook our food," she said. "It can be Texas, or it can be Pine Creek. Home means living from here" — she pressed on his hand — "where God's Spirit enables you to love and be loved."

He leaned forward and kissed her, his hand resting in that vulnerable place between them. Each heartbeat beneath his palm added impetus to his desire, a desire that grew beyond words. Desire for her, absolutely, but that fell short.

Eternity in his heart. The longing Cam liked to preach about to prove that man's greatest desire could only be fulfilled by his Creator.

He kissed her with greater fervency. She held on so well. Held on to home, to family, to the back of his shirt.

He wrapped his arms around her, tugged her closer, and put his cheek on the top of her head. "I won't say we'll never return to Texas, but I have things to do here, like make peace with my scars." The healing had just started, and it couldn't be completed in Texas. "I want to make a home with you here."

She drew back, narrowed her eyes, and squeezed his left arm. "Since we're saying what we want, I still want to study those scars."

"You can study every inch of me if you marry me."

Her face flamed. Laughing, he tugged the tie from her

braid and ran his fingers through her hair.

She offered him a smug look. "For making me blush, you can come inside and help me finish packing." Smiling, she took off toward the house.

At the door she stopped and stared ahead. Resting a hand on the doorjamb, her shoulders rose with a deep breath. "Would you mind going inside and getting rid of . . ." Her voice cut off, as if she'd choked on the words.

He stepped around her and nodded. She didn't want any signs of Matthew.

She called after him. "I don't ever want to see that nightgown again. Do something with it, anything, but I won't wear it."

"Fine by me."

She backed away from the open door, and a moment later he heard the creak of the rocking chair. He marched across the room and swiped the honeysuckle blossom off the floor. If she wasn't moving off the dairy, he'd dig up every honeysuckle vine on the property.

"You can get me a new one as a wedding present," she said. "Something pretty."

"What for?" He grinned. "I'll keep you warm."

The back and forth of the rocking chair stopped. He imagined her face, redder than a moment ago.

The rocking started again, and she called, "I think we'd better get married sooner rather than later."

"That's the best idea I've heard in months."

Luke propped his arms behind him and stretched his legs across the wool blanket. Picnic baskets dotted the field behind the church where Pine Creek's population had swelled to three times its normal size for the Fourth of July festivities.

"Are you ready?" Mary's tender voice slipped under the cheers of the baseball game.

Luke nudged her foot and smiled.

Only one thing would make him more ready for his three o-clock installation, but Johnston had assured him that a few false accusations wouldn't intrude on Pine Creek's celebration of a new, highly anticipated sheriff.

A few false accusations. Johnston's way with words outshone poets, politicians, and pastors alike. If Luke were brought in on those false charges, Johnston might serve well as an attorney.

"You did right, telling Johnston."

He angled his head sideways, meeting Mary's gaze. "I know, but when's it going to end?"

He'd not expected they'd want to move ahead with the installation. Then again, Johnston wouldn't let something like allegations against his favorite candidate deter him.

"You're innocent?" he'd asked.

"Of course."

Johnston had shrugged. "We got a town to run. We don't have time to let unfounded suspicions get in the way."

And so he'd called an immediate vote after church. Apparently, Pine Creek had agreed.

"How do you like Mr. Millwood?" Mary's gaze followed her papa around from blanket to blanket where he introduced the new dairyman to families.

"He's got more energy than a litter of puppies."

Mary laughed. "I think some of it has rubbed off on Papa."

"Nah." Luke reached across and took Mary's hand. "Any new energy your papa has is coming from us. I think he could have milked a hundred cows after I asked him for your hand."

Helen ran to their blanket and dropped a handful of squished daisies onto Mary's lap. "Save these for me. Jed Pearson called me a cry baby, and I have to chase him." And with that, she took off, red-faced and already breathing hard.

Luke plucked a daisy from Mary's lap and began pulling the petals off. "He loves me." He tossed the petal onto her lap. "He loves me." He tossed another petal. "He loves me."

"Surely you're not mocking me."

He laughed. "Surely you know that I know it was me all those years ago."

She lifted her shoulder in a small shrug. "I'll never tell."

The sound of a clearing throat reminded Luke of the hordes of townsfolk around them.

"Luke Thomas." Marshal Swensson smiled down at him. "I hear you're going to be installed as Pine Creek's first sheriff in a few hours."

Luke rose. "It's going to be a pleasure working with you. I've appreciated the kind way you've treated me, all things considered."

"A man's innocent until proven guilty, and if my hunch is correct" — he waved an envelope — "this is the relief you've been waiting for. Came a few days ago, but business has kept me from delivering it. I hope you'll forgive me."

Luke tore into the missive with the formal Ranger insignia on top. Mary stood and peered over his shoulder.

Dear Luke,

I apologize for the delay, but more was occurring than I was at liberty to discuss. After receiving multiple depositions and examining several issues brought to our attention, your name has been cleared and all charges dropped. The witness who'd raised allegations against you was Ranger Langston Brooks, whose own loyalty we'd been secretly investigating the past eighteen months. We were able to catch him, along with the final Fowler brother, in a robbery in East Texas.

The Rangers offer you a formal apology and seek your return to duty as soon as your healing is complete and you can make your way south. In addition to welcoming you back, I'd like to enlist your services in training new Rangers. Consider it a promotion, with appropriate pay increase to be discussed when I see the whites of your eyes. Make it soon. We've been down a good man for too long.

Captain R. Finch

Luke smiled and fought off the watering in his eyes. "The charges have been dropped."

"That's wonderful." Marshal Swensson clapped him on the shoulder. "Guess this is your own Independence Day."

The marshal wandered off, and Luke read the short missive again, each word removing another stone from the burden he'd adapted to carrying.

"Luke?" Mary touched his elbow.

He turned and cupped her cheek. "I'm not even considering it. Nothing could tempt me away from here." He pursed his lips to fight the trembling of his jaw.

Mary shielded her gaze from the sun. "You were that worried?"

His breath came out shaky. "I didn't know how it'd be possible that they'd convict me, but those weren't lightweight allegations. The consequences would have been serious."

He shoved the note in his pocket. "Let's go find my family." He put his arm around her and led her between the blankets.

She reached and held his hand where it hung down around her shoulder, careful not to pull on his splinted fingers. "We're not going to be like Barrett and Claire, are we?"

He followed her gaze to where Barrett was serving Claire a plate of food. Claire started to get up for something, but Barrett held her back. "What about them?"

"Now that they're married, their banter's been replaced with over-sentimentality. Have you noticed? He waits on her like she's the Queen of England, and she's lost some of that snappiness with him that defined their relationship."

He'd bet that snappiness came out in ways only Barrett saw. "Don't worry. I'll still argue with you, tease you, and tell you when you're wrong."

Mary turned her face up at him. "Good. I don't want to lose our fun."

He laughed and pulled her closer to his side. "Believe

me, darling. The fun's just starting."

Dear Reader

Now that you've read about Mary and Luke's coming home, I hope you'll share with me your story. Tell me about your heart. Has it found its home? Saint Augustine wrote in his *Confessions* that our hearts are restless until they find rest in Christ.

You can connect with me or drop me a message through my website or social media profiles:

www.sondrakraak.com
Facebook: Sondra Kraak Author
Twitter: @SondraKraaak
Pinterest: Author Sondra Kraak
Instagram: SondraKraakAuthor.

Also, if you have a passion for Christian historical romance and love to gab on social media, please consider joining my Trek Team. You'll have the opportunity to receive advanced reader copies of my upcoming releases as well as join me in promoting my stories. Find more information and apply on my website.

If you missed Claire and Barrett's story, *One Plus One Equals Trouble,* be sure to go back and catch it.

Finally, will you join me for another journey in Pine Creek? Cam needs a woman. Bless his tender preacher's heart. He's not going to get what he expects. He's going to get a woman who thinks she can match him hammer-strike for hammer-strike. A woman with money and influence. In other words, he's going to get the challenge of his lifetime. And hopefully, you'll get a great read from it!

P.S. If you were waiting for him to wake up and see sweet Grace for the gentle-loving soul she is, sorry. But don't despair. Grace will get a nice surprise.

Invitation To Leave A Review

Reviews are an author's treasure! An honest review of *Two Ways Home* on Amazon.com would be a great gift to me. Feel free to copy and paste that review onto Goodreads as well. Thank you!

Praise for One Plus One Equals Trouble

"I settled in for this story and just had to keep reading! Kraak skillfully blends her beautiful, lyrical style with her humorous wit and masterfully creates a story that is at once easy to read and yet full of depth—a rare combination."
   --Jennifer Rodewald, author of *The Carpenter's Daughter*, *Reclaimed*, and *Blue Columbine*.

"Oh my goodness! This book has been recommended to me so many times recently and I TOTALLY SEE WHY!! The chemistry, the flirting, the KISSES… the intense pursuing!!! Be still my KissingBook-loving heart! One Plus One Equals Trouble by Sondra Kraak is going in my faves category."
   --Meez Carrie, from the blog *Reading Is My SuperPower*

"Someone hand me a fan! This book is chock full of romantic tension and witty banter. If you enjoy books by Karen Witemeyer and Regina Jennings, then you'll love this debut by Sondra Kraak. Can't wait to get my hands on her next book!"
   --Sarah Monzon, author of *The Isaac Project* and *Finders Keepers*.

"It's my personal preference as a reader to have unanswered questions that keep me interested in the story, and Ms. Kraak is very skilled at delivering the intrigue."
   --Lesley Ann McDaniel, author, *Crescent Cove* series

Acknowledgements

Thank you, Jesus Christ, for leaving your heavenly throne and making your home among us. Because of your work on the cross, we can join you in a forever home.

Thank you to my husband, Nate, for putting up with my moaning and groaning when this story took longer than I anticipated and the characters would not work out their issues. We've done home together for a dozen years now, and it's been a glorious adventure.

Thank you to my daughter, Faith, for asking me about Luke, pestering me about Luke, spying on my story, and giggling about romance. I'm grateful we share a love of story and writing.

Thank you to my son, Silas, for crawling into bed each morning and cuddling with me. Your sweet spirit brings me joy and pours over into my writing.

Thank you, first readers Marci, Mary Ellen, and Katrina.

My critique group (and Fiction 411 team) provides awesome support, encouragement, and brainstorming power: Janette Foreman, Gwendolyn Gage, and Amy Drown. A special thank you to Amy for beta reading and giving plot feedback that changed my story. The ending is better because you asked me the hard questions.

Thank you to my first critique partner, author Jennifer Rodewald, for your mounds of encouragement and for not letting me get away with mediocre.

Roseanna White, my cover designer, has done it again! Your graphic eye is amazing, and even more so, your professionalism and gracious spirit.

To my editor, Robin Patchen, I hope I've learned a bit more on this, my second book, so that next time your job will be easier. Thanks for answering my grammar questions, strengthening my verbs, and pointing out inconsistencies. It's a relief to put forth a book knowing that it's been through strong editing.

To the Blue Ridge Writers, I enjoy the fellowship we share and the wisdom you all offer.

Thank you, readers, for taking the trek with me down story lane. Your enjoyment of my stories is what makes my job as a writer so delightful.

About the Author

A native of Washington State, Sondra Kraak grew up playing in the rain, hammering out Chopin at the piano, and running up and down the basketball court. After attending Whitworth University in Spokane, Washington, she moved to North Carolina to work for a small non-profit ministry. It was in the backroom of that office, amidst the clamor of copy machines and printers, that love blossomed. She married her mountain man in 2004, and they spent the first season of their marriage in New England where Sondra attended Gordon-Conwell Theological Seminary.

Now settled in the foothills of the Blue Ridge Mountains, she works part-time at her church doing worship ministry and leading Bible studies. Life at home with her husband and children is full of Yahtzee, backyard football and baseball, reading parties, activities involving food, and magically multiplying loads of laundry. She writes historical romance set in the beautiful Pacific Northwest through which her passion and delight is to provide readers with stories that not only entertain, but nourish the soul.

Her debut novel, *One Plus One Equals Trouble*, was an ACFW Genesis semi-finalist (2015) and the winner of the Blue Ridge Mountains Christian Writers Conference Unpublished Women's Fiction Award (2015).

Made in the USA
Charleston, SC
27 January 2017